JOSIE BONHAM

The Marquess's Christmas Runaway

First published by Pitcheroak Press 2020

This novel is entirely a work of fiction. The names,
characters and incidents portrayed in it are the work of the
author's imagination. Any resemblance to actual persons,
living or dead, events or localities is entirely coincidental.

Josie Bonham asserts the moral right to be identified as the
author of this work.

First edition

ISBN: 978-1-913856-04-5

This book was professionally typeset on Reedsy.
Find out more at reedsy.com

Chapter One.

Cheapside London, December 1806.

Georgie lay on the hard, narrow bed fully clothed including her travelling cloak and boots. Even with the attic room's only blanket wrapped tightly around her she was still cold. Night time was the worst. A tell-tale scrabbling around the edge of the room made her shudder. Her head rested on her travelling bag, which had been thrown into her prison after her. Better than no pillow at all and it kept it away from the rats. She couldn't go on like this for much longer.

Her hand found the gold chain she had managed to hide in the secret pocket of her cloak. It must be quite valuable. Someone would check on her in the morning. If it was a footman, the chain might be enough to persuade him to help her escape. James, in particular, hadn't liked having to incarcerate her up here and a footman could easily find another job in London. If only she had thought to enlist James's help, she might have escaped the first time. She should have realised Cousin Mary's maid was spying on her. Just her luck that Cousin Algernon had been at home to stop her leaving.

The sound of doors slamming down below jolted Georgie out of her uneasy half sleep. That would be Algernon coming home

1

foxed again. She stretched her stiff limbs and drew the blanket more tightly around her. Sure enough, she heard the sound of someone staggering upstairs. Erratic footsteps carried on and Georgie froze. Algernon was climbing the attic stairs. A flicker of light showed under the door. Georgie sat up and threw the blanket off. The footsteps stopped nearby and were followed by the sound of the heavy key turning in the lock of her prison door.

Algernon stumbled into the room and very deliberately rested his candlestick on the windowsill, sending dancing shadows all around. Georgie blinked in the light.

"You might as well marry me, Georgie, and get this over with. M'mother won't relent." Algernon's words came out as a slurred mumble and he rocked from side to side.

The smell of alcohol wafted towards Georgie. Her heart thumped. This was her chance. She grabbed the handle of her travel bag at the same time as Algernon lunged towards her and caught hold of the end of the bed to steady himself.

Georgie jumped up and edged towards the door.

Algernon followed. "Oh no you don't. It's time I sampled the goods to make you see sense."

Georgie swung the bag at him as hard as she could. It caught him on the shoulder and he fell onto the bed, hitting his head on the bars of bedstead. He ended up lying across the bed on his stomach, breathing, heavily, but apparently unconscious. Whether from the knock to the head or the alcohol he had consumed she wasn't sure. There was no time to lose. She snatched up his candlestick and slipped out of the room, closing the door behind her.

Every creak of the attic stairs was agony but Georgie reached the floor below, where the family bedrooms were, without incident. There was enough light from a couple of wall sconces to manage the rest of the way. She slipped into Algernon's bedroom and extinguished the candle flame, leaving the candlestick on the floor by the door. With her breathing so ragged she feared immediate discovery, Georgie ran lightly down the main stairs and gently tried the front door. Luck was with her. It was one of those mornings when Algernon had left it unlocked.

Georgie closed the door gently behind her and ran down the short flight of steps to the street. It was still dark, except for faint moonlight. After a few deep breaths of the cold night air, she pulled up the hood of her dark grey cloak and walked towards the main road. Cousin Mary had sent her on so many errands, in the time she had been forced to live with her, that Georgie knew the location of every obstacle to be avoided and was able to stay in the shadows close to the houses. There didn't seem to be anyone about to see her but it was best to be careful. In all likelihood Cousin Mary would have her obnoxious lawyer friend send his people out to try and find out where she had gone.

Georgie picked up speed as soon as she was well clear of the house until her breath came in heavy gasps, releasing white tendrils into the early morning air. There was always the chance that she had been spotted leaving by one of the servants. She hardly dared to look back but she kept a wary eye out for anyone who might recognise her. The street seemed deserted, without a pedestrian or carriage in sight. It must be too early even for any merchants, who owned a lot of the houses in the area, to be on their way to their places of business. Even if she had been spotted leaving there was still a chance of escape if she could find a hackney. There wasn't much she

3

wouldn't do to avoid being captured.

The main road came into view and Georgie was relieved to see a fair number of carts rumbling past the end of the road. Probably on their way to markets but that meant there might be hackneys abroad soon. She redoubled her efforts. There was less shelter here. Sleet froze her cheeks and settled in dips in the uneven pavement. She ignored her burning lungs and threw herself around the corner. Her boots slipped on wet slush, taking her onto the cobbles of the main road. The side of a stationary cart caught her in the midriff and knocked the last remnants of breath from her. She grabbed at it and somehow stayed on her feet. The carter gave a string of oaths.

"Watch what you're a doing Miss. If we'd moved off then you'd a been under the wheels." He shook his head at her in reproach but what she could see of his face, above the thick muffler wrapped around his neck and over his chin, seemed friendly enough.

Georgie gulped in more air and nodded, unable to speak. The traffic started moving again and the driver of a carriage arriving behind shouted at them to move on. Georgie tried to step away but was obliged to catch hold of the cart again as her feet scrabbled to gain purchase on the wet footpath. The carter stood up and waved a fist at the coachman.

"Give over. Can't you see as how the young miss is winded?"

He jumped down from the cart and picked up her valise. "You better ride with me for a bit until you can breathe again."

Georgie didn't argue. He threw her bag onto the bales of hay filling the back of the cart, and helped her on to the seat. She took the reins from him and risked a glance around. There was no sign of pursuit. Her heart hammered. The few minutes it took for the carter to walk around, addressing a few pithy

4

comments to the complaining coachman on the way, seemed like a lifetime. Her breathing eased as they moved off. They were going in the right direction even if progress was slow. The traffic thinned out and the carter turned and tilted his head towards her.

"Can you talk now, Miss

"Yes. Thank you so much. I was in such a hurry I slipped."

"I could see that." He raised bushy eyebrows. "Where is it you're in a rush to get to?"

Georgie breathed deeply. She had no choice but to trust him. "Fetter Lane. If you would drop me before you go off the route, I'll happily pay you."

"I have to deliver this lot to Smithfield." He jerked his head towards the back of the cart. "I can take you all the way. By the weight of that bag it's the White Horse you want."

"Yes please. It's my aunt you see." A sob broke from her, quickly suppressed. In a way it was the truth, if Aunt Anne was still alive she would be living safely with her.

"Bad news, eh. Don't worry, Miss. It's early yet. You'll be in plenty of time for a morning coach. Folks won't be too keen to travel in this weather, so there should be seats going."

Georgie peered behind whenever her rescuer wasn't looking. The sky was starting to lighten up and she kept her hood pulled forward, covering most of her face. No one seemed to have the slightest interest in them. If she had got away without being seen it would be hours before anyone checked on her.

* * *

The red brick façade of the White Horse coaching inn came into view. Georgie gasped at the size of it and the press of people

5

milling around watching the coaches leave. They pulled up nearby. The noise of constant arrivals and departures was deafening. Georgie tipped the carter and he lifted her valise down. She winced as she picked it up. Her ribs felt bruised and her shoulder ached from running with the heavy bag. The carter gave her a cheery wave before moving off. Luck was favouring her so far. Would she get a ticket for the Canterbury stage coach?

Her ears roared for a moment and the noise receded. She gave her head a shake. She was not the sort of female to faint away at the slightest thing. Everything came back into focus and she carried on. It took her some time to pick her way through the melee and find the coach booking office.

The elderly clerk scratched his head. "Kent you say, Miss?"

"Yes please."

"Hmm. The Canterbury coach is fully booked. There might be another way to route you." He licked his lips and rubbed his hands together, not meeting her gaze.

Georgie had heard about the practice of sending people a roundabout way to charge more and stood her ground. She had no choice with the meagre contents of her purse.

"I'll ride on the outside if I have to but I must get to ..." She paused. It wouldn't do to give too much away. "To Canterbury, this evening." She could tell the guard on the coach that she wanted to get off before Canterbury.

A porter came in staggering under a pile of packages. He dumped them in an alcove. "That's the last lot from the Cambridge mail coach."

"Good." The clerk sighed. "Do you know if there is any space on the Canterbury stage?" He nodded at Georgie. "She's only a slip of a thing."

Georgie held her breath.

The porter smiled. "They're loading up. The coachman was moaning because someone hasn't turned up. Can't say as how I blame them; we'll have snow for sure soon. You're in luck if you can afford an inside seat, Miss."

The clerk named a price that sounded high, but she had enough to cover it with a little left over. The landlady at the Golden Cross would surely put her up for a few nights and wait for payment. Her funds wouldn't stretch to lodgings as well as coach fare.

She handed over the fee and the porter picked up her valise.

"Follow me. They're nearly ready to leave."

Georgie trotted after him. He dropped her valise by a coach and shouted up to the driver.

"This is the last one. Hope the snow holds off for you."

Georgie shivered. Snow was all she needed but, as long as she made it to the safety of the Golden Cross, heavy snow that stopped travel later on would help her. If she stayed hidden from Cousin Mary for five more days she would be free. It was certainly cold enough for more snow. The outside passengers were muffled up in so many layers of clothes it was difficult to tell what sex they were. She scrambled into the coach and a plump woman made room for her on the forward facing seat.

She sank back onto the seat. The gap was so narrow it was difficult to avoid the knees of the man sitting opposite. Nausea threatened to overcome her as the smell of onions wafted across from him. It must be because she hadn't eaten for so long. She mentally added up how much money she had left. It should be enough to buy something to eat at one of the stops. The coach pulled away. She was so tired she drifted into an uneasy sleep, only for the memory of Algernon's wet lips on

7

hers to plague her dreams.

* * *

She was back in Cousin Mary's shabby drawing room, fighting Algernon off with all her strength. Her throat constricted with terror and in desperation she kicked out at him with her sturdy walking boots. Algernon's yelp brought his mother running. She breathed easier when he flounced out of the room, declaring he didn't want to marry a shrew who went around kicking people.

"What do you think you are doing, attacking my son." Cousin Mary glared at her. "Running away too, after all I've done for you, you ungrateful wretch."

Georgie stood tall and faced her. "How can you expect me to stay here with your son trying to seduce me at every turn." Somehow, she kept her voice steady.

Cousin Mary's face went bright red. "You'll marry him or starve, my girl. I'm not letting your fortune slip through our fingers." She stared at Georgie, her eyes cold, hard pebbles. "I'll have you put in the attics until you see sense." Her voice rose to a screech. "James, William. In here, now!"

The two manservants came running and Georgie was carried, kicking and screaming, up to the attics. She was thrown into a dark room with the tiniest of windows. The door slammed in her face.

* * *

Georgie woke up with a start. The man who smelled of onions was grumbling loudly and she realised they were stationary.

She felt clammy despite the cold. Cousin Mary hadn't found her, had she?

The plump woman patted her shoulder. "Don't look so worried, dear. It's only some silly lads overtaking us for fun, not highwaymen."

The coach started up again and Georgie saw a curricle in the ditch as they pulled out wide. Her conscience was troubling her about leaving Algernon with a possible head injury, but she wouldn't have had another chance to escape. He'd been so foxed he'd landed softly and besides he should have stood up to his mother and stopped her from trying to starve her into submission. The plump lady opened a bag and the smell of fresh bread made her stomach rumble. Three days without food had left her feeling weak.

She managed to buy a scalding hot cup of coffee and a small piece of bread and cheese at one of the longer halts. Her mouth fell open at the price. She wouldn't be able to afford anything else. She didn't have time to finish the food but she took it back on the coach with her. It relieved the worst of the hunger pangs. They were in a battle to outrun the weather. The sleet of London turned to light snow during the second half of the journey. Georgie could hear shouted curses coming from the coachman as he was forced to slow down in places.

The light began to fade and Georgie shivered as she watched the flakes of snow falling past the window. They were definitely getting bigger. She drifted into an uneasy slumber and woke with a start when her head knocked against the side of the coach. It slowed and then lurched onwards. A glance out of the window confirmed that snow was lying in a thin layer on the road. At least they weren't far away now. They rounded the sharp bend that lay before the Golden Cross. She tensed when the coach slithered across to the other side of the road. Fortunately, there was nothing coming in the other direction.

The coach slowed and turned into the yard of the inn. She was the only passenger to alight. The guard threw her valise down and the coach was on its way as soon as the ostlers had changed the horses. She crept in around the back and made use of the necessary house. Then if anyone saw her they wouldn't be surprised she hadn't gone in the front way. The back hall was deserted. Was it her imagination or was it dirtier than she remembered? The floor looked as if it hadn't been swept for a while and surely that was dust on the skirting board. How strange. She put a hand on the wall to steady herself as a wave of dizziness hit her. If the place had changed hands she was in trouble.

Chapter Two

Max Lovell, Marquess of Hargreaves, put his cue away. "Three losses are enough for one day. Well done."

Simon Pyrce shook his head. "That's the first time I've beaten you at billiards in as long as I can remember. You're losing your touch, Hargreaves. With the ladies too." He slapped Max on the back. "Must be the shock of missing out with the merry widow to old Villiers."

Max grunted. "I thought I had been discreet."

"You were, old boy, only those of us who know you well would have guessed you were interested in that direction."

"I hope you're right." Max drew in a sharp breath. He ought to be used to being the butt of gossip.

"Don't look so blue-devilled, no harm done and you never had a chance if it was a ring she was after."

"No, I suppose not." How had he misread the signs so badly with Lydia? "Villiers has done me a favour. I'll be damned if I ever let another woman trick me into proposing."

"Not still worried about that old scandal, are you?" Simon gripped his shoulder. "Come on, I've ordered a late luncheon to be laid out in the breakfast room for those who want it. Some estate reared beef and a good claret will soon set you straight."

Max shook his head. "I think I'll go for a walk."

"What and have people saying you're skulking around because you lost out? Besides all the ladies will be having tea and cakes in Mama's drawing room by now."

"You're right. The truth is, I'm bored with a bachelor lifestyle but I don't know for the life of me what to do about it."

Simon grinned at him. "It's our looming thirtieth birthdays. I'm in an even worse fix. Mama is trying to get me to join her in London for the season. She has a long list of potential wives. Why not share the pain with me?"

"What, Almacks, balls, drives around Hyde Park with all of the Ton watching my every move. No thank you." Max shuddered and allowed himself to be led to the breakfast room.

Sure enough, the room was empty. Max relaxed and followed Simon to the buffet table. Simon's uncle, the Earl of Welford followed them in with a lady on his arm. Max stiffened, it was Selina Lovell, his widowed aunt by marriage. All his interest in roast beef disappeared.

Selina dropped the Earl's arm and sidled up to him. "Ah, Max. I've been trying to catch a word with you for days."

Simon raised his eyebrows at him and Max's lips twitched. "I'm surprised we have anything to talk about, Aunt."

"Oh, but we do, Max, as you very well know. Cuthbert is your heir and it's about time you recognised him as such." She smiled up at Welford. "It would suit me very well if you invited Cuthbert and me to stay at Hargreaves for the Christmas festivities."

Max stood stock still but he couldn't stop his nostrils flaring. "Oh, but it wouldn't suit me at all, Aunt." His voice was a silky drawl.

Welford took Selina's arm but she shrugged him off and moved closer to Max. "Face it, Max, you will never recover from Lavinia's betrayal and find a wife. Be sensible and accept that Cuthbert will be the Marquess of Hargreaves one day."

He ought to walk away but Selina was the outside of enough. "I am less than five years older than Cuthbert and far more clean living, so that is by no means certain."

"What?" Selina's voice rose. "Clean living, you. We all know you were after a liaison with Lydia Winters until Marmaduke Villiers snatched her from under your nose with the offer of a ring on her finger."

Max lifted his chin. "You go too far, madam." He turned and stalked out of the room.

A sprinkling of people out in the hallway melted away as he strode past them. Deuce take it, how many people had been listening to that exchange?

Simon followed and pulled him into the library with a hand on his arm. "Good, there's no one in here." He shut the door firmly behind them. "I'm sorry, Max. Uncle asked me if he could invite a friend to keep him company. I left my secretary to take the details and send the invitation. Didn't realise it was Lady Lovell until she arrived or I would have warned you."

Max sighed. "It's not your fault. Selina has been spoiling for a fight this age."

"Still, I'm sorry you were subjected to that. Uncle has known her since they were children. He always says that she would have got over her disappointment at not being the Marchioness of Hargreaves if your uncle hadn't died young."

"I doubt it. The woman is pure evil. I'm sorry Simon but I'm going home. I shall lose my temper completely with many more of her barbs. That sky looks like snow to me. I'll use the weather as my excuse and people can say what they like. Give my regards to your Mama."

* * *

Max ordered his curricle to be brought around and ran up the stairs. He changed into a pair of buckskin breeches and a thick jacket as fast as he could. All the rest of his things went into his travelling bags in a jumbled heap. Jepson would complain, even more than he had about being left behind, when he saw them. What did it matter? All he wanted to do was show this place a clean pair of heels, regardless of the fact that Simon was one of his oldest friends. He couldn't be in company with Selina for two minutes without his hackles rising but she had really surpassed herself today.

With his bags packed, he shrugged into his greatcoat and drew on a pair of driving gloves. It was a cold afternoon and the road conditions might slow them down but even so he should be home in an hour or so. Lord he was in a coil but the time to worry about that was when he was safely home. He knew the house nearly as well as his own and ran down a set of servants' stairs to avoid bumping into any of the other guests. He wasn't in the mood to exchange idle chit chat. Simon's efficient grooms led his curricle to the side door at the same moment that he walked through it. He threw them a crown and climbed in.

There was a light dusting of snow in places but the roads weren't as bad as he feared until he reached the Canterbury road. He pressed on and the Golden Cross came into view within threequarters of an hour of setting off. His horses seemed to be straining a bit. He should have taken more care of them, instead of letting his anger spill over into his driving. It might be best to stop here and rest them. His grooms would wonder what was up with him if he arrived with them in a distressed condition, exactly the sort of speculation he hated.

He could dine here too. Having missed his roast beef earlier he was sharp set and it would save him having to deal with his taciturn new housekeeper. Lord, if it had been anyone else but Cook who had recommended her he would have let her go by now.

Max turned into the inn's yard and a groom rushed forward to take his curricle from him.

He jumped down and handed the reins to the groom. "I'll need them in an hour or so but rub them down well and rug them up, will you?"

Max strode into the taproom, where the landlord was serving ale to a couple of customers

"Not busy this evening then, Pleck?"

Pleck looked up and smiled. "Good evening, my lord. Too much snow in the air for country folk to want to stay out. What can I do for you?"

"Can you rustle me up an evening meal?" He grinned. "You're right about the weather, the sky looks full of snow to me. Something cold will do."

Pleck scratched his head. "There's cold beef, cheese and fresh baked bread but that seems hardly fitting for you, my lord. I'll ask the cook to stay a bit longer if you like."

"Cook? Is Mrs Pleck unwell?"

"It's her mother what's ill. Gone to look after her." Pleck grimaced. "It's hard without her but what can you do?"

"I'm sorry to hear that." Max watched a flurry of snow drift past the window. "Cold beef and cheese will be perfectly

15

acceptable. I don't want anyone getting stuck in snow on my account, including myself. I came home early because I didn't like the look of the weather."

Pleck looked relieved. "I'll have the maid set it all up for you in the coffee room. It's empty and there's a roaring fire.

"Excellent. I'll have a bottle of your best claret too."

"I'll bring that myself, my lord. There's a good brandy that will warm you up while you're waiting."

Max nodded and strode off to the coffee room. A few drinks might take the edge off his anger. Pleck followed him with the brandy. Max stripped off his driving gloves and greatcoat. He poured a generous measure of brandy and walked across to the fire with it, where he tossed it back. That was better. Warmth inside and out. Lord he was in a coil. Could he cope with taking up Simon's offer of sharing his matchmaking Mama for a season in London? It might be less excruciating than letting his sisters loose. He wandered back to the brandy decanter and poured another measure. He had to find a wife somehow before he was goaded into strangling Selina, but in the full glare of the Ton?

He shook his head and tossed back his second brandy. Yes, he could do it if he had too. He was a Lovell for heaven's sake. The trouble was, after the scandal of him jilting Lavinia, the sort of parents likely to produce a daughter he might be happy with would look at him askance. The last thing he wanted was a bride dragooned into marriage by ambitious parents with an eye on his title. He couldn't afford another scandal. Didn't want another scandal for his family's sake.

He smashed a hand down onto the mantelpiece and was obliged to rescue a candlestick, narrowly avoiding getting burned. And he didn't want to get tricked into marriage by some chit who didn't care a jot for him as a man either. He wanted a good marriage like those of his parents and sisters.

* * *

There was only one customer in the Golden Cross's main room when Georgie went in and he was engaged in conversation with Mr Pleck. Georgie's tight shoulders relaxed. He was still the landlord then. Neither man looked her way. She found the alcove she was looking for and carefully parted the russet coloured drapes, letting them close softly behind her. She hefted her valise onto the window seat and sat with her back against it to ease the stiffness in her spine and shoulders from long hours on the road. All she had to do was to wait for Mrs Pleck to appear. It had seemed so simple when she managed to buy a ticket for the stagecoach. Now it felt rather too uncertain for comfort. The two male voices came nearer and she heard the slap of a tankard being deposited on a table.

"There you go, Sam. I wouldn't take too long to drink this or you will be stopping the night." Mr Pleck sounded tired.

There was a loud laugh. "No thanks with you cooking breakfast, now you've sent your cook home." The man's voice was pleasantly low pitched, possibly a tenant farmer? "Have you heard from Mrs Pleck?"

Georgie tensed.

"Yes. We had a message the other day. Her mother's in a bad way. I don't look to have her back before Christmas."

The rest of the conversation became a jumble of words. What was she to do with Mrs Pleck not being there? Mr Pleck was well enough but he wouldn't want to take her in with his wife away. He probably wouldn't even recognise her. They hadn't been here since the spring and Mrs Pleck had always looked after them. She stood up and pulled the curtain apart a few inches. The room appeared to tilt for a moment. She concentrated on her breathing until it steadied. She had no choice but to at least speak to Pleck.

She wanted to see his face before she approached him to judge his mood. A door opened and the noise of two sets of footsteps disappeared into the distance. She stepped out into an empty room. A quick glance up and down the corridor showed the place to be deserted, apart from Mr Pleck disappearing into the kitchen. The door to the coffee room stood open and she was drawn towards it. The room was tidier than the main one but not the polished perfection Mrs Pleck had always presented. The remains of a meal languished on the large table in the centre.

There was a window enclosure to match the one in the main room. Flakes of snow landed on the glass as softly as if they were lambswool and slid down. She closed the heavy, wine-coloured drapes behind her, leaving the barest gap to watch for the return of the occupant. There seemed an enormous quantity of food for one person but only one place was set. She could smell cheeses and pickles and her stomach rumbled so loudly that anyone entering the room would surely hear it.

No one came and there was no sign of Mr Pleck. Perhaps the room's occupant had cut short his meal worried about the snow? Hunger drove her forward and she made her way to the table. The food was plain but wholesome and she ate her fill. She was chewing on a piece of beef when footsteps sounded coming towards her. The tall figure of a dark haired, youngish man loomed in the doorway.

"What have we here? Don't run away my little brown

18

nymph."

His deep and well-modulated voice made her shiver. She gave up any idea of trying to escape and squared her shoulders before facing him. He had a presence that made her catch her breath. Some town buck on his way home for Christmas by the look of his expensive, drab coloured greatcoat. He was looking around the room as if searching for something. His scowl made her shrink back.

"Well? Have you nothing to say for yourself?"

She forced her gaze to his face and shook her head. His substantial figure blocked her path to the door and a quick glance around confirmed there was no other exit. He grabbed her wrist before she could dodge past him and she jumped at his touch. A surge of awareness ran through her. He wasn't exactly handsome and yet he was the most attractive man she had ever met. His eyes narrowed and the smell of alcohol hit her as he pulled her close.

"A rather drab bird for your game, are you not?" His voice sounded derisory.

He looked her up and down in a manner which scared her. He must think her a country doxy. Her breath came in shallow pants and she opened her mouth to scream. Before she could, he clamped strong fingers on either side of her chin and turned her face towards him. Dark blue eyes with a hint of grey considered her. He gave her a lopsided grin.

"Quite pretty though and you look clean."

He relaxed his grip and she tried to break free. He grabbed her arm and pulled her to him. She couldn't stop herself from relaxing into his arms. He held her close against his hard body, which was probably just as well as her legs didn't want to support her. Her lips parted as his tongue nudged at them. She could feel the tension in his already taut muscles tightening as he explored her mouth. She regained her senses with a shudder and made another attempt to pull away.

"Ah, you want payment first." He slapped a golden guinea down on the table.

A rush of heat exploded in her cheeks. She pushed past him and he staggered. He put out a hand to steady himself and she dodged towards the window seat. She couldn't afford to leave her valise. She hefted it ready to hit him but he lifted a pair of gloves from a side table and inspected them. She must have been so hungry not to notice them.

"Ah, my missing gloves. Too cold without them in this snow. Oh yes snow. I had better get off." He fumbled in his pocket and threw another guinea at her. "Here take this for the disappointment."

She relaxed as he turned on his heel and walked out. He was foxed and not the threat she'd first thought him. Her breathing eased. By tomorrow he would have forgotten about their encounter. A door banged in the distance. Good he had gone. She shuddered but picked up the guinea from the table and hunted for its fellow on the floor. She hated herself for doing it but she couldn't afford to be proud. Two guineas would keep her for a while.

She couldn't stop here now. He was so bosky he might come back and tell everyone she was a whore. But where to go? There was no help for it. She would have to go straight to the Armstrongs, even though taking in a runaway ward would put them in an awkward position with the church if it came out. They were too kindly a couple to turn her away and after her birthday Cousin Mary would have no legal hold over her. The vicarage at Benfort was several miles away. Would she make it through this snow in the dark?

She didn't dare draw attention to herself by ordering a carriage and Pleck might not agree to risk one of his animals in this weather in any case. She remembered a footpath through the fields. All she had to do was follow the hedges and turn by those big hay barns just before Benfort village. It was far shorter than by the road. It would be cold but she would have to manage. She had lost weight since she'd been forced to move in with the Huttons, when Aunty Anne died, even before her three days of starvation. Her rough woollen gown hung on her. Why not put more clothes on underneath her cloak? Then her valise would be lighter too.

There was no sign of Mr Pleck. Fingers fumbling in haste, she managed to don two more dresses and an extra pelisse and threw her thick travelling cloak over the top. She wrapped the last of the beef in a handkerchief and added a piece of bread. She stowed it in the bag and added a small flagon of what smelled like lemonade from a side table. Even with that the bag was lighter than before. She took a deep breath and made her way outside, stopping to listen for footsteps several times.

She found the path she was looking for and breathed easier. She had been brought up largely in the countryside and the velvety darkness didn't trouble her now she had the hedge to follow. Every time the moon peeped out through the scudding clouds the snowy fields sparkled as if sprinkled with diamonds. At any other time, she would have found the scene entrancing. The hoot of owls as she plodded past a spinney was strangely comforting and the trees offered some respite from the biting wind.

* * *

A couple of hours of trudging along, slipping and sliding through snow several inches thick in places, left her exhausted. The snow was falling so heavily now it would be easy to lose her way. She cried out with relief when she saw the outline of the barns looming in front of her. There was no question of going any farther tonight. She prised open the door of the largest barn and staggered inside. Relief swept through her when she saw the hay loft. She left her valise by the ladder and went back and shut the door, stamping her feet as she walked to regain some feeling in them. Her eyes gradually adjusted to the dim light as she found her way back to the ladder. It felt sound and she lifted her bag and climbed up, checking every rung as she went.

The cold was going to be her biggest problem. She pulled off her damp boots and burrowed into the hay. Her feet started to warm up, tucked underneath all her skirts, and the sweet smell of the hay was soothing. Oh goodness, would there be rats? It would be safest to eat her food now. When everything was eaten, she pushed the bag well away from her. Now all she had to do was survive until the morning.

Chapter Three

Max opened eyes that felt full of grit. He turned over onto his back. It was barely light and his head felt like it was being hit by hammers. He groaned as the door opened and his valet edged into the room.

"I'm sorry, my lord, but Hadley from the home farm is below. The snow is drifting several feet deep in places and he's lost some cattle. He wants to know if he can borrow men to try and find them."

Max lifted his head with difficulty. "We had better oblige him. He can't afford to lose cattle. Round up some of the younger footmen and tell them to meet me down at the stables in half an hour."

Jepson retreated. Max forced himself out of bed. Every step towards the window sent a pain shooting through his head. He pulled the heavy red drapes apart. Everywhere he looked was covered in a sparkling white coat. He closed his eyes against the brightness. He only had himself to blame for his current condition. He had better get out there and help. A tramp across the fields might clear his head. With Jepson's help, he shaved and dressed. The butler was hovering in the hallway as he went down to the breakfast room.

"Some hot coffee, if you please."

After two cups of coffee Max felt more human and managed to force down some ham and eggs. He strode down to the stables, taking care to keep to the main paths to avoid drifts of snow. The footmen were waiting for him. He divided them into four teams and added a groom to each one. Each team was sent to cover an area adjacent to the home farm. He collected his two wolfhounds and went to find Hadley.

The dogs ran around in circles and he let them have their heads until one of them fell into a drift. By the time he had helped to free the dog his head was spinning. He called them to heel and set off again. The obvious place to shelter the cattle was in the large barns that belonged to the estate. He reached the field they were in, near to the home farm, and sure enough Hadley was there. Hadley touched his cap and Max gave him a nod which he quickly regretted.

"Good of you to come, my lord. We've run out of space near the farm. If you're agreeable, the best place for any cattle we can find is in the hay barn."

"That would be best. I'll go and check it over."

Max summoned the dogs and made for the barn. He stopped short when he reached the door. The snow in front of it was shallower than elsewhere, as if it had been pulled open before it finished snowing. He whistled to the dogs. They ran towards him and milled around sniffing at the door. Was somebody in there? He wrenched the door open and sent the dogs in first. They scampered to the foot of the ladder leading to the hay loft and barked.

"Quiet." He leaned his head back with a groan and studied the top level of the barn. It looked like some of the hay had been disturbed.

The dogs stopped barking but stayed by the ladder whining.

"Come down now unless you want me to send for the magistrate," Max shouted, rubbing at his throbbing temples.

He jumped back as a valise landed at his feet.

A pair of boots appeared at the top of the ladder followed by a black clad rear. Max gaped as its owner hitched up her skirts and revealed a glimpse of shapely calves above well worn boots.

"Who the hell are you?" His voice rose.

The woman lost her footing and tumbled into his arms. The dogs barked enthusiastically and the girl, for she looked no more than that, gave a cry. Max dumped her on the ground in a flurry of skirts. He caught a glimpse of brown wool under the black. A memory came back to him of a tavern wench in brown.

"What are you up to, girl? You could have frozen to death in here. Pleck throw you out, did he?" Max grimaced. He would have to rescue her but if she talked about his advances of the evening before it would be a further stain on his reputation.

She tried to run. Max caught her by the shoulders and studied her. A pair of frightened grey eyes looked out of a heart shaped face. She was never a tavern wench. Max felt heat flood his cheeks as he remembered the stolen kiss and the guineas he had thrown at her. Lord, he must have been foxed. Foxed and angry but it was no excuse for insulting any woman like that. He felt her tremble. Was it the cold or fear?

"If I let go of you will you promise not to run away? I've got the devil of a headache this morning."

She stared at him for a moment and then nodded. He whistled at the dogs and they moved on either side of her. He released her shoulders.

"You have nothing to fear from me today. I'm sober now."

He managed what he hoped was a reassuring smile. "Who exactly are you?"

"I'd rather not say."

She was definitely not a tavern wench with that voice. "Then you leave me no choice. I'll have you taken up before the magistrate."

"Oh, please don't do that." She stood her ground but there was desperation in her eyes.

Her whole body started shaking and he put out a hand to steady her. She flinched and twisted away from him. The dogs started to growl. He called them to him. Nausea swept over him for a moment. He hadn't drunk so much since his youth.

"I can see you're running away from something." He laughed. "We have that much in common. I mean you no harm and if you tell me who you are and why you're here I'll do my best to help you."

He waited and watched a myriad of emotions flit across her face. Eventually she sighed and raised her eyes to his.

"I'll tell you my circumstances but I don't want to tell you my name."

"Hmm. You look sensible enough. We'll start with the explanation and then I'll decide about the magistrate. First I need to get you somewhere warm."

He picked up her bag and took her arm. She looked too exhausted to protest and started walking with him. They were barely outside the barn when she stumbled and he had to catch her before she fell.

"I'm sorry. My legs don't belong to me." She clung to his arm and stared at her feet, looking anxious.

He picked her up and threw her over his shoulder. She needed warmth and she needed it quickly. He secured her with one hand on her rather delectable derriere and picked up her bag with the other.

"Put me down." He felt her fists hitting his back.

"Quieten down, woman. I have to get you to the house before you freeze to death."

She stopped beating him and he sent the dogs on ahead. With luck someone would come to meet him. His head felt it every time he stumbled but he trudged onwards. She was so cold against his shoulder he feared for her safety. He pushed on with every muscle aching and his breath coming in painful gasps. There was no sound from the girl now and she was completely still. The side gate of the Hall's gardens came into view and he staggered towards it. Fortunately, it was open and wide enough to get them both through without too much manoeuvring.

Max whistled at the dogs, gambolling about in snow drifts up ahead, to go back to the stables. He missed his footing on the slippery path and fell backwards. It took all his strength to twist sideways in mid-air and lift her up so that she wasn't squashed underneath him. He landed on his back in a snow-drift with the girl sprawled across his chest. His sudden frisson of excitement was doused by difficulty drawing breath.

She managed to roll off him. "Are you alright?"

Her voice sounded shaky. Max nodded too winded to talk. The dogs came running, followed by two grooms. He sat up with an effort and forced in a few deep breaths.

"Right. You two carry this lady to the house for me. I'll follow with the bag."

The girl tried to protest.

"If you're not cold, I am. The sooner we reach the house the better." Max nodded to the two grooms.

* * *

Georgie's heart hammered as the two men made a seat for her with their arms. Such a public arrival was the last thing she wanted. At the same time, she was so cold she ached. They trudged through the snow and a huge building with honey coloured stone walls and tall chimneys came into view. Shapes under the thick white blanket in front of the house suggested extensive formal gardens, bounded by walls of the same stone breaking out of the snow in places. Who exactly was she being rescued by? The grooms went to take a side entrance but the man told them to go to the main one. This entailed a climb up an imposing flight of grey stone steps, protected by a curving balustrade at either side. Oh no, this must be Hargreaves Hall. The door was opened by a wooden-faced butler before they reached it.

Her rescuer dumped her valise in the hall and caught hold of her as the grooms put her down. "Steady on now." He held her up. "Barton, fetch the housekeeper."

Georgie felt the room swinging around her. She had no choice but to hang on to the man she suspected was the Marquess of Hargreaves himself. Despite the pain in her legs, as feeling started to return, she was intensely aware of him. He was tall and there was a vibrancy about him she had not come across before, but then she hadn't met many members of the aristocracy.

The butler returned with a rounded, red-cheeked woman who bristled when she saw her. Georgie was only too aware what the woman was thinking. She staggered and the man held her tighter. He had undone his greatcoat and her head was resting against his shirt. He wasn't wearing a cravat. She

28

buried her face into his chest. The smell of fresh masculine sweat mixed with a tang of oranges and lavender which met her was strangely appealing.

It wasn't enough to distract her for long. What was going to happen to her now? She shivered and tears trickled down her cheeks. As if sensing her distress he picked her up and carried her into a sitting room. He laid her down on a sofa and turned to the housekeeper, who had followed them in.

"She's been out all night in this freezing weather, Mrs Powell. Can you make up a bedroom and fetch a maid for her and some footmen to fill a hot bath. Oh, and make sure there's a good fire as well."

Georgie sat up and raised her head. She risked a look at the woman. Outrage was written in every last inch of her. She didn't feel strong enough to do battle and she closed her eyes for a moment. She opened them to see the Marquess, if that was who he was, disappear leaving her alone with the housekeeper. The woman looked her up and down.

"Well Miss, you're lucky we have so much snow or Lord Hargreaves would have had the constable out." She sniffed. "That's what a wanton like you deserves. I saw you throwing yourself onto His Lordship's chest. We had better get you warmed up but just you mind your step my girl. This is a respectable house."

Georgie tried to ignore the disapproval in her harsh voice. Her rescuer was the Marquess of Hargreaves then. She might be cold but that didn't stop a hot blush flooding her cheeks. The man had represented safety, nothing more, when she had drawn closer to him. She said nothing and allowed the housekeeper to lead her up a staircase. She was back in charge of her legs, although they ached, but it was a relief when they reached the top. To her surprise, the housekeeper stopped at a bedchamber in the guest quarters. Her mouth dropped open as she looked around a lovely room with pink damask hangings.

"This is too good for the likes of you, but the fire was already lit."

Oh dear, they must be expecting guests. Georgie decided to maintain her silence. It seemed the best defence. A young maid came in with a hot brick to heat the bed. She peeped at Georgie and smiled. The smile faded when the housekeeper turned round.

"Martha will look after you now, Miss." She walked out with another sniff.

Martha grinned at her. "Is it true, Miss?"

Georgie stared at her. "Is what true?"

Martha jumped up and down. "Ooh. It is isn't it? You have a lovely voice. I can't wait to see old Ma Powell's face when she finds out."

Georgie's shook her head in bewilderment. She was too tired to enquire further. There was a knock at the door and two footmen came in carrying a tin bath. They were quickly followed by several more with cans of hot water. Martha proved to be a willing and efficient helper. Georgie climbed into the hot bath and settled down. She had no idea what Martha was talking about but she was too content to care. This was her first bath since she had moved in with the Huttons. They had offered her a home when she was left alone in the world and then treated her far worse than anyone else of her acquaintance treated their lowliest maid.

The warmth gradually seeped into her bones. She didn't know what the future held but, for now, she was going to enjoy her good fortune. Every day here was a day a closer to her birthday. Her eyes began to droop and she asked Martha for a towel. She didn't want to fall asleep in the bath. Once she was dry Martha produced a pretty nightgown and robe.

"These belong to one of the master's sisters. His valet sent them for you."

Georgie's hands flew to her face. Was the Marquess trying to turn her into his mistress? He would hardly give her his sister's things in that case. Would he?

"Martha, I need my clothes, I must speak with the Marquess."

Martha giggled. "That would upset Mrs Powell. He's gone to bed and he said you need to rest too. Would you like something to eat now?"

Georgie glanced at the bed. It did look comfortable, food and then sleep sounded wonderful. "Yes please."

Martha pulled a small armchair up to the fire. "You sit here and get warm, Miss. I'll bring you a tray."

Georgie curled up in the chair and watched the flames dance in the fireplace. A fire in her bedroom was something else she hadn't had for a long time She demolished everything on the tray Martha brought up, including two cups of hot chocolate. She was being treated as an honoured guest. She sighed. Perhaps she could avoid facing the Marquess again until tomorrow. By then there would be just three days to go until she reached her majority. He said he meant her no harm but what did he mean by harm? There was no point worrying. She pulled back the covers on the bed and climbed in without even removing the robe. She still wasn't as warm as she could be but the flannel wrapped hot brick inside helped.

Chapter Four

Max turned on his back and stretched. He lifted his head and the room stayed steady. He sat up and lowered his legs to the floor. Everything was still. His pocket watch said five o'clock. Had he really slept for seven hours? That would explain why he felt so much better. Jepson tiptoed into the room as if he had been waiting in the dressing room listening for the sound of movement. Knowing Jepson, he probably had.

"Have Eliza and Nat made it through with their brood?"

"No, my lord, but the roads are clearing. I think we will see the Overtons tomorrow."

"Good. I'll get dressed now but nothing too formal. I'll have supper in the library I think."

He might as well enjoy a few hours peace. Jepson coughed.

"What is it Jepson?"

"Mrs Powell was wishful to know what to do with the young person you found, when she wakes up." He waited with his head slightly tilted, eyebrows raised.

Why was Jepson looking so curious? Max groaned as it all flooded back. His life was full of complications and it all came back to Selina Lovell. She was obsessed with her son's position as his heir. If her machinations hadn't driven him away from the house party early, he wouldn't have come across the girl. On the other hand, if he had stuck to his original plan, he might have struggled to get home at all this morning with the snow. The girl herself might not have survived. What was she running away from? He looked up at Jepson.

"Let her rest today, she must be exhausted. Tell Mrs Powell to have food sent up to her whenever she wakes up."

Jepson hovered, moving his weight from right to left and back again. What was the matter with the man?

"Was there anything else Jepson?"

"Er, we were wondering who exactly the young lady was, my lord."

Jepson couldn't meet his eyes. Good Lord. Did he think he would have some of his sister's clothes sent to his mistress in his own house? Max jumped up and Jepson took a step back.

"She refused to say who she was. So, I'm afraid I can't enlighten you."

Jepson finally met his gaze and Max read disbelief in his eyes. He opened his mouth to give him a pithy set down and then closed it again. Jepson was nothing if not loyal. He couldn't stop his jaw tightening but tried to keep his tone level.

"Out with it, Jepson. What do you know that I don't?"

Jepson coughed and stuttered. Max clenched his fists and waited.

"The thing is, my lord, one of Hadley's men saw her as she was carried up to the house." Jepson stopped and looked at the floor.

"You find me all ears. I take it there is some significance to that statement."

"The fellow said she arrived on the Canterbury stage my lord and...."

33

Max's patience finally snapped. He stalked across to the window and stared out into the gloom before heading back towards Jepson.

"Whilst that is an interesting piece of information, it doesn't help me provide you with her name."

"He also said he saw you kissing her in the Golden Cross." Jepson squared his shoulders. "I got this off the head footman and I thought you ought to know what was being said, my lord." Jepson kept his eyes lowered and fidgeted with the buttons on his waistcoat.

Max stared at him. "You did right. Is there more?"

Jepson hesitated. "There is talk that you were seen leaving the Golden Cross just before the stage arrived so Headley's man must have been mistaken."

Max groaned. "Or that he saw me kissing someone else."

"I'm afraid so but the maids are convinced he saw a different man. They have taken it into their heads that the girl is your betrothed, come to meet you after a lover's quarrel. The stage was late and you decided she had changed her mind and you went home."

"What do the rest of you think?"

"Mrs Powell thinks the girl is no better than she ought to be my lord."

"Hmm, and what about you?"

"I don't think she's a woman of easy virtue but I don't think for a minute you are betrothed to her my lord."

"No, I'm not, Jepson," Max stroked his chin and laughed, "although in my current circumstances that might not be such a bad idea." He ignored Jepson's look of enquiry.

"I was wishing I hadn't found her a minute ago, but I'm not sure she would have survived. The stage makes sense; she's

34

running away from something. She's well-spoken and I'm sure she is nothing more than a lady in trouble. I'd be grateful if you would try and quash talk of anything else."

"Of course, my lord."

Jepson nodded and disappeared into the dressing room.

* * *

Max pushed away the remains of his solitary meal.

The butler entered the library. "Would you like port now, my lord?"

"Not tonight, Barton. I'll have a pot of tea."

"Very good, my lord. I'll send a footman to clear the table."

Max moved over to the fire and relaxed into his favourite chair. Eliza would know what to do about the girl. He ought to marry her. With that sort of gossip about her, she would be ruined if her name came out. She was a taking little thing but there was probably an irate father somewhere. Had she been abandoned by a clandestine suitor? She didn't look old enough but then Sally's daughter, Cecilia, who had always been his favourite niece, had needed rescuing from that excuse for a soldier at barely seventeen.

Did he want a bride that young? A young bride would give him more chance of an heir though. Lord, what he wouldn't give for an heir. It would get Selina off his back let alone keeping the Hargreaves estates out of Bertie's clutches. He jumped up and strode around the bookshelves. This was cold hearted nonsense. Surely there was room for love somewhere? Still he had more chance of that with a filly with the gumption, however misguided, to try and help herself out of her difficulties than the girls his sisters paraded in front of

35

him.

He sighed. He'd always known he would have to do his duty someday but with his thirtieth birthday approaching and Selina's latest antics there was no hope that his sisters would leave him to find his own bride. Even Eliza had dropped hints. If he'd listened to Eliza he would never have gone to that house party. He hadn't expected Selina to be so brazen as to try and force him to invite her and Bertie for Christmas, in front of witnesses. He shuddered as he remembered the amusement on the sea of faces in the hall when he walked out of Simon's breakfast room.

He didn't mind his friends ragging him, but he did object to family matters being aired in front of some of the biggest gossips in the Ton. The episode would be fine fodder for the scandal sheets, especially after his precipitous departure from the house party. He had to marry sometime and he'd had enough of Selina's obsession with Bertie's chance of inheriting the title. After this he would only have to dance twice with a girl for speculation on an engagement to run wild. Perhaps his runaway would be the solution.

He stopped short. The poor little thing deserved better than having him tell her what to do. On the other hand, she would be lucky not to be compromised by this escapade and his duty as a gentleman was clear. Any irate father would be soothed by the prospect of a marquess as a son-in-law. He needed to talk to her as soon as he could.

* * *

It was dark when Georgie woke up. She sat up in bed and wondered what to do. Someone scratched at the door.

"Come in, Martha."

The door opened but instead of Martha the Marquess entered. Georgie gasped and pulled the covers up to her chin.

"What are you doing here? I thought you said you meant me no harm."

He shut the door and advanced towards the bed.

"I don't mean you any harm but I need to speak to you." He frowned and raised his voice slightly.

Georgie cried out. "You're not going to send for the magistrate, are you?"

The Marquess shook his head. "If you must know, I am the magistrate." He carried a chair over to the side of the bed and sat down. "We have quite a problem."

He studied her face.

Georgie bit her lip. She shivered at his gaze. "I suppose you want to know how I became stranded in your barn?"

"Yes, that would be helpful."

Georgie hesitated, he had a right to know but would he want to return her to the Huttons and wash his hands of her? "If I tell you I will be one and twenty on Christmas Eve would you mind if I leave the rest of the explanation until then?"

"As it happens, I would mind very much."

"I rather thought you might." Georgie sighed. "You have probably worked out that I am running away from my legal guardian. She was trying to force me to marry her son. When I resisted, she locked me up with nothing more than water."

"Ah. Was that why you stole what was left of my meal? You were taking quite a risk."

Georgie nodded. "I'd had nothing to eat for nearly four days, apart from some bread and cheese at one of the inns on the way here."

She looked up at him. He certainly seemed more awake than he had in the morning. She glanced away quickly, with a flush in her cheeks, at the admiration in his eyes.

"I see. What do you intend to do when you are one and twenty?"

"Collect my inheritance and travel up to Yorkshire to live with my old governess."

Instead of answering, the Marquess stood up and paced the room. Georgie watched him anxiously. At least he hadn't immediately insisted on returning her. Her head started to thump with the tension of waiting for his answer. She grunted with frustration and he turned and walked back towards her.

"I have a proposition to make you."

Georgie's cheeks became unbearably hot. She started forwards forgetting to hang on to the bedcover. His eyes dropped to her bosom which added to her confusion. He shifted his gaze and sank into the chair beside her.

"No, no, no. I don't mean what you think I do."

"What do you mean then?"

"I'm offering you my hand in marriage."

Georgie's mouth fell open. "But you don't even know me. If you're worried that you have compromised me it was entirely my own fault." She studied his face. Was he being chivalrous or was it a trick to get her into his bed?

The Marquess laughed, but he didn't look amused. "I have compromised you and I need to put it right."

Oh dear, he sounded angry. Did he think this was an elaborate plot to ensnare him? "I am not the sort of minx who sets out to trap a man into marriage. I'll be quite happy to buy a cottage and live quietly with my governess as companion."

"I have my own reputation to consider, Madam." He glared

at her. "The truth is there was a witness to my outrageous attempt to kiss you at the Golden Cross. It was completely out of character I assure you. You would oblige me by accepting my offer of marriage, thereby saving your own reputation as well as mine."

"You would marry a woman you don't even know simply to keep up appearances?"

His eyes narrowed as he looked at her. "Is there anything about your background that would make you an impossible match for me?"

Georgie looked away. He was considering her as if she was a mare to breed to his best stallion.

He slapped a hand on his thigh and grimaced. "Am I to take your silence to mean you would not be a suitable bride?"

"No, it's not that."

His eyes narrowed as he studied her. "Have you been lying to me and there's a suitor waiting for you somewhere?"

"I'm not in the habit of lying." Georgie's voice deepened. "There is no suitor except for the obnoxious cousin I'm running away from!"

The Marquess ran a hand through his hair. "I'm tired of these games. Just tell me who you are."

"If you must know had I been born a boy I would have the title of Baron now. I'm a suitable, although not brilliant, match for a marquess but I don't want to marry you or anyone else."

"Look, I'm not keen on the idea of marrying someone I don't know either. The fact is I need a wife. I too have some unpleasant relatives and it's about time I set up my nursery, unless I want Cousin Cuthbert running tame. Will you marry me?"

He sounded exasperated. Hardly the devoted suitor of her

dreams. Georgie studied him. She opened her mouth to refuse and then closed it again. Was it such a bad idea? He was tall, with a passably handsome face and an athletic build. He was older than her but not by many years. Besides which he had probably saved her life and he was very keen to find a wife. He seemed quite high in the instep at times so perhaps the housekeeper taking her for his doxy had upset him. She was startled when he laughed.

"Touché. Now you have studied my points what do you say? I should have realised you were an innocent yesterday but I convinced myself that you responded to me when I kissed you. It's a poor excuse but I would never have kissed you like that had I been sober and not in an appalling fury about something." His expression softened. "For my part I find you quite delightful,"

His eyes dropped to her bosom and she remembered the bed covers and drew them up under her chin. He smiled and met her gaze.

She looked away. "I'm surprised you remember anything from yesterday."

He laughed. "The Lovells have notoriously hard heads, but mine hasn't been given such a test since my Oxford days. The more I think about it, the better this idea seems. You need a place of safety and I need a wife. Many a marriage has prospered with nothing more than a mutual admiration."

"You said something about us both being runaways earlier. Was that why you got so foxed yesterday?"

"I see I am going to have to tell you the whole. Cuthbert Lovell is a charming wastrel. His mother, my aunt Lady Selina Lovell, managed to get an invitation to a house party I was at. She set about trying to persuade me into inviting her and

Cuthbert here for Christmas. I suspect Cuthbert is in dire need of funds. When she started making remarks in front of other people to try and force my hand that was too much. I made my excuses to my host and left."

The Marquess jumped to his feet and paced the room. "I was so angry at being put in that position. The truth is, of course, that as my heir I should be taking an interest in Cuthbert but he would run through even the Lovell fortune inside a year or two. My sisters have been urging me to find a wife for years. After this latest start from Madam Lovell they will be determined to push me to the altar."

"So you've decided to pick the first eligible female who comes along?"

"I'm offering you the protection of my hand because I have compromised you as a result of my fit of temper. I am a man of honour. I am pointing out to you the advantages to myself." He smiled at her.

Georgie shivered. When he smiled passably handsome was definitely an understatement.

"Are you still cold?"

She shook her head.

"There is nothing to be afraid of. I would treat you well. I would also keep you safe. Can you be certain that reaching your majority will be enough to keep you out of your cousin's clutches?"

"Surely once I have contacted the lawyers after my birthday they will look to my safety?"

"They may act with exemplary care but not all lawyers are honest. What do you know about the ones handling your inheritance?"

"Nothing – but they have been the family lawyers forever as

far as I know."

"Anyone unscrupulous enough to lock you up without food is not likely to give up easily. Can you be sure that these lawyers would resist an offer of payment out of your funds if they helped force you into marriage?"

"Oh, I hadn't thought of that."

Georgie's mind whirred. She had overheard Cousin Mary's lawyer friend telling her about some awful things he had done with great pride. How safe would she be from someone who happily devised ways to defraud his hapless clients? Her biggest fear was that his team of investigators would find her whereabouts. Perhaps reaching her majority wouldn't be enough to save her if they did. She knew Cousin Mary to be ruthless after all.

The Marquess took her hand and rubbed her palm with his thumb. "Am I such a bad bargain you would rather take your chance with them?"

Georgie felt a pulse beat in her neck as heat rushed to her cheeks. "It's not that. It's all so sudden I don't know what to think."

The Marquess smiled at her. "If I add that I have seven sisters and a lively dread of what their matchmaking might entail won't you take pity on me?"

Georgie gasped. "Seven sisters!"

His smile widened into a grin. "I'm afraid so."

A marriage without love went against everything her family had taught her. Perhaps love might grow afterwards and she was so tired of being frightened. Only marriage would protect her from Cousin Mary and her schemes. It would be wonderful to feel safe and the Marquess did make her feel safe in a strange way, despite the manner of their first meeting. Georgie took a deep breath. She might regret it but why not?

"Yes. I will marry you." There she had said it. Her heart skipped a beat. Only time would tell if she was right to trust her instinct that he was a decent man.

"Thank you. I promise I'll treat you with respect. One of my sisters is expected with her family as soon as the roads are passable. They were due today. We need to get our story straight before she arrives." He sank onto the seat.

"Why can't we tell her the truth?"

"It's complicated." He paused. "There is more than one version of the story in circulation."

"Oh. I think I understand what Martha was talking about now."

"If you mean the version that you are my betrothed and I was waiting to collect you from the coach but missed you because of the delay then yes." He sighed. "The truth is I would hate my sister to find out how I insulted you." He looked at the floor but he couldn't hide the flush staining his cheeks.

"I still think we should tell her everything." Georgie said softly.

"Perhaps. You haven't told me your name." He grinned at her. "Now we are betrothed it might be useful for me to know."

"I'm Georgina Sherborne. I lived in Benfort with my aunt until she died last spring."

"If you've been living less than five miles away why haven't we met before?"

"We hardly move in the same circles, do we? Besides, when my aunt died, I was sent to live in London with my Hutton cousins."

"The ones you ran away from."

Georgie nodded. Her head was throbbing and she was hungry

again. The Marquess sat staring at the floor and she lay back against the pillows. He jerked upright.

"I wonder if you were recognised. The story of an engagement between us wouldn't seem so fantastical then. Who were your aunt and uncle?"

"Mr and Mrs Weston, my uncle was a clergyman."

The Marquess ran a hand through his hair. "Eliza might have known your aunt. The Overtons live the other side of Benfort."

"That wouldn't be Lady Eliza Overton would it?"

"Yes. She's my youngest sister."

Georgie smiled. "I've met her two or three times."

"Ah that makes things a lot simpler." He grimaced. "You're right though, we will have to tell Eliza the whole since she knows you. We should be able to brush off any scandal with her help." He looked relieved.

Georgie stiffened. He seemed a lot more worried about his reputation than hers. Was she doing the right thing?

"You look tired. I'll send Martha up with a tray. We'll talk again in the morning."

He stood up and bowed to her before turning on his heel and marching out.

* * *

Georgie watched him go. Had she really just agreed to marry him? There was so much she didn't know about him. Why had he had a meal at the inn when he lived nearby? Although he couldn't have been expected at home that evening and having met Mrs Powell that was understandable perhaps. There was a knock at the door and Martha entered.

"Miss, did you say yes?" Martha stared at her with eyes too big for her face.

There was no going back now. She smiled at the girl. "Yes, I did."

Martha carefully laid the tray she was carrying on the chair. Her face was alight with mischief. "That will upset old Ma Powell."

Georgie tried not to smile. She sympathised with Martha but Mrs Powell had some justification for her attitude. She would reserve judgement on the woman and it wouldn't do to encourage Martha to be disrespectful.

"Thank you, Martha," she said, in what she hoped was a quelling voice.

The maid bobbed a curtsey. "It's no trouble, miss." She ran out of the room before Georgie could say more.

* * *

The next morning Georgie came to with a start to find Martha opening the drapes. Light streamed through the window and she pulled herself into a sitting position.

"What time is it?"

"Nearly eleven o'clock, Miss. I'll go and fetch your clothes."

How had she managed that after sleeping for most of the day yesterday? She sipped at the hot chocolate Martha had left for her. Martha returned with the best of her dresses. The brown velvet was old but at least it was good quality.

"I've washed and pressed this for you, miss."

"Thank you. I'm sorry for the extra work I've caused you."

Martha grinned. "I'm not. I'm from the village and when the Overtons didn't arrive yesterday old Ma Powell would have

45

sent me home on half pay."

Georgie drew in a sharp breath. That wasn't very good. Really what did she know about the Marquess? Was he simply careless or had he taken on a dragon like Mrs Powell to save him money? She pursed her lips. She had the impression he liked to think himself dutiful but especially when it coincided with his own interests. Perhaps that wasn't entirely fair. At least in part he had been trying to put her at her ease.

"I think I will have breakfast in bed please, Martha."

"Yes, Miss." Martha skipped out.

She was a coward but she needed a few more hours to herself to adjust to her situation. Lady Overton had been kind and gracious in the past but would she be influenced by Mrs Powell's attitude? The Marquess looked the sort of man who generally got his way but it would be uncomfortable if Lady Overton took a dislike to her. She leaned back against her pillows.

If she had asked him to help her obtain her inheritance and keep her safe until she was established, without marrying him, he would have done so she felt sure. He was a proud man and now she had agreed to his proposal he would probably be too angry to help her if she changed her mind. The truth was he fascinated her and part of her wanted to marry him. The wanton part that couldn't forget his kiss and his firm body pressed against hers.

The sensible part had serious doubts. A shudder ran through her. He would keep her safe if only to protect any future heirs. He couldn't have made it any plainer that his main interest was to get himself an heir. How would he act if she failed to provide at least one son? She shivered. What had she done?

46

Chapter Five

Max left the dogs at the stables and walked up to the house. The snow had melted in places and he stopped to inspect the drive. Jepson was right. The roads would be passable today. A coach followed by another turned in past the gate house and excited shouts reached him.

"Uncle Max, Uncle Max. We're here."

Max smiled and waved at his tussle headed nephew, hanging out of the window of the first coach. "I can see that, brat."

He strode after them and arrived at the steps in time to lift Master Overton down from the coach and swing him onto his shoulders.

"You've grown again, Peter. I won't be able to do this for much longer."

He ran up the steps with a giggling Peter holding onto his head.

"Faster, faster, Uncle Max."

Max trotted through the door, held open by one of the footmen. He untangled Peter's arms and threw him up in the air. He caught the boy and lowered him to the ground only for Eliza to throw her arms around him.

"We're so glad to be here, Max. Peter would have been inconsolable if we hadn't been able to spend Christmas with you."

"We thought we would be here before you." She pushed him at arm's length. "You look strained. How was the house party?"

Max's smile turned to a grimace. "Selina was there and she made a complete pest of herself. I'll tell you about it when you're settled."

Eliza studied him. "I'll see Peter and Judith to the nursery and come straight down."

Peter pulled at his mother's skirts. "I don't want to go to the nursery. It's for babies. Now I'm a man, in proper breeches, I want to stay with Uncle Max."

Max ruffled his hair. "Judith needs you to keep her company. Do as your mother says and I'll come and fetch you down later."

Peter stamped his foot but stopped when Max caught his eye. He pulled a face, "Awight, Uncle Max."

Eliza led Peter away, throwing Max a grateful look. Max took Nat with him to the library. He poured them both a brandy and handed Nat the larger of the two.

"Thanks, Max. I need this. You're not drinking much."

"I had far too much the other day. I'm happy with the result of that though."

He took a sip. Yes, he was happy with the result. Miss Georgina Sherborne was the answer to his problems. She was too thin but lovely. A memory of her sitting up in bed, wearing that revealingly overlarge nightgown, had a painful effect on him. He looked up to see Nat watching him over the rim of his glass.

"I had better wait until Eliza is here before I tell you or I'll never hear the end of it."

"I'm intrigued. I'm glad the roads cleared enough for us to get through."

Max walked to the window and stared at the sullen sky. "I hope we don't have any more snow."

He wandered around the room. It might be best to set off for Canterbury as soon as he'd told Eliza. A quiet family wedding on Miss Sherborne's birthday would be best. Eliza came in and shut the door behind her. She almost ran across the room to sit by her husband. Max flopped down in the chair opposite them.

"I think Bertie must be well and truly in the suds. Selina wouldn't leave me alone at the Pryce's. When I refused to have her and Bertie here over Christmas she made such a fuss, at luncheon the day before yesterday, I made my excuses and came home. Several people outside the breakfast room had obviously been listening to it all."

Max could see Eliza bouncing in her seat with impatience. Oh Lord, had she heard about Miss Sherborne from one of the maids? "I wasn't the only runaway."

He saw Eliza shoot a glance at Nat, who had lost his usual relaxed air and was sitting up straight studying him.

"I rescued a young woman who was fleeing a plot to marry her off to her guardian's son and I've asked her to marry me."

Eliza jumped up, looking anxious. "But Max what do you know about her." Her voice shook.

Max smiled. "She'll be one and twenty on Christmas Eve and she's from near here, although I hadn't come across her before. She's met you."

Eliza flopped back in her seat. "She has? Oh, you wretch, tell me her name!"

"Miss Georgina Sherborne and she lived with her aunt, Mrs

Weston, at Benfort."

Eliza sat thinking and Max curled his hands into fists as he watched her. He was surprised how much Eliza's answer mattered to him. At last she spoke.

"Oh yes, I remember them. Mrs Weston is," she looked up at Max, "I presume that should be was, a quiet but interesting woman."

"Mrs Weston died last spring rather suddenly and Miss Sherborne was placed with some cousins called Hutton." He uncurled his fists.

"Miss Sherborne seemed prettily behaved. I believe the Westons brought her up from when she was quite young."

"Do you know anything else about them?"

"Not really. I do know the Westons were well thought of in church circles."

Some of the tension left his shoulders. "There doesn't seem anything to stand in our way then." For once Eliza seemed lost for words. She turned to look at Nat.

Nat considered for a moment. "Except the fact that you hadn't even met her before yesterday, was it?"

Max took a turn about the room. He stopped at the fireplace and stood facing them with the warmth at his back. "Think of the advantages. She's young and attractive and she is prepared to accept my offer to ensure her safety."

"But Max how do you know she is telling the truth?" Eliza said. "She could have taken herself off in a temper over something. Worse she could have set all this up to trap you."

Max glared at his sister. "I thought you'd be pleased. My marriage will keep Selina at bay and you've all been on at me for years to find a bride."

Nat held up a hand. "Calm yourself, Max. Eliza, I think

it would be difficult for the girl to have set herself up to be rescued by Max. I grant you we only have her word about her reasons for running away from her guardian."

Max ran a hand through his hair. "I was hoping to leave her in your charge and ride in to Canterbury for a marriage licence."

Eliza's mouth gaped open. "A marriage licence? When do you intend the wedding to be?"

"Christmas Eve, her birthday. A quiet family wedding at the church in Hargreaves."

"Why so soon?"

"I got completely disguised at the Golden Cross on my way home. I was so angry with Selina. Miss Sherborne had arrived on the stage from London. I took her for a tavern wench and kissed her. We were seen. I won't have the girl ruined."

* * *

Georgie heard what sounded like two coaches pull up in front of the house. She climbed out of bed and ran to the window. The Marquess scooped a small boy out of the first coach and ran up the steps with him on his shoulders. That must be his nephew. They disappeared into the house. He liked children, that was a point in his favour. A tall man and a dark-haired lady, who she recognised as Lady Eliza Overton, followed them up the steps.

Georgie came away from the window. Her stomach clenched. She was betrothed to the Marquess of Hargreaves and she didn't even know his first name, what would his sister make of it. Her palms felt damp and yet she shivered. Was she doing the right thing? There was the awful Mrs Powell to worry about as well. If she hadn't been attracted to the Marquess her answer would have been easy. She could live quietly in Yorkshire and not worry about a ruined reputation. Wasn't that what Aunty Anne would have expected her to do?

She sighed. It was too late now she had given him her word. She laughed. It wouldn't be much fun for him having seven sisters all matchmaking but had he thought this through? She flopped down on the bed. Wouldn't his sisters want him to make a brilliant match? She rubbed her temples and rang for Martha. If Lady Overton appeared upset, she would offer him the chance to withdraw in exchange for a promise to keep her safe from the Huttons.

Martha bounced in. "I can't wait to dress you, Miss. Will you let me be your maid? My mother has taught me how to look after clothes and I've managed to spend time with some of the lady's maids learning about hair, whenever the family have come to stay." She scowled. "That is before Mrs Powell became housekeeper."

Georgie sighed at the beseeching glance Martha gave her. Presumably she would be able to choose her own maid if she married the Marquess, but she had better make sure Martha was up to it first.

"I can't promise anything. Let's see how things go."

Martha's face glowed. "Thank you, Miss. I won't let you down. Ma will be so pleased if you take me on."

Martha chattered away as she helped Georgie dress. She didn't seem to require answers so Georgie let her have her head. Martha worked surprisingly quickly and she was soon in the dress.

"There you are, Miss. The gown is a bit loose but it's a good cut. Now for your hair."

It wasn't long before Martha stood back, satisfied. "I think I've remembered that style well."

Georgie stared at her reflection in the looking glass. Martha had clever fingers and had worked wonders with her heavy chestnut brown hair. The velvet gown was a link with her previous life in Benfort. She was as ready as she would ever be to face Lady Overton. She dismissed Martha and made her way downstairs.

In the hallway, doubt hit her in the chest. She forced a deep breath into frozen lungs. She should have waited to be summonsed. No! She held her head high and walked towards voices coming from what was probably the library.

"But Max, if you marry that quickly you won't have time to become acquainted with her?"

That must be Lady Overton. She should announce her presence but she felt compelled to listen.

"It's my duty to marry her and it suits me very well to arrange the wedding as quickly as possible. That way Selina won't have time to stir up any trouble."

"I know what you mean but, even if the main part of Miss Sherborne's story is true, how can you be sure she didn't recognise you and set out to trap you?"

Georgie stood, petrified, as the door opened and the Marquess marched out. He was looking behind him.

"Enough, Eliza. My mind is made up."

She wasn't fast enough to sidestep him and they collided with a thump. The heat of mortification suffused her cheeks. A pair of strong arms embraced her as she nearly fell. Her legs trembled and she was forced to stay in his arms. She glanced up at him and was surprised to see a smile spread over his face.

"I seem to spend a lot of time keeping you on your feet."

Her pulse raced and her cheeks felt hotter than ever. His smile was surprisingly sympathetic. Gently, he put her from him and threaded her arm through his.

"There is something I need to ask you. Eliza thinks I'm quite mad."

* * *

That was unfortunate timing. He didn't want her crying off. Max led her away from the library and into an elegant sitting room, decorated in shades of rose, cream and gold.

"This was my mother's room. Won't you take a seat?" He was tempted to sit down next to her on the pink brocade sofa but she looked so stricken he draped himself over a chair opposite. "She loved warm summery colours. What do you think of it?"

She scanned the room. "It's very welcoming."

Good, she had relaxed a little. "I'm of a mind to hold the wedding ceremony on your birthday."

"But what about the banns?"

Good, she hadn't changed her mind. Perhaps she hadn't heard anything.

"If I leave you now, I should be able to get Canterbury and back in time."

"A special licence?"

Even better, she was intelligent. He had never understood the fashion for silly women.

"A bishop's licence is all we need if we name the church. Once we are married your worries about your cousin will be over." He smiled at her.

"But do you want to go ahead if your sister disapproves?"

Max hesitated. Miss Sherborne must have heard at least some of what Eliza had said. "She doesn't disapprove of us marrying but she was hoping for a big family wedding."

He moved across to sit by her and took one of her hands in both of his. "You do trust me, don't you? I will have settlements drawn up for you but that will have to be after Christmas."

Her hand moved in his and a frown wrinkled her brow. "Why the haste?" She sounded a little uneasy.

"Precisely because it avoids a big family wedding. Apart from making you feel safe of course."

"Are you sure you want to go ahead, my lord?"

He tried for a jovial tone. "I'm very sure my little brown nymph. If you had met some of my other sisters you would want to avoid a family event. There is Selina to reckon with as well. She might try and cause trouble if she knew about our wedding in advance."

* * *

He gave her a smile which almost robbed her of breath. He had such a strong effect on her but she must be mad to give herself to him with so little knowledge of his character.

"So you see, my dear, you would be rescuing me twice by agreeing."

Georgie nodded and looked at the floor. It seemed his mind was made up and she couldn't in all conscience back out now if he was content to go ahead.

She glanced up at him and took a deep breath. "Very well, my lord, if that is your wish."

He took her hand and raised it to his lips. A shudder ran

through her and she felt her cheeks redden. Would he think her a wanton if he knew the effect he had on her?

"Come, let's join the others in the library." He helped her to her feet and threaded her arm through his.

The walk to the library seemed far too short. Lady Overton didn't sound pleased about their hasty marriage. Did she think she had set out to trap her brother?

The Marquess stopped before they reached the library door. "Now we are betrothed you must call me Max."

"My family have always called me Georgie."

"Then I'll call you that." His words, spoken near to her ear, were almost a caress. Georgie felt a shiver of excitement run through her.

Max led her through the door and settled her in a chair in front of a roaring fire. He stood next to her and turned to face the other two.

"Georgina has agreed to a wedding on her birthday, if I can obtain a licence in time."

Georgie forced herself to look at the Overtons. Lord Overton seemed unperturbed and Lady Overton surprised her by smiling.

"You will soon learn that when Max has made up his mind it's difficult to move him! Are you sure you are quite happy with such haste?"

"I don't mind if you would rather postpone it. Whatever you think is best."

"The timing is between you and Max. I merely wondered if there was anyone you would like to invite to share it with you."

"All the people I cared about are dead now. There is my governess who lives in Yorkshire but a visit to her later, perhaps in the spring, should suffice."

She felt Max's hand squeeze her shoulder. "A trip to York-shire when the weather improves would be excellent. I have an estate up there which is overdue a visit."

"Thank you, my lord." She risked a glance up at him to see him scowling.

"You need to call me Max, my love."

She forced a smile and nodded. "Of course, Max." Why was he pretending they were a love match when his sister knew the truth? "It will take me a while to become accustomed ..." She trailed off. It would be more than calling him Max she would need time to adjust to.

He dropped a kiss on her forehead. "I expect it will. Now if you will excuse me, I'll set off for Canterbury. I'll leave you in Eliza's capable hands."

He bowed low to the room in general and was off. Georgie suppressed a surge of panic. At least he represented safety. She watched his retreating form until he was out of the room.

Lord Overton coughed and stood up. "If you will excuse me, ladies."

Georgie looked at the floor. What must Lady Overton be thinking of her? She glanced up. Her expression seemed more one of sympathy than anything else.

"Are you alright, my dear?"

"I think so, my lady, although the last few days have been difficult and I feel as if I am in something of a dream." Her cheeks reddened. "Not that I'm blaming His Lordship, Max that is. I'm not sure how I would have made it to the vicarage at Benfort. I knew it would be cold in the barn overnight but not that cold."

"Why did you not stay at the Golden Cross?"

"I was going to ask Mrs Pleck to shelter me until my birthday but then I overheard she was away." Georgie lowered her eyes and hoped her cheeks weren't too red at the memory of Max's kiss. "We always hired a carriage from them when we went travelling. We would have a meal there when we came back and she always waited on us herself. I didn't think Mr Pleck would remember me so I decided to try my luck at the vicarage straight away. The Armstrongs were friends of ours and I had intended to enlist their help once I was one and twenty."

It was only partly true. Max's kiss and his assumption about her had made it too dangerous to approach Mr Pleck. Her hands flew to her cheeks. What would Lady Overton think if she knew about her response to his kiss? He had been kind about it but Mrs Powell's accusation stung. She felt like a wanton. A hand came to rest on her shoulder.

"My dear, I didn't mean to upset you. You must have had a terrible ordeal. It was unfortunate Mrs Pleck was away."

Two dark blue eyes regarded her. Brother and sister were very alike. She took a deep breath. "Did Max tell you he saw me in the inn the day before he rescued me? I didn't know who he was. I hope you will believe me when I say I'm not the sort of female to set out to trap any man."

It was Lady Overton's turn to blush. "I was afraid you might have heard that. I'm sorry, but if you knew how many traps have been set to try and snare Max you would understand why I had that thought."

Georgie studied her. She seemed inclined to be friendly. "He told me about his problems with his heir's mother and his seven sisters pushing him towards the altar."

Lady Overton smiled. "So, you took pity on him and agreed to a marriage?"

"That did play a part. That and the way he made me feel safe."

Georgie felt suddenly weak and a sob escaped her. She found herself gathered into a perfumed embrace.

"My dear, I hope you will forgive me for doubting you. I can see, now that I have spoken with you, that Max knows what he is about rather more than I gave him credit for. Come, I'll send for some tea and then we had better look through my clothes to see what can be altered to fit you."

Lady Overton rang for a maid and Georgie tried to compose herself. It was silly but she felt bereft without Max to protect her. Did Lady Overton believe her? Even if she didn't, there was nothing she could do. Was she making the best of the situation by befriending her? She drank her tea in silence before handing back the cup.

"That's better. There is nothing like tea to fortify one I find. I'm sorry we have started off badly together, Miss Sherborne. I do hope we can still be friends?"

Lady Overton smiled a little tremulously at Georgie. Unless she was an extremely good actress, her offer of friendship was genuine. Georgie smiled back. "I would like that. It's kind of you to offer me some of your clothes but I'm still in mourning for my aunt."

"Of course, I should have offered you my condolences. When did she die?"

Georgie sighed. "At the end of May."

"I imagine you saw her almost as a parent so I can understand you wanting to wear dark colours for a bit longer although it would be perfectly acceptable for you to wear something paler now."

"I suppose you're right."

"Forgive me for asking but is the gown you're wearing one of your own?"

"Yes, this is the only gown from my former life I managed to bring with me."

"I've seen you in it haven't I? You've lost an awful lot of weight."

Georgie sighed. "There was never enough to eat at the Hutton's, although they seemed to manage. They starved me for three days before I escaped."

"Max said something of the sort. You have had a bad time. Come, let's see what we can find for you."

Georgie allowed herself to be led up to Lady Overton's dressing room. "I hope I wasn't given the room meant for you Lady Overton."

"No, you weren't. Another sister and her family were due to join us but only if the weather was kind. They live farther away so I don't think we will see them. I expect you have been given one of their bedchambers."

A maid appeared. "Ah Betty, how many dresses did you pack for me? Is there anything that could be altered to fit Miss Sherborne without too much difficulty?"

Betty held her head on one side and screwed up her face. Her features relaxed as she smiled.

"Yes, my lady. Are you thinking of something for Miss Sherborne to be married in?"

Lady Overton nodded.

"I'm sure I packed your cream satin evening dress. That might be suitable."

Betty rushed off to fetch the dress.

"Since we are about to become sisters, Miss Sherborne, would you oblige me by calling me Eliza?"

She felt a flush stain her cheeks. "Of course, if you wish. My family always called me Georgie."

"Georgie it is then."

Betty came back with a glorious satin gown draped over her arm. Georgie gasped. She had never worn anything half as fashionable. The gown was a vision of fine primrose muslin over a cream satin body, trimmed with blond lace around the hem.

Eliza smiled. "We don't have much time Betty. Would you be able to alter it to fit by Christmas Eve?"

"Yes, my lady. I could probably do another one too."

Eliza waved away Georgie's protest. "Two would be excellent if you can manage it Betty. See if one of Max's maids can help. A darker colour for the second one as Miss Sherborne isn't quite out of mourning for her aunt, which is why we are having a quiet family wedding."

"Leave it to me, my lady. I shall enjoy doing it." Betty rushed out.

"You will want something to wear on Christmas day Georgie. When the weather is better Max will have to take you to Town to replenish your wardrobe."

Georgie shuddered. "I've had enough of London after living there with the Huttons for months."

"You will have nothing to fear with Max by your side."

"I hope not. At least Cousin Mary won't be able to marry me to her son, Algernon." She shuddered.

Eliza took her hand. "Did he scare you?"

"Not him so much, except the time when I ran away. He was foxed and I'm sure he was even more afraid of his mother than I was. He must have been to go along with her plan to make me marry him. The maids all thought he was chasing a young widow from Gracechurch Street."

"I don't see that your Cousin Mary could harm you once you're of age, especially when you're married."

"I know, but there is something sinister about her lawyer friend." Georgie shrugged. "As you say, I'll be safe with Max. I might even enjoy London."

Georgie tried to imagine what it would be like to spend time in the capital with Max. Would he become bored with her? Did he have a mistress in London? Rumours of him being rather wild had reached as far as Benfort. What had she done agreeing to this? Sought safety over all else that's what she had done. She refused to be downhearted. She would be a good wife to him and perhaps it would work out well? Unless, of course, she didn't bear him a son. She pushed the thought to the back of her mind as Betty returned with Martha in tow.

"Now, Miss, we had better measure up and see how much we need to take these in."

Georgie stared as she saw the second gown being carried by Martha. It had a green satin body with an over-dress of a deeper green crape. The style was simple with almost a Grecian look to it but the overall effect was stunning. She was entering a world of which she knew very little.

Chapter Six

Max strode up to his bedchamber and rang the bell for Jepson. He walked around the room as he waited for him to arrive. Where was the man? He rolled his shoulders to try and remove the knot of tension that was settling at the back of his neck.

At last Jepson appeared, looking flustered. "I'm sorry, my lord. I wasn't expecting you to need me at this time of day."

"Of course not. Something urgent has cropped up and I need to go into Canterbury. I will stay overnight."

"I'll pack your bag as quickly as I can, my lord."

Max made a few suggestions as Jepson selected clothes and packed them into his valise. He tried not to sigh as Jepson worked meticulously. This couldn't be rushed if he wanted his clothes to arrive in Canterbury without too many creases. Eventually, Jepson declared himself finished.

"Thank you. You've worked wonders. Have one of the footmen take it down to the stables to be loaded onto my curricle."

"You don't want me to accompany you, my lord? I always keep a travel bag packed for myself."

"No. I'll only be away for the one night and I think you deserve a holiday."

Jepson was silent as he helped him to change into travelling clothes. It would be quicker with only his tiger up behind. He would also have more privacy. His mind strayed to the purchases he intended to make for Georgie. She was a taking little thing and it wouldn't do to expect her to wear someone else's nightgown on her wedding night. Max felt his pulse quicken at the thought of Georgie in a frivolous nightgown.

Then again, he didn't want to frighten her. Something frivolous but not too revealing would be best. He ought to buy her a bridal gift as well. A string of pearls perhaps? He would have to be careful to shop where he was less likely to be recognised. Damn he should have asked Eliza. Jepson helped him into his greatcoat and he wrenched his mind back to the journey he had to make before he could shop for presents. The sooner he was there the better it would suit him but a few more minutes wouldn't hurt. He tore down the staircase and stopped a passing footman.

"Do you know where Lady Overton is?"

"I believe she's in the library, my lord."

He found Eliza selecting a novel. Nat was reading in an armchair in front of the fire. They looked so comfortable together that Max caught his breath. Would his marriage work out as well as theirs?

"Can you write down some names of good, but lesser known shops in Canterbury? A decent jeweller too."

Eliza sighed and walked over to a writing desk set by a window. "I can see there is no point asking you to slow down Max."

"It's better this way and Georgie will feel safer once we're married."

"There is that to it, I suppose." Eliza blotted her list and handed it to him.

Max tucked it into a pocket and kissed her cheek. "It will all work out, you'll see. I'll be off."

Nat rose from his chair. "I'll walk with you to the stables if you don't mind, Max,"

He said nothing more until they were away from the house.

"Eliza has remembered seeing Miss Sherborne in the gown she's wearing today. She said the girl has lost a lot of weight since she saw her back in the spring and she's convinced her story is true. I think she's taken to her."

Max turned to look at his friend. "That's good, but you didn't follow me down here to tell me that."

"I can see why you feel you must save her reputation but the thing is the poor girl has been through a lot. Don't you think it might be best to give her more time to adjust?"

Max sighed. "I meant what I said about getting the deed done before Selina has time to make trouble. Once we're married it will be easier for me to protect Georgie from the inevitable unpleasantness from that quarter."

"I suppose so. She did seem rather lost just now though. What if she changes her mind after the ceremony?"

"I'm sure she won't do that. Think of all the benefits she'll get from the union."

"Max, this isn't a business arrangement."

They reached the stable and Max's curricle was waiting for him with a groom holding the horses' heads.

"Of course, it is. I'm sure we'll become good friends and nothing more is needed to make a success of it."

Nat gave a roar of laughter. "For a man with seven sisters you have a lot to learn about women. I wish you joy but promise me you'll be kind to the poor girl."

Max bristled at the anxious look Nat gave him. "Of course, I will. If you must know I'm extremely grateful to her for solving my problem."

Max jumped up into the curricle and signalled to the groom to let the horses go. They pranced and sidled for a moment as his tiger jumped up behind. He waved a whip at Nat in acknowledgement as they moved off. Their conversation lingered as he drove along. He wasn't being unfair to Georgie, was he? No, of course not, she was grateful to him for giving her a safe haven. He couldn't see her giving him much trouble as a wife.

* * *

Max took rooms at the Blue Boar in Canterbury, rather than stay in one of the more fashionable hotels where he was more likely to meet someone he knew. He sent his tiger with a message to the Archbishop of Canterbury's office as soon as he arrived. There was a small, rather gloomy, sitting room attached to his bedroom. The worn, dark brown, leather armchair by the window was comfortable enough and he read the newspapers the manager of the hotel had sent up to him whilst he waited for a reply. He jumped when there was a knock at the door.

"Enter."

The messenger touched his cap and grinned when Max handed him a generous tip in exchange for the sealed note he carried. The door had barely closed behind him before Max tore the missive open. He let out a relieved breath as he scanned the contents. The Archbishop would receive him in the morning. That would give him time to return to Hargreaves Hall in the light. His horses should be rested enough to drive them back by then.

Everything seemed to be going to plan. Yet somehow Nat and Eliza had unsettled him with their advice to wait. But surely this was best. Georgie would be entirely safe from her cousins as his wife. He wouldn't rush her once they were married so he couldn't understand what they were worried about. In truth he couldn't believe his luck. All his problems solved and a grateful wife who would be easy to please. It wasn't the love match he'd dreamed of but he felt sure they would be friends. In many ways that might be easier.

He ran down the stairs and walked out into the street to look for the jewellers Eliza had recommended. He found it quite quickly. The shop was busy. Max pulled out his card and an assistant ushered him past several wooden counters, each with a salesman dealing with a customer, into the private office of the proprietor.

"What can we do for you, my lord?"

"I'm looking for a good quality string of pearls suitable for a debutante." He had so many nieces that would sound believable.

"Of course. I'm sure we have exactly the right thing." He rang a bell and instructed the assistant who came in response to bring a selection of pearls.

Max suspected there had been some sign language going on and he would be shown the most expensive. Good, Georgie deserved a treat. He accepted a glass of wine and selected a string of pearls. His conscience hit him when he remembered that Cecilia was making her society debut after Christmas and he selected a second string.

"I'll have these as well. It's an expensive business being an uncle."

There was a knock at the door and an assistant entered, carrying a rosewood jewellery box.

"May I leave these with you for safekeeping, sir? My customer took the emerald set."

Max's eyes flicked to the box. It would be lovely to buy Georgie something special. The shop's proprietor must have seen his glance. He opened the box to display a glorious set of diamonds. The man lifted the necklace up and it glittered under the light of the chandelier directly above them.

"These are the best diamonds I've seen in a long time, my lord."

"I'll take those as well."

They would look wonderful on Georgie. Max felt colour flood his cheeks. He had to buy them even though it would look like he had a mistress in keeping. Something he'd never done near home, preferring to keep his amours to the anonymity of London. Thinking of which, it was fortunate he had paid off his latest mistress in the autumn, at the start of his unsuccessful flirtation with Lydia Winters. He was ready to leave his bachelor days behind him.

Max left the shop after arranging for a draft on his bankers in Canterbury. The proprietor promised faithfully to have the jewels delivered to the Blue Boar that evening. He sauntered along the street. Finding women's clothing was going to be harder. He turned a corner and came across exactly the sort of shop he was looking for. A linen draper that advertised some ready-made items. All of the assistants appeared to be male, which was a relief.

Inside he could see no one he knew and none of the assistants paid him particular attention. It seemed he hadn't been recognised. Wooden cupboards, arranged like shelves, lined the walls. Their round holes each holding a bolt of cloth, with the last few inches projecting into the room. The smell of cotton reminded him of the nursery. He enquired for ready-made garments and was ushered over to wait behind two other men in a separate part of the shop. There seemed to be quite a selection available. What size would Georgie be? He would have to guess.

When it was his turn to be served, he pointed to a collection of gossamer thin nightgowns and various items of matching underwear. His pulse quickened at the thought of Georgie wearing them. He picked up a nightgown that looked about right and measured it against his hands. Thinking back to when he had lifted her and allowing for all the clothes she had been wearing, it was at least two sizes too large. She was bound to put some weight back on now she was being properly fed. The assistant gave him an odd look and he replaced it on the counter.

"That should be perfect for my wife." He felt his cheeks heat up and was grateful for the poor lighting. "I forgot to pick up her list which had her measurements. I'll take two sets of the whole range."

The assistant's expression changed to a beaming smile. "Thank you, sir."

He needed something more modest for their wedding night, or he would struggle to keep his promise not to rush her.

"She asked me to buy some warm nightgowns for her niece. I'm sure they needed to be two or three inches smaller."

The assistant fetched some in a thicker fabric and laid out three.

"These should be the right size then, sir."

69

"I'll take all three."

Max paid cash and opted to take the package with him to avoid giving his name. He sauntered back to his hotel feeling rather pleased with himself. The poor little thing had been through a lot. He must be kind to her.

The next morning Max received a message from the Archbishop's Secretary putting their meeting back to the afternoon. The door closed behind the messenger and he paced about his sitting room. Why the delay? It was probably nothing to worry about. Christmas was not a good time to approach an Archbishop after all. He already had some gifts for the family put by but perhaps he would buy some more presents for the children. He had better see what he could get for the Fordhams as well, in case they managed to make it through to the Hall. He spent the next few hours wandering around the shops.

What to get for Georgie? He would give her the pearls as a wedding gift but it was probably too soon to give her the diamond set. He could save that for her first ball with him. Had she ever been to ball before? There was so much he didn't know about her. It might panic her if he gave her the underwear and flimsy nightdresses straight away. She was probably quite an innocent having been brought up in an ecclesiastical family.

He checked his pocket watch. There was still another hour to go before he needed to make his way to his appointment. He stopped short on the pavement and apologised profusely to the man who bumped into him from behind. He stiffened and screwed his hands up into fists. Could Georgie be known to the Archbishop? It was a possibility he hadn't considered. He moved forward away from the press of people. It was fortunate that Georgie had already met Eliza. If the Archbishop, or whoever interviewed him, wanted to know more about the details of their courtship he would have to play on that relationship.

His attention was caught by a shop that seemed particularly busy and he moved towards it. Most of the customers were women but he could see a few men. He wandered inside. The most popular counter held a selection of painted fans. They were quite delightful, perfect presents. He selected one each for Georgie, Sally and Eliza, in different designs.

He marched back to the Blue Boar and unloaded his parcels. He tidied his windswept appearance as best he could and regretted not bringing Jepson with him. So much rested on his interview at the Archbishop's office. Selina would do her best to cause a scandal to try and stop the wedding if she got wind of it. He paced his bedroom until it was time to set off for his appointment. His shoulders felt tight and a pulse jumped at his temples.

Chapter Seven

Georgie exclaimed at the quality of Martha's stitching when she brought the green gown for her to try on.

"My mother worked in a dressmaker's shop before she married, my lady. She's taught me everything she knows."

Georgie sighed. "I'm Miss Sherborne."

"Not for long and I thought it would be a good idea to practice. I don't think His Lordship would be best pleased if I carried on calling you Miss Sherborne after the wedding."

Betty glared at the girl. "Martha, remember what I've told you."

Martha turned bright pink and stared at the ground. "I'm sorry, Miss Sherborne. I should do exactly what you tell me and not comment on my betters."

Georgie was distracted by the sound of an arrival. She rubbed at her temple. She hoped Max had got his marriage licence, at least then she would be out of this state of constant worry. Any more days of wandering aimlessly would be too much to bear.

Betty cut into her thoughts. "That sounds like His Lordship. Why not put on the green gown to meet him, Miss Sherborne?"

Georgie opened her mouth to protest and then shut it again. Why not? Martha had left a bit of growing room but it was a much better fit than her brown dress. It might help her feel more confident.

A scant ten minutes later she descended the stairs. Her heart skipped to a faster beat when she saw Max standing at the bottom. He seemed disinclined to say anything. She forced legs that somehow seemed distant from her to negotiate the last few treads. Max caught her hand and raised it to his lips. She shivered and recognised the warm feeling that spread from her hand right and thrummed through her body as desire.

Max was the most attractive man she had ever come across. How would a girl like her hold his interest for any longer than it took to give him an heir? Heat flooded her cheeks and she was glad of his support when he threaded her arm through his.

"Come. Let's go and tell Eliza and Nat the good news." He patted a pocket with his free hand. "I have the licence here and I made a detour to the vicarage on the way home. Mr Wright will marry us tomorrow morning."

Georgie allowed herself to be led into the library where Nat and Eliza were sharing a sofa in front of the fire. She saw them spring apart as they entered and her heart ached. That was the sort of relationship she wanted. Would she be able to achieve it with Max? She sank into the seat he showed her to.

Max stayed on his feet. "The marriage is arranged for eleven o'clock tomorrow morning. I don't think the vicar was best pleased but he cheered up when I offered to pay for the repairs needed to the church roof."

Eliza laughed. "Oh Max, it is Christmas. You surely didn't expect him to be full of joy at fitting in an extra service." She jumped up. "If you will all excuse me, I had better go and organise the servants. Georgie, I will be so glad when I can hand over the role of Max's hostess."

Georgie smiled at her. "Would you like me to come and help?" Anything to get away from Max's unsettling presence.

"That's a good idea if you feel up to it. There's a lot to learn and I'll give you as much help as I can over Christmas."

Both men stood as they left the room. From wanting to escape, Georgie felt bereft once she was away from Max. It would be mortifying if he knew what effect he had on her. She hoped Eliza wouldn't notice her hot cheeks. Eliza led the way to the housekeeper's room. Georgie stiffened. She had managed to avoid Mrs Powell but, once she was running the household, regular contact would be necessary. This was going to be uncomfortable but at least she had Eliza with her.

Eliza stopped and pulled her into a sitting room. "You look nervous. I had forgotten, but Betty told me you had a bad start with Mrs Powell."

Her cheeks so hot it was a wonder she didn't set the room on fire, Georgie nodded. "I'm afraid so. I'm sure she thought I was a woman of easy virtue."

"I can't say I've ever liked the woman. I don't remember how Max came to employ her. An agency I suppose. Don't be shy. If you aren't at ease with her after a week or two you must talk to Max. If necessary, he will pay her off and you can select someone else."

"She couldn't entirely be blamed and it seems harsh to dismiss her for making a mistake that many people might have made."

"It's your decision but if you're still not entirely comfortable with her in a few weeks then think hard. Your relationship with the housekeeper of your main country seat is probably your most important one after your marriage."

Georgie nodded. "I'll remember that. I know I have a lot to

learn and I can see the sense in what you say."

"Your sense of fair play does you credit. Now I warned the servants to be prepared for a wedding tomorrow. The best servants will cope with anything. However, it's always better if you can give them some warning of possible future events."

Georgie barely heard the last of Eliza's words as the room circled around her at the thought of her wedding the following day. She squared her shoulders and forced herself to concentrate. Eliza knew what she was about and Georgie learnt a lot in the next hour. Eliza was bred to run a house of this size. Would she ever be able to manage to the same standard? Eventually Eliza declared that they could do no more and it was time to prepare for dinner.

"That gown looks lovely on you, much better than it did on me. You could wear that for dinner."

Georgie nodded. "Your maid persuaded me to put it on."

Eliza laughed out loud. "Betty is a treasure. You will need a maid now yourself."

"I think I will ask Max if we can take on Martha as my maid."

"That's a good idea. Martha has been working hard to learn everything she can from Betty. Let me give you one more piece of advice. When it comes to household matters you are in charge. Don't ask Max, tell him."

* * *

Max helped himself to brandy. He sat in the chair next to Nat and crossed his legs. Georgie had looked stunning in the green dress.

"The Archbishop saw me himself. He remembered Georgie and her family. I had to fudge things a bit by implying Eliza knew the family better than she did and not correcting him when he assumed that was how I had met Georgie." He swallowed a large mouthful of brandy.

"In the circumstances you did the right thing. I think you're right about Selina. Even if it is too late to try and stop the wedding, I wouldn't put it past her to cause trouble out of spite." Nat laughed. "She's never forgiven you for being born. Perhaps you ought to consider hiring bodyguards."

"I don't think she would go to those the sort of lengths, but all the same I might just do that." Max thought for a minute. "A lot of people work at the archbishop's office. I'm sure several recognised me. I'll have some grooms posted on the route to church. I don't think Selina is that unhinged but I'm sure she's had people spying on me before now."

Nat nodded. "As a former soldier I think that's wise. I've got pistols with me and I'm the obvious choice to escort Georgie to church."

"Thank you, Nat. I don't suppose you've brought Bright with you?"

Nat grimaced. "It never occurred to me he might be needed. I gave him some time off to visit his daughter. Both coachmen and the two grooms I brought with me were trained in security by him though. I'll have them all armed to be safe."

"Good. Besides armed grooms watching the route I'll have Barton discreetly warn the footmen who will be in church to keep watch." Max shook his head. "I can't believe it will all be needed but it's best to be safe."

The bell rang for dinner. Max hung back and hovered in the hall waiting for another glimpse of Georgie walking down the stairs. She was wearing the same green gown that had sent his pulses racing before. Now she had her hair piled high on top of her head. Why hadn't he noticed before what magnificent hair she had? He'd got himself a better bargain than he knew when he offered his name to protect the reputation of an exhausted waif.

He walked forward and offered his arm. She seemed to jump at his touch. He studied her face. Huge grey eyes lifted to his. Was she nervous about the wedding night? He must make time to talk to her tonight.

"You look quite delightful, Georgie."

The smile she gave him seemed rather uncertain. She was definitely nervous but then perhaps brides were supposed to be nervous on the evening before their wedding.

Eliza kept up a steady flow of cheerful conversation during the meal. Georgie visibly relaxed. She seemed to be getting on well with Eliza now which was a big relief. Eventually the meal was over and the ladies left the men to their port. Max suggested to Nat that they re-join the ladies after just one. In the sitting room he drew Georgie away from the other two.

"Is there anything you want to talk about before tomorrow? I know you're not getting the wedding that most young women dream of but I promise I will make it up to you afterwards." He took one of her hands in both of his.

She seemed to tremble. He gave her what he hoped was a reassuring smile.

He lowered his voice. "Are you worried about the wedding night? I promise I won't rush you."

Her cheeks adopted an adorable shade of pink. "Do you know Max, I hadn't thought about that? I've watched Eliza orchestrate an impromptu wedding feast. I've never had any training in running a big household. I hope I don't let you down."

A chuckle escaped him. How his friends would laugh to hear she was more worried about running the house than her wedding night.

"There is no need to worry about the house. You have Mrs Powell to help with that sort of thing."

She looked dubious.

"What is it?"

"That's my problem; I don't think Mrs Powell likes me."

"Why doesn't she like you? She's paid to like you." He laughed. "I don't think she likes me very much."

Georgie hung her head. "Of course, Max. I'm not making a good start, am I? I will try and do better."

Oh dear, he had made a mull of that. How to reassure her?

"I'm sorry, Georgie. I didn't mean to sound so sharp. I'm sure you will learn how to go on very quickly."

She looked as if she was about to say more but Eliza came across to them.

"I don't want to sound too motherly but it's going to be an exhausting day tomorrow. Perhaps you ought to retire early, Georgie?"

Max turned and walked across to the fire to hide his annoyance. It was going to be difficult to have much conversation with Georgie until they were on their own. He heard her agree with Eliza. They excused themselves and went out together. Max felt a stab of embarrassment. Was Eliza going to check if his bride was aware of what would be expected of her on their wedding night? He ran a finger around the inside of his neck cloth. It felt rather too tight. Perhaps he should have warned Georgie about his reputation as a rake but it was too late now.

Chapter Eight

Georgie sat patiently as Martha dressed her hair. The cream gown was beautiful. It was the sort of gown she had dreamed of owning in what seemed another life. She could barely remember her mother but she longed for her aunt, the generous aunt who had offered her a season in London. Perhaps she should have accepted but it hadn't seemed fair when Aunt Anne's means were modest. If she had found a husband, then at least her aunt would have been at her wedding.

At last Martha had finished. There was a knock at the door and Betty came in. She handed Georgie a small wooden jewellery box.

"The Marquess sent this for you, Miss Sherborne. It's a wedding present and he thought you might like to wear it for the ceremony."

Georgie opened the box and gave a gasp of delight. Nestled in amongst the deep red silk lining was a beautiful string of pearls. Martha took them off her almost reverently.

"These will be perfect with your dress, Miss." She fastened the pearls around Georgie's neck.

Georgie studied her reflection in the looking glass. Even a few days of being well fed had improved her figure and given her roses in her cheeks. She felt as ready as she would ever be to face the future. It was too late now to worry if she had made a mistake. Max was a maiden's dream. He was certainly hers but she knew little of his character. Yet something had made her accept his offer. She could only hope her instinct had been correct.

Eliza scratched at the door and came in. "Max has already gone to the church. Nat will escort you and give you away if you are happy with that."

Georgie took hold of Eliza's hands. "Thank you so much, both of you. You've been so kind."

In response Eliza gave her a quick hug. "It's been nothing and don't forget we will always be here if you need help."

"Thank you. There is one thing. Mrs Armstrong. How will I explain the wedding to her?"

"Don't worry about that. I'll think of something to say. It's time for me to be off now. Betty will take you down to Nat when you're ready."

Martha put the finishing touches to her hair. "You're ready now, my lady. I'll go and fetch Betty."

Georgie felt surprisingly calm as she waited. The scent of the lavender Martha had sprinkled in her bath water enveloped her in a soothing cloud. Betty knocked at the door and led her downstairs. Lord Overton smiled at her as she placed her hand on his arm. He led her outside and handed her into a large, old fashioned landau.

"This carriage has been used to take all the Lovell brides to church. I believe it was made for Max's mother."

Georgie settled into the comfortable, light green squabs. Her composure nearly deserted her when they reached the church. It seemed as if all the people from Hargreaves village had come out for the wedding. There were even some from Benfort. She gave them the brightest smile she could muster. She would have to get used to being the centre of attention as a marchioness. A stab of fear hit her. If so many people knew could Cousin Mary have found out? Her eyes darted around the crowd.

There was no sign of the Huttons or their scary lawyer friend. Some of the Benfort folk were waving at her. She relaxed and waved back. They must have come with the carrier; his cart was tucked behind the church. Their presence was a real comfort even though it made her think of her aunt again. Lord Overton helped her to alight. She smiled her thanks and the crowd cheered as they walked through the gate to the church. Georgie froze at the sounds of a scuffle outside the church. Lord Overton bundled her back into the coach. The driver pulled out a pistol and the groom on the box jumped down and joined her inside the coach, also carrying a pistol.

"Get down, Miss Sherborne. Keep your head below the window."

After what seemed an age, Lord Overton returned. "You can come out now, Georgie. False alarm. Just a scuffle between a couple of villagers." He smiled at her. Forgive me for overreacting. My ten years in the army have left me seeing danger lurking in every shadow."

He helped her out and they made their way back to the church. Georgie couldn't help noticing that the armed groom followed them rather than stay with the coachman. Had she been traced by Cousin Mary? Most of the people inside were servants from Hargreaves Hall. She couldn't see all the pews but there was no sign of the Huttons. She let out a breath as her gaze alighted on Eliza, near the front with her two children, and Mr and Mrs

Armstrong in the pew behind. Mrs Armstrong gave her a lovely smile as she walked up the aisle. Whatever Eliza had said to her must have worked.

They were nearing the altar and Georgie broke into a smile when she saw Max. He was exquisitely turned out in a tightly cut navy jacket and snowy cravat. He smiled back and she faltered momentarily. Lord Overton patted the hand that rested on his arm and they took their places. It was unlikely that the Huttons, or their lawyer, were there, after the scuffle outside Max would have had any strangers removed to be safe. She still couldn't help but strain her ears listening for any disturbance. She made the right responses in the right places until the Vicar of Hargreaves pronounced them man and wife. She felt giddy with relief.

Max leaned over and placed a kiss on her cheek. The Overtons were smiling at them and so were the Armstrongs. A tremor went through her at the enormity of the step she had taken. She managed to smile at Max. She had always loved the marriage vows. Now she had made them she must try and make this strange marriage work. She walked back down the aisle on his arm. How seriously would Max take his vows?

Max nodded to a group of footmen standing near the church door with Jepson and Barton. Two footmen rushed to open it. It was then that Georgie noticed the row of hampers lined up and the large money bag carried by Barton. They went outside to cheers and she looked back to see Barton walking amongst the assembled crowd distributing largesse. She glanced up at Max who grinned down at her.

"I left a message with Mr Wright, our vicar, yesterday that anyone attending the wedding would receive a Christmas present."

Mr Wright walked behind them to the church door. Max thanked him and waited for him to talk to Georgie.

"Well, my dear, I must admit I was a little surprised at the timing of the wedding but I understand His Lordship's worries about the weather closing in. Mrs Wright and I are thrilled to welcome you to the parish." He beamed down at her.

Georgie smiled back. "Thank you, Mr Wright. I'm delighted to be here."

The Vicar bowed in acknowledgement. Max put a hand under Georgie's arm and shepherded her towards the gate. Georgie looked around and saw the footmen distributing foodstuffs amongst the crowd. She shivered in the cold wind.

Max wrapped an arm around her. "It is something of a Lovell tradition to distribute food and money to locals attending a family wedding. It seemed particularly appropriate at Christmas."

"What a lovely idea."

Further conversation was impossible over the cheers of the crowd as they walked through the gate to the coach that was waiting for them. Georgie found it comforting that Max had traditional values and was prepared to help the poor. Her pulse quickened as Max helped her into the coach. Now they were married it didn't have to be an open carriage.

He climbed in beside her and called to the driver to move on. Georgie opened the window and leaned out to wave at the crowd. Once they were out of sight she quickly closed it. Max put an arm around her and pulled her close. She was intrigued by the scent of his cologne. He smelled of Christmas with hints of spice and oranges.

"Max what was that incident outside the church all about? I was terrified the Huttons had found me."

"I don't think so. A couple of men who weren't from Hargreaves or Benfort villages were hoping to share in the community presents. The locals didn't take kindly to it. Don't give it a thought." He didn't meet her gaze.

Georgie sighed. "What a relief." Could she believe him though? He was making light of it but he didn't look convinced himself.

Max hugged her close. "This is almost as cold as the morning I found you."

Georgie pulled away a little and put her head to one side. "No, it's not. I have never been as cold as I was on that morning. I was trying to move around when you found me but it all seemed so much effort. Looking back, I should have pressed on to the vicarage in Benfort the night before."

Max gave her a lopsided grin. "Ah yes, but if you had you might not have met me."

Georgie found she couldn't look at him. Was she glad or sorry? The truth was she didn't know. Max gave her a quizzical look. She tried to think of an answer but was saved when they pulled up at the front of Hargreaves Hall.

* * *

"What the devil." Max watched a line of coaches making its way to the stables. "I think you are about to meet more of my family, Georgie. Sally and Wakeley must have made it through."

"Oh dear, I think I'm in a bedroom meant for one of them."

Max frowned. "Your things will have been moved to the marchioness's suite next to mine."

Georgie's hands flew to her mouth. "I wasn't thinking." Her

cheeks went pink.

She seemed nervous. He was going to have to control himself until she relaxed. In any case with all his family around he felt awkward about bedding his new wife. His problem was his groin didn't agree with him. He was in for an uncomfortable few days.

The door of the chaise opened. He climbed out past Georgie and then turned to help her. Instead of taking her hand he put both of his hands on her waist and lifted her down. She was feather light. Much lighter than she had felt when he carried her back in the snow but he hadn't been in very good shape that day. She was wearing fewer clothes too. He wished his family to the devil. All he wanted to do was throw her over his shoulder and take her up to his bedroom. He sighed. Duty came first.

Max tucked Georgie's arm through his and they walked up the steps to the front door. Georgie seemed quiet. He glanced down at her and smiled. Serious grey eyes met his and she gave him a faltering smile in return. He loved the way the shade of grey of her eyes changed with her mood. The door remained stubbornly shut when they reached the top of the stairs. Most of the servants would still be at the church. Eventually a harassed looking footman opened it.

"Thank you, Evans. Can you tell me who has arrived?"

"The Earl and Countess of Wakeley. Lady Cecilia, Viscount… "

"Ah, so my sister has arrived with her family. There is no need to tell me the names of my niece and nephews."

The footman looked at the floor. "I'm sorry, my lord."

Max saw Georgie frown. She was right; he shouldn't take his frustration out on the footman.

"You have nothing to be sorry about, Evans. Have a message sent to my sister and her husband that we will be in the marchioness's drawing room. Then tell the servants who have stayed behind to report to Mr Barton as soon as he is back."

"Yes, my lord." The footman scurried off.

"I trust that is satisfactory, my dear. It will give us a few moments to ourselves."

"Of course, Max. I hope there will be enough food for them all." Georgie bit her lip.

Max propelled her towards the sitting room with a hand at the small of her back. "Don't worry I had food delivered from Canterbury for the presents at the church and for the wedding feast. We had originally catered for the Fordhams."

Georgie laughed. "That's good. I would hate to run out on my first event as a marchioness."

That was better. More like the spirited girl he had rescued. He looked around the drawing room.

"When we go up to London you can choose new furnishings for this room and make it your own."

Georgie walked to the window and didn't answer him for a moment. What was troubling her?

She turned towards him. "There is no sign of them coming back from church yet. I think I had better go and warn Cook that there will be more people at the wedding breakfast."

Max watched her almost run out of the room. The domestic arrangements seemed to be troubling her. She was clever and would soon learn what was required. Then they could relax. He should be pleased that she seemed determined to take up the reins of the household quickly. Wasn't that exactly what he wanted, someone who would be a good marchioness but not make too many demands on him personally? So why did he feel so piqued that she was more interested in running the house than she was in him?

There was a rustle of silks and his sister Sally entered. Max took a deep breath and resigned himself to an inquisition.

"You made it through the snow then, Sally?"

Sally laughed and took a seat on one of the sofas. "We did but I think the weather is going to close in on us. You will be stuck with us until after twelfth night I expect." She raised her eyebrows at him.

Max moved away from the window and sat next to her on the sofa. "How did you find out?"

"Rollo rode in to Canterbury to see what the roads were like and bumped into a friend of his. It's all around the local clergy about you obtaining a marriage licence. Then we saw the crowd as we drove past the church. The question is who is she?"

Max saw Georgie return out of the corner of his eye. She halted in the doorway and he waved at her to come forward.

* * *

Georgie straightened her back and moved forward. At least she didn't have to meet all of Max's sisters at once.

Max stood up to greet her. "Georgie, this is my sister, Sally, Countess of Wakeley."

He led her to the sofa. "Sally, this is my wife Georgina. You may know her as Miss Georgina Sherborne."

Sally jumped to her feet and enveloped her in a hug. Georgie tried to smile as Lady Wakeley stood back to look at her better. At least she seemed disposed to be friendly.

"Georgina Sherborne. My word you've grown into a beauty."

Georgie felt heat rush to her cheeks. "I'm sorry, Lady

Wakeley, you have the better of me. I'm afraid I can't place you."

"Your aunt and I worked on a charity committee together a few years ago. I remember meeting her in Canterbury when she had you with her more than once." She turned towards Max. "Why don't you leave us to have a little chat before the others arrive?"

Georgie felt like begging Max not to go. Instead she inclined her head to Lady Wakeley. "That would be lovely."

She nodded at Max who seemed reluctant for a moment. Then he smiled at her and she caught her breath at the affect his smile had on her insides. When would she lose this stupid sensitivity to him?

"Why not, Georgie has quite a few of you to get to know."

She found it hard to take her eyes off his retreating figure. This wouldn't do. She forced her attention to Lady Wakeley. Shorter than Eliza, she had the same dark colouring and blue eyes as her sister. Were all the Lovells so attractive?

"There's no need to look worried my dear. I was sorry to hear about your aunt's death and I wish I had posted straight down to see you then but I was rather distracted at the time."

Georgie couldn't think of an answer.

"I should explain. Anne confided to me once that if anything happened to them the only relatives to take you in were rather ramshackle, since your family were estranged from the cousin who inherited the barony. From the bits of the story I've heard, about you being on the stagecoach, I assume they were worse than she could have imagined."

She gave Georgie a beaming smile that put her in mind of Max. "I have to say though that the result of my neglect has been fortuitous. You're just the sort of sensible girl to curb

Max's wild ways. It's about time he settled down."

Georgie was full of questions but the sound of arrivals interrupted them. "There will be a wedding feast in the formal dining room as soon as everyone is back, Lady Wakeley. Cook was nearly ready when I checked. She said there was enough for an army so there should be no problem with your family joining us."

"That sounds promising." Lady Wakeley laughed. "I'm sure Eliza knew we would get through if we possibly could. We would have been here yesterday evening if we hadn't agreed to wait for Rollo to come back from Canterbury before we started out. No one wanted to miss Christmas at Hargreaves Hall."

The door opened and Eliza swept in. "Sally, I'm so glad you made it."

"That wasn't too difficult but looking at the sky we're in for more snow. I was telling Georgina I think we will be with you until twelfth night and probably beyond."

Eliza released her sister from the hug she had wrapped her in and plopped down on the other side of her. "I'm afraid we will too. It will be lovely for the children but not ideal for a newlywed couple to be doing so much entertaining immediately."

Georgie raised a hand to a burning cheek. "Perhaps we should make our way to the dining room?"

Eliza jumped up and ran to her side. "I'm so sorry to put you to the blush. You will soon get used to our blunt ways."

Lady Wakeley screwed up her face. "As to that, Eliza, that wasn't very tactful even for you." She turned towards Georgie and smiled. "You will have to forgive Eliza she was always the scatter-brained one. Now that we're sisters I hope you will call me Sally."

"Thank you, Lady... Sally. I'm generally known as Georgie."

"Georgie it is then. Now come along. Let's not keep everyone waiting."

Georgie felt swept along on an irresistible tide as they walked to the dining room. She looked down to hide a smile. If some of his sisters were as masterful as this, no wonder Max had almost begged her to marry him.

Barton was in the entrance hall when they left the wing of the house that was home to the marchioness's drawing room.

"His Lordship has given Mrs Powell leave to spend a few hours with a sick friend in the village, my lady, but everything is in hand. Would you like me to announce the wedding feast?"

"Yes please, Mr Barton. Would you thank all the staff for their hard work when you have a moment?"

Barton bowed low. "Of course, my lady."

Georgie caught smiles of approval from both ladies. It was much easier to be positive in her new role with Mrs Powell out of the house. She might have to follow Eliza's advice and consider replacing her. She heard Max's voice coming towards them together with the sound of young children. Lord Wakeley appeared to be carrying Judith. They were a delightfully informal family. How she longed to be a proper part of that family.

"Georgie, my dear, Peter has something to ask you." Max shepherded forward a suddenly silent young man.

Georgie bent down to the boy and smiled at him. "What would you like to ask me?"

Peter looked around at his uncle and then back at her. "Uncle Max said you would like me and Judith to come to the wedding feast."

Georgie's lips twitched as she watched Max turn around to

hide a grin. "He's quite right, Peter, as this is a family occasion everyone should be here."

Max smiled his thanks over Peter's head. Peter tucked his hand in hers. "May I sit with you, Auntie Georgie?"

Max squatted down by him. "I'm afraid that place is for me, Peter, but your cousins are here and you will want to sit with them."

Georgie glanced around. She didn't even know how many children the earl and countess had.

"That's a point," Sally said. Where is everyone else?"

"I think the young people all went off with Nat to look for the best places to pick holly and mistletoe," Max said.

Georgie noticed a slight hesitation before the word mistletoe. Unless she was mistaken there was a blush to his cheeks. Eliza was right. It was strange being newly married and it was awkward having other people around to witness that. There was the sound of an outside door opening and closing and a few minutes later Nat arrived with four young people in tow. There were three teenage boys and a young woman who was probably the eldest.

Sally stepped forward. "Georgie, let me introduce the children. In age order we have Cecilia, Rollo, Timothy and Neil. Now I suggest we all follow your uncle and new aunt to the dining room."

Max smiled and held out his arm for her. She noticed that some of the large formal dining table had been taken out. When they were seated they were close enough to make conversation comfortable. It was a merry meal. She had Max on one side of her and Lord Wakeley on the other. The young people opposite were holding a lively conversation which she would have liked to have heard more of. She noticed with approval the way the bigger boys included young Peter. Judith was seated on her father's lap but seemed to be taking in everything that was happening. She also had a healthy appetite.

A wave of longing hit her. What would it be like to be part of a family like this? She had a vision of a row of little boys all looking like their father. Would she be able to give him sons and how would Max feel if she didn't? She had found the courage to escape her cousins. Now she must reach out and find the courage to try and win Max's heart. She mustn't think about what it would be like if he rejected her. Surely the prize was worth fighting for?

Chapter Nine

Georgie was rather quiet but she seemed composed. Perhaps she was a naturally quiet person. She had handled Peter well. She must have realised the little rascal had twisted his words. They were such an informal family it was good that she had allowed the children to attend the meal. He tried to concentrate on his food. Looking at Georgie did uncomfortable things to parts of him that he was glad were hidden. He would never survive until after twelfth night. Somehow, he would have to pretend that his family were nowhere near once they were alone at night.

"Uncle Max, will you come and help us collect greenery this afternoon?" asked Neil.

Max turned to Georgie. "I know it's old fashioned but we have always kept to the customs of decorating on Christmas Eve. Are you happy with that?"

Georgie smiled at him. "I am, with one condition."

"Which is?" Max held his breath. The children loved decorating the hall for Christmas. As his marchioness it was her right to order the household. It was a pity he hadn't had time to discuss this sort of thing with her beforehand. He could see everyone's eyes on her.

"That you take me with you. It sounds like fun."

Everyone started talking at once.

"Quiet," said Max. "Yes, of course, we will. Any member of the family who wants to collects holly, laurel and so on from the woods nearby on Christmas Eve. Cecilia is usually the best at it."

Cecilia wouldn't meet his eyes. Had she been about to excuse herself from collecting until she realised Georgie was going? She was growing up fast.

"Cecilia always manages to find the mistletoe," Neil said.

Max glared at him. "Perhaps we won't bother with mistletoe this year."

"Uncle Max, you can't have Christmas without mistletoe," Rollo said. He exchanged glances with Tim who grinned. "The servants would be so disappointed."

Max ignored the comment. His jaw tightened. This was going to be a difficult Christmas.

The footmen arrived with the last course. Once they had eaten their fill Sally looked across her husband to Georgie.

"This is the point we would normally leave the gentlemen to their port," she said. "I think they will be prepared to forego that today as the light will be fading in an hour two."

Half an hour later the foraging party assembled near to the stables. There was a biting north wind and Max turned up the collar on his greatcoat. Eliza and Nat appeared, each holding one of Peter's hands. Max put his arm around Georgie shoulders. She had changed into the brown velvet gown with a thick cloak over it. A warm hat covered her brown curls. She looked adorable with her nose tinged with pink.

"We'll have to go without Cecilia if she doesn't come in a minute, " he said. "We'll all freeze standing here."

"The rest of you carry on," Rollo said. "We'll wait for Cecil."

Max sighed. Unless he had missed his guess there would be an awful lot of mistletoe this year.

"Thank you, Rollo. Right, I spotted a good place for laurel and holly the other day." He selected baskets, some with shears inside, from the ones he had borrowed from the gardeners. He handed a small basket to Peter and full-sized ones to the other three.

"I'm sure I can manage two that size Max," Georgie said. "We won't have time to come back before dark."

Nat took an extra one as well. Max tied a pair of long loppers over his shoulders and checked that they were all ready.

"Follow me."

He managed to link an arm with Georgie. Her cheeks were quite pink but that could be the cold. Even with Peter in tow, it only took him ten minutes to find the spot he remembered. He pointed. "It must be a good year for berries."

They were on the edge of the home woods and holly bushes had taken advantage of the light there to produce a blanket of bright red.

Peter jumped up and down in excitement. "Look holly with lots of berries."

Georgie seemed taken with the little boy. That was another plus. If he was blessed with sons, he wanted them to have a loving upbringing. He had seen too many boys at school damaged by cold parents. He passed the shears to her so she could help Peter select which branches he wanted. She didn't disappoint him. Even whilst he was helping Nat cut longer branches of holly with the loppers he watched her. She tactfully helped Peter choose branches small enough to fit into his basket.

"Uncle Max, look how much I've got. I'm the best collector."

Max moved across to Peter and inspected his basket. "That's very good indeed Peter. You've got lots of lovely berries" He remembered all the children's things he had bought in Canterbury when he was kicking his heels. "I'll find a prize for you later."

"Thanks, Uncle Max. What about Aunt Georgie, she helped me?"

Max smiled down at Georgie. This time he was sure that she blushed. "I think I can find something for her as well but it might take some time. I'll give it to her later."

He felt a blush heat his own cheeks and backed into the shadow of the bushes. He'd forgotten that he was giving Georgie nightwear. Georgie seemed not to see anything amiss but Nat gave him a quizzical look.

"I did a lot of shopping in Canterbury on the free morning I had before I could see the archbishop. That's where I found the string of pearls I gave Georgie as a wedding present."

"I thought so," Eliza said. "Did you use that jeweller I recommended? The pearls were absolutely perfect."

"Yes I did. I bought a string for Cecilia as well to mark her come out. I'll give it to her tomorrow."

It was the work of moments to top up Nat and Eliza's baskets. Perhaps he could have some time alone with Georgie.

He turned to Eliza. "I think we've got enough holly there. The boys will gather plenty of larger branches of greenery. You can take Peter back to the house with the holly if you like. Georgie and I will try and find some laurel."

Eliza agreed readily, after a sharp glance at her husband. Nat gave him a salute and picked up three baskets, leaving Eliza to carry Peter's. He ignored Nat's grin. At least his embarrassment had cooled his ardour. That didn't last long when he glanced down at Georgie and she gave him an uncertain smile. He longed to take her in his arms but he didn't want to rush her. Besides which he wasn't sure he could stop at a kiss. It was weeks since he had parted from his latest mistress and Georgie was so sweet.

He put one basket inside the other with the shears inside and hitched the loppers over his shoulder. "Let's look for this laurel it's too cold to stay out much longer."

"It's nothing to how cold I was when I woke up in that barn."

Despite his load Max managed to put an arm around her and pull her close. "I know. You were so cold when I picked you up, I was afraid I wouldn't get you to the warmth of the house in time. Come on."

He took them down a path that led into the heart of the woods. Rain and snow struggled to penetrate here and fallen leaves crunched under their feet. It grew darker until they could barely see where they were going. Georgie tripped on a root and he steadied her and tightened his hold. The shoulder carrying the baskets was aching but he didn't want to let her go. He pushed on and the trees began to thicken until they came to the large clearing he was looking for.

"Here we are. There is usually some laurel and holly in here."

They dropped their baskets and did a quick circle of the clearing. Georgie looked more relaxed out here than she had in the house. He was tempted to forget about the greenery but soon gave up the idea. They had better fill the baskets or the boys would want to know why not. They reached a row of laurel bushes, some so tall they were almost trees. He gave Georgie the clippers and left her to try her luck with the lower branches.

He set to with a will with the loppers. Physical effort might help to take his mind off his current frustrations. Sweat trickled down his back by the time his baskets were filled to overflowing. He threw the loppers over his shoulder and made his way back to Georgie. She had done pretty well with the clippers.

"This is an even better spot than I remembered."

He put his baskets down and helped her fill her second basket. He loved the way the tip of her tongue peeped out when she was concentrating. She reached up for one last branch. He took it from her and squeezed it into the top of the basket. Her face was framed by a shaft of golden light and she smiled at him. He took the clippers out of her hands and dropped them next to the baskets. It seemed the most natural thing in the world to embrace her and lower his face to hers.

He hesitated as his mouth neared hers. She reached up and threaded her arms around his neck. Their lips met and he felt as if he had been thumped in the chest. He took a great gulp of air and then applied himself to the kiss. He teased her lips with his tongue and her mouth flew open on a gasp of surprise. He pressed his body even closer and deepened the kiss. Excitement jolted through him as she responded, tentatively at first but with growing confidence. He had better stop this while they still could but he didn't want to.

She stiffened in his arms. Damn he'd lost his discipline and rushed her. Then he heard the sound of voices. Ah she must have heard them before he did. Reluctantly he unpeeled his body from hers and pulled her into the edge of the woods.

"That sounds like the boys. Are you alright? I hope I didn't frighten you? Let's take a minute to compose ourselves."

The voices sounded louder. "I think we had better go back to the baskets Max or they will guess." Her voice petered out.

"You're right."

He took her arm and they almost ran back to where they had left everything. She bent down and picked up the clippers and he did the same with the loppers. He was eyeing up the baskets when Rollo came into view.

"We thought we had better come and see if you needed any help, Uncle Max."

"As you can see, we have done very well with our laurel hunt. You can help us carry it back."

Neil and Tim joined them and as they were all empty handed he distributed baskets and tools amongst them. He held out his arm to Georgie.

"What thoughtful nephews I have, Georgie."

She laughed, a lovely musical sound, and tucked her arm in his.

"You do indeed. I was wondering how we were going to manage those heavy baskets."

The light was fading fast by the time they neared the house. Max sent Rollo to return the tools to the gardening stores. When they reached the house Cecilia and her mother were sorting piles of greenery in the main hall.

Sally inspected the baskets as Neil and Tim put them down. "Excellent. We have a good selection now. Cecilia even managed to find some hawthorn, ivy and rosemary."

Max noticed several branches of mistletoe. At least now they had kissed properly as man and wife it should be easier to cope if they were caught under a branch.

The next couple of hours were a frenzy of activity. The hall and the dining room were filled with greenery and the boys took some down to the servant's hall for their party that evening. He had no time for those fashionable folks who thought proper Christmas celebrations were vulgar. Simply watching the enjoyment on the faces of everyone helping, not just the young people, made him happy.

Max changed out of his outdoor things and went to look for Nat. They found the library unoccupied.

"Thanks for checking no one had followed us here, Nat. I didn't want to alarm the family and they would have thought it strange if I cancelled the greenery hunt."

"I could see no signs of anyone. A shame the men managed to get away. You did say there were two strangers didn't you."

"Yes, Barton was adamant that everyone else at the church was from here, Hargreaves village or Benfort."

"Good. One of my grooms has stayed in Hargreaves village to see what he can find out. I've given him plenty of money. He'll follow them if he can get a lead. Bright says he's a good investigator."

"Thank you. It would be good to find out who they were. I suspect Selina was hoping they could stop the wedding."

"That seems most likely but we can't rule out a kidnap attempt on Georgie I suppose."

Max shook his head. "Perhaps, but how did they find her?"

"Guessed she made for Kent and got lucky in Canterbury? Rollo had heard about you getting a marriage licence."

"I suppose so. If there was that much talk the bride's name might have been mentioned too. I ought to have thought of that. Georgie should be safe now that we're married but I hope your man turns something up."

"Me too. I don't like loose ends. It will be easy to keep a watch out now it's snowing again. At least we can enjoy Christmas." Nat grinned at him.

"Don't you start. I'm going to have enough trouble with

the boys. I've never seen so much mistletoe. I'm going to ask Barton to have the yule log brought into the hall and then I'll find Georgie."

"I think she will be in the dining room."

Max soon found Barton who dispatched a footman to summon the grooms with the massive yule log that would burn at least until the end of Christmas day. He went into the dining room where Sally was presiding over the refurbishment of the paper Christmas decorations the footmen had retrieved from the attics. Ribbons and pinecones were strewn across the table in front of Sally. He could hear the boys arguing over where to hang the last of the greenery in the hall. Georgie was chatting away to Cecilia. She seemed to be having a wonderful time and enjoying the company of the Fordham youngsters. Of course, at one and twenty, she was nearer in age to all four of them than she was to him.

Max raised a hand and waited until everyone went quiet. "The yule log should be arriving at any minute. Follow me to the hall if you want to see it lit.

Peter spotted him and came running across. "Uncle Max, have you found my prize yet?"

Max laughed. "I'll go and fetch it, after I've lit the log, if your mother tells me you have been a good boy."

"Oh he has, Max. He even helped me entertain Judith when we got back."

Max picked the boy up and threw him in the air. Peter giggled when he pretended to nearly drop him.

"Right you are, Master Overton. Be good for a few moments longer and you shall have your prize. I bought some more fancy paper as well, Eliza, so you can make some new decorations."

He smiled at Georgie, who had glanced their way. "You

won't believe the size of the log we manage to fit into the hall fireplace. Come and watch me light it. We like to make it a bit of a ceremony."

He held out his arm and led her into the hall, with everyone following behind. Half a dozen grooms staggered in with the yule log and manoeuvred it into place. One of the grooms spread the contents of a large box of wooden splinters under and around the end of the log that was fully in the fireplace. Georgie watched, looking fascinated.

"The splinters are all from last year's log. It's my job, as head of the household to use them to light this year's."

Barton handed him a lit candle and he bent down to apply its flame to the splinters. Once they were crackling merrily, he stood back and watched until he was sure the log was well and truly lit. He looked around the hall. His niece and nephews might be growing up quickly but from their faces they still enjoyed the rituals of Christmas.

Peter joined them. "Don't forget my prize, Uncle Max."

"I'll go and get it now." Max ruffled Peter's hair.

Georgie smiled at him and went to join the chattering group of young people around Cecilia. He left the hall and ran lightly up the stairs. Georgie was more talkative with the young people than she had been with him. Was he imagining a certain restraint between them? There was no doubt she had been badly treated by her cousins but could she have recognised him in the inn? He pushed the thought to the back of his mind. She seemed too straightforward a person to concoct a plan to ensnare him.

Chapter Ten

Georgie sensed as much as saw Max stroll in and talk to Peter. She tensed when he smiled at her but managed to smile back. Everyone seemed to be engrossed in what they were doing. Which was just as well, since a smile from Max sent shivers down her spine. She bent her head over the decoration she was teasing into shape on the dining room table. Every time she saw him it made her think about that kiss in the woods. It must be the hint of red in her hair that made her blush so readily.

"Max has some more paper for us," Eliza said." He'll bring it down in a minute with something he's got for Peter."

Sally put the finishing touches to the decoration she was working on. "That's good, a few of these are past repair."

Georgie helped Cecilia fix a bow to a string of pinecones. "Max said he is taking me to London when the weather is better. Will you be there? It would be lovely to see some familiar faces."

Cecilia gave a little cry and made to rise but her mother waved at her furiously.

Georgie caught her hand. "I'm sorry I didn't mean to distress you."

Cecilia didn't answer and looked over to her mother. What

on earth had she said to discompose the girl so much?

"I see Max has told you nothing of Cecilia's situation," Sally said. "He's loyal I'll give him that, but you need to know. We might need your help."

Georgie looked from mother to daughter in total bewilderment. She still had Cecilia's hand and it quivered in hers. She came to a quick decision.

"Cecilia, if you want to tell me what's troubling you I shall be happy to help." She glanced across at Sally. "However, it's your decision. I promise I won't ask Max if you want to keep whatever it is private."

Sally snorted. "There's not much chance of keeping it private. You are right though, Georgie, it is best that Cecilia tells you her story when she's ready."

Georgie gave the girl's hand a squeeze. "I'm sure what happened to you can't have been as bad as my adventure. It will be me who needs help in London."

Max came in and Georgie put her mouth close to Cecilia's ear. "We can talk about it after dinner if you like."

Cecilia nodded and gave her a half smile.

* * *

Dinner was a strange meal. It felt as if their wedding hadn't really happened. They had reverted to a normal seating pattern with Max at the head of the table and Georgie at the foot. Rollo and his father were seated either side of her. Her glance kept wandering to the sight of Max laughing with his sisters at the other end of the table. He would develop a disgust of her if she kept gazing at him adoringly.

She concentrated on the conversation around her until Lord

Wakeley coughed.

"I think my wife is trying to attract your attention, my dear," he said quietly.

She felt a warm colour spread into her cheeks. Everyone had finished and, as Max's hostess, she must direct the ladies to leave the men to their port. It felt strange but she squared her shoulders and signalled to a footman. He was very young and she couldn't remember seeing him before.

"Perhaps you would let Mr Barton know we are ready for tea?"

The boy stood stock still and seemed unsure of what to do. He stammered something she couldn't catch and blushed scarlet. Hadn't Max said something about a party for the staff today?

"Is Mr Barton presiding over the staff party?"

"Yes, my lady."

"Perhaps you could tell whoever is left in the kitchens that we require tea in the drawing room?"

He nodded and ran out.

Georgie raised her voice. "Ladies, tea will be served in the drawing room shortly. We'll leave the gentlemen to their port."

She waved the others on and stopped by Max's chair. His nearness had the usual effect of leaving her breathless and with legs that didn't quite feel her own.

"Max, Mr Barton is at the staff party. When we have been served tea should I send a message for the staff still working to go and join them? It would be a shame for anyone to miss it?"

Max gave her a smile that lit up his eyes and had her surreptitiously holding onto the table for support.

"That would be kind of you, Georgie," he smiled again," and

exactly what my mother would have done."

"Good. I'll leave you gentlemen in peace then."

She smiled around the room, without looking at Max. Once she was outside she drew in a deep breath and made her way to the drawing room. The young footman came out from the servants' quarters and nearly dropped the tray he was carrying.

"I'm sorry if I startled you. I've agreed with His Lordship that once we have our tea tray you may tell all the servants still working that they may join the party downstairs."

The boy's face glowed. "Thank you, my lady."

He followed her into the room and set the tray down on a side table. She smiled at the sound of running footsteps as soon as the door shut behind him. After helping her aunt at church functions, preparing and serving tea came naturally to her. At least there was one aspect of her new role she didn't need instructing on.

Sally accepted a cup and settled onto a chair near the fire. "It's ironic after our parent's heroic struggles to produce an heir that so many of the next generation are male. At least it means we can all have a seat near the fire."

Eliza laughed. "Very true."

Georgie sat on a sofa a little away from the older ladies and Cecilia took the space beside her with a shy smile.

"Thank you for standing up for me this afternoon, Lady Hargreaves."

"Oh, please call me Georgie."

Cecilia gave her a tentative smile. "I would be honoured."

"I love how informal this family is. I've visited places where people call close relatives by their title. This is so much more comfortable don't you think?"

Cecilia nodded. "I'm glad Uncle Max has married you and

not one of the horrors Mama and my aunts were considering for him."

Georgie struggled to know how to answer but Cecilia ploughed on.

"He saved me you know. Not many uncles would have gone to the trouble he did and afterwards there was not a word of disapproval from him."

She drank her tea down in a few gulps and sat staring at her hands.

Georgie finished her own tea. "Do you want to tell me about it?"

Cecilia raised a face which was now bright red. "Yes please."

The door opened and Max entered followed by the rest. He caught Georgie's eye and started to walk towards her. She shook her head at him. Cecilia didn't appear to have noticed the men come in and she needed the release of telling her story. Max's brows shot together in a frown. She would have to explain later.

"I thought Hugh loved me," Cecilia almost whispered." I told Mama I didn't need a season as he was going to offer for me and I would accept."

There was silence for a few moments. Cecilia seemed to have been transported to a different place, her eyes unfocussed.

"What was her reaction?"

"She was furious. Told me he was a fortune hunting rascal and I was never to speak to him again."

"Ah I see. That didn't leave a spirited girl many options did it?"

Cecilia caught her hand. "I knew you would understand. We waited for my father to go away, so there was less chance of pursuit. Hugh hired a coach and two horses from an inn in the next town. The horses were real screws as my brothers would say."

"And Max happened to visit and set off in pursuit."

"Yes, it was awful." Cecilia dashed a hand across her eyes. "Hugh was more interested in the size of my dowry than me. He seemed angry when I didn't know how big it was. We stopped at an inn for supper and I overheard him book a room for the night. He started kissing me as soon as we were in a private room waiting for our meal. I said we should wait until we were married and he said he wanted to see if I was worth marrying or whether he would be better to ransom me."

Georgie gave her a clean handkerchief and held her hand until her tears stopped. "I pushed him off just as Uncle Max charged in. Uncle Max floored him with one blow, and carried me out to his curricle. I was so shocked my legs wouldn't seem to move."

Cecilia started crying in earnest. Georgie rocked her in her arms. Sally and Eliza joined them.

"I'm sorry, Georgie," Sally said, looking harassed and concerned at the same time.

"I don't mind. I think talking about it will make Cecilia feel better."

Sally moved forwards and Eliza waved her back.

"I'll look after her, Sally. Don't worry, Cecilia, you aren't the first girl to be tricked by a rogue and you won't be the last. You can relax now you've told Georgie. I told you she would be kind. There is nothing to upset you now. Let me escort you to your room."

Sally stared after them. "I made a complete mull of dealing with her first tendre."

"Your instincts about the man were obviously right."

"We girls learnt to pick out fortune hunters at a hundred paces. Where there is money there will always be plenty of them. I should have warned her when she was a little younger." Sally stiffened. "I shouldn't be burdening you with this on your wedding night. Thank you for being kind to her."

* * *

Max moved away with a sigh and fell into conversation with Nat. They both looked up at the unmistakable sound of sobbing. Good Lord, it looked like Cecilia was telling Georgie the story of her ill-fated elopement. It was their wedding night damn it. Christmas was not a good time to get married.

Nat threw him a sympathetic look and he grimaced. His expression softened when he studied Georgie comforting Cecilia. She would definitely be a warm parent, if they ever got the chance to try their luck at becoming parents that was. He tried not to grind his teeth in frustration. He bore Cecilia no ill will over her escapade but she could have picked a better time to unburden herself.

An unwelcome suspicion hit him. Georgie hadn't encouraged Cecilia's confidence to avoid spending time with him, had she? She'd welcomed his kiss in the woods but she was still young and could be feeling overwhelmed. No, it was more likely she was finding the presence of his family as inhibiting as he was. In his case desperation was definitely overcoming his embarrassment. How soon could he suggest they retire?

At last Sally and Eliza took a hand in dealing with Cecilia. He relaxed when Eliza went out with the girl. Perhaps now he would be able to talk to Georgie. He spotted the three Fordham boys chatting together. They kept glancing from him to Georgie. Knowing that trio they were probably taking bets on how long it would be before he took his bride to bed. This was going to be a long night.

He walked over to Georgie and sat down beside her. She was so engrossed in her conversation with Sally it was a few moments before she noticed him. He felt like a volcano simmering on the edge of erupting. He burst out laughing. This was ridiculous.

"I see you have been well and truly accepted into the family, Georgie. Thank you for helping Cecilia. Has she been telling you of her adventures?"

"Yes. She did have a bad experience. I'm glad you were able to rescue her."

"The poor girl was most unfortunate in her choice of suitors. If he hadn't been such a nipfarthing as to make do with only two horses, and a pair of screws at that, I would have arrived on the scene too late."

"I'll be eternally grateful to you Max," Sally said. "If I had handled it better it probably wouldn't have happened."

Max stroked his chin. "I rather fancy if she hadn't gone willingly, he would have kidnapped her."

Georgie shivered. "Is he still a danger to her do you think?"

"Oh, he won't be able to do her any more harm."

Georgie stared at him.

"Don't look so alarmed. He wasn't worth risking having to flee the country for. As far as I know he is alive and well, on a ship bound for the colonies. He certainly sailed with the ship. I had a group of men watch him around the clock and stay in the harbour with spyglasses trained on it until it was no longer visible."

"Oh well done, Max," Sally said. "Do you mind if I tell Cecilia that? She is afraid of seeing him again."

Max stretched his features into a smile. "By all means, Sally. No one harms my family without facing the consequences."

"Thank you, Max. You are more like father than I had realised. I'll send these boys to bed."

"It might come better from Wakeley," Max said as gently as he could.

Sally might have had a fright but she hadn't learned the lesson of not riding high spirited young people too hard. She flushed but nodded and went over to talk to her husband. That was another thing in Georgie's favour. She didn't show any overly managing tendencies like some of his sisters. Indeed, she had been prettily deferential over the matter of releasing the servants to their Christmas party. He settled into the sofa by her and took her hand. It definitely fluttered a trifle. He had her attention now.

He chuckled, "I trust the memories of our wedding day will have us laughing in the years to come. I apologise for you being drawn into family problems quite so quickly."

"Oh, I don't mind. When I was younger I helped my aunt and uncle with the parishioners all the time. I rather missed that when we moved to Canterbury."

"I thought you moved to Benfort?"

"That was after uncle died when I was nineteen. He was given a position connected to the cathedral when I was sixteen."

Max closed his eyes for a moment. Some of the archbishop's staff must know her. No wonder they had given him such a grilling.

"Ah, so you must know some of the people at the cathedral."

"Yes quite a few, although most of them not all that well.

That was another reason for hiding in this area. Once Christmas was over, I was hoping to find some of my old friends to help me with the lawyers."

"Why not go straight there?"

"Cousin Mary wouldn't let me go out without her and I had no access to writing materials. I had no idea who would be there now. I made a couple of friends of around my own age but they were both engaged and I don't know where they moved to."

"Once my secretary is back from leave, I'll have him try and trace them for you."

Georgie smiled at him. "That would be lovely. Thank you for taking the trouble."

Max laughed. "It's no trouble to me. My poor beleaguered secretary will do all the work."

He glanced around the room. "I have a suspicion that my nephews are planning to ambush us with a bunch of mistletoe. You look tired. I suggest you go up to bed first and I will stay a while longer to foil them. I'll not have them put you to the blush." He sighed. "I can remember when they were as sweet as little Peter."

"It has been a long day. I think I would like to rest now."

She didn't meet his gaze. He leaned towards her to shield her from the view of his nephews.

"I bought a few things for you in Canterbury. I hope you don't mind. They will be waiting for you."

As he expected, she blushed adorably. "Thank you, Max."

Her voice was huskier than normal and he was tempted to consign his nephews to the devil and go up with her. At the same time he wouldn't have her, or him, made a spectacle of. He sat back and nodded with as much apparent unconcern as he could muster when she said goodnight. He leaned back so his face was in the shadows beyond the flickering light of the fire. She walked out with a great deal of grace. Yes, she had the makings of a fine marchioness.

Once she had left, he jumped up and watched his nephews, led by Rollo, smirking in a corner. He walked across to Nat, slowly.

"Would you like a game of billiards, Nat?"

Nat looked surprised but agreed readily enough. They went out and Max silently pointed at a branch of mistletoe that had appeared above the drawing room door.

When they were out of earshot he grinned at Nat. "The work of my Fordham nephews hoping to embarrass the newlywed couple."

Nat burst out laughing." They should know better than to try and outwit their uncle." He patted Max on the back. "Damned awkward for the pair of you though, having the whole family with you."

"I know. It was something I hadn't thought of. Come on let's have that game. Georgie looked exhausted. A few minutes to herself will give her time to rest."

It was an hour later when he made his way upstairs. He ran up the last few stairs when he was sure no one was looking. He had told his valet not to wait up for him. It was a bit of a struggle to remove his tightfitting coat and boots. The coat would survive but he was in for a scold over the boots. He threw his clothes over a chair and shrugged into his dressing gown, not even bothering with his nightgown. At last he could make her his. Heart thumping, he almost ran to the connecting door between their suites.

Chapter Eleven

Georgie stretched out and turned over. She felt so much better for a rest. How long would Max be? He was a man with a tight control of his emotions but would he lose some of that control in the marriage bed? She shivered with anticipation. His kisses had made her aware of her body in a way she had never been before. Would she be able to satisfy him? There had been enough rumours, even in Benfort, to realise that he was experienced with women. To be fair to him though, there had never been any talk of affairs around Hargreaves Hall or, worse still, disappearing maids.

She turned onto her back and sighed. She was nervous enough without all this waiting around. How long was he going to be? She threw the covers back and shivered. With the curtain around the bed pulled back, she could see that the fire had burnt itself out. She glanced at the window and jumped out of bed. The drapes were thick but surely that was light creeping in around their edges? She grabbed her robe and rushed to the window. Outside the grey light of dawn was reflecting off the landscape. She looked more carefully. There had been heavy snowfall overnight.

That was one worry less. They would be cut off for a while so Cousin Mary wouldn't be able to descend on them, if she had managed to trace her. That incident at the church was a bit of a coincidence considering. She would have to deal with her at some point, but preferably not under the gaze of a sizeable part of Max's family. She wrapped her arms around herself to try and keep in some warmth. It must be past the time the maids would normally light the bedroom fires.

There was nothing for it but to climb back under the covers. She pulled them over her shoulders and propped herself up against the pillows with her knees drawn up under her chin. Oh heavens, she must have fallen asleep waiting for Max. What must he be thinking? It was kind in him to have left her to her slumber but he must have hoped for more on his wedding night. She groaned. Would he have taken offence thinking she was faking sleep to put him off?

"Are you alright, Georgie?"

Georgie jumped and the covers fell to her waist. "I didn't hear you come in. You startled me."

Max laughed gently, "I'm sorry. I crept in. In case you were still asleep."

His voice sounded even deeper than normal and his eyes were focussed on her new nightgown. Her chest felt tight as she took a deep breath to steady herself.

"I'm so sorry, Max. What must you think of me?"

He raised his eyes to her face. "Nothing more than that you were tired. It's rather cold in here. I told the staff not to disturb us this morning. I'll soon get that fire going."

She watched him lay the fire and bend over the tinder box. His face was a study in concentration as he applied a spark to the twigs at the centre. Her body seemed to have warmed up simply from his presence in the room. The twigs burst into flames and he stood up after a few minutes, when the logs started to smoulder.

"There that should do it. May I join you in bed as we wait for it to warm the room?"

Georgie nodded and dropped her robe down over her shoulders. Max leant over her and gently pulled it back up. She shuddered as his hands brushed her arms, sending a wave of longing through her.

"Let's lie together and talk for a bit. I don't want you to be cold."

He climbed in beside her and her heart hammered in her chest. He lay down and pulled her into the crook of his arm. At last she understood why so many girls allowed themselves to be seduced despite the danger they put themselves in. She let her head rest on his broad chest and he stroked her hair.

"That's better. You will soon feel warmer. It's me who should apologise for my behaviour last night."

"But to fall asleep on our wedding night..." She tried to sit up.

"Relax, Georgie. I was so embarrassed by the antics of my nephews I went off with Nat to play billiards. It was more than an hour later when I came into you. After the time you have had of it over the last few days, I'm not surprised you drifted off to sleep."

The rhythmic stroking of her hair had a hypnotic effect and she gave herself up to the pleasure of the moment. Her hand came to rest on his chest. She could feel the heat of him through his robe. A shudder ran through her when she realised that was all he was wearing.

"What's the matter, sweetheart?" His voice was little more than a husky whisper.

How could she explain that she wanted to rip his robe off

and explore every inch of his hard, masculine body?

"Georgie, don't you feel ready for this? We can stop and wait until the family have gone if that will make you more comfortable."

"No. That is I don't want to stop. That's the problem." Oh heavens why had she said that? Now she would have to explain. She blushed as she remembered Mrs Powell's disapproval of her.

Max chuckled. "We're married now so why is you wanting this a problem?"

His free arm gathered her closer and stroked her back and her buttocks. She was lying partially on top of him and she could feel the hard ridge of his arousal against her thigh.

"It's just.... Well you know."

Instinct was telling her to roll completely on top of him. Her face grew even hotter. What would he think of her if she did?

"No I don't or I wouldn't be asking." He sounded a little cross.

She took a deep breath and tried again but for once in her life she was tongue-tied.

Max gave out a string of oaths and she tried to move away.

"I'm sorry, sweetheart. You're feeling nervous and I've rushed you, haven't I?"

She could have cried with frustration. What should she tell him? Then common sense kicked in. She couldn't live a lie and her only option was to tell him the truth. If he found her brazenness repulsive, he would have to learn to live with it.

"No. I was feeling excited rather than nervous."

Max sat up and stared down at her. "Then what in heavens name is the problem?"

She turned her face away. "I want you so much I'm afraid of

117

how I will react. I don't want you to be disgusted by me."

He lay back down and pulled her close. One hand stroked her back. "Oh Lord, you're not blaming yourself for the way I mistreated you at the inn are you? I vaguely remember saying something recently about you reacting to me when I kissed you."

"Not exactly but I am afraid you will think me a wanton if I'm too enthusiastic."

"But darling I want you to be enthusiastic." He laughed. "If you're not I will have failed you as a lover. Can you be the only woman not to know of my reputation in London?"

"Of course, I've heard about that but women are supposed to be demure not wanton."

He kissed her neck and she arched her back. "That's better. Forget all that nonsense about women not enjoying coupling. It's just stories told to girls to try and keep them safe from marauding boys. I can't think of anything worse than a wife who endures, rather than participates in, lovemaking."

"Oh. So I don't need to worry."

"Do what comes naturally. I'll help you. Are you shy about undressing?"

"Not really, but I expect it will feel strange at first."

He threw back the covers and stood up. She watched his hands as he untied his banyan and when he let it slip to the floor she gasped. His body was strong but lean and reminded her of the statues in the gallery of a stately home she had visited with her aunt. Aunt Anne had laughed but hurried her away from them all the same. The flickering light of the fire softened his features. She tried not to look at all of him but couldn't resist. A moment of panic hit her. How was this going to work?

"Don't look so worried. Your first time may hurt a little but it won't last long. Trust me to look after you."

He pulled her to her feet and kissed her until she felt dizzy. She snuggled closer and returned his kiss with the fervour she had managed to restrain in the woods. He put his hands either side of her waist and massaged the bottom of her breasts with his thumbs. She threw her head back with pleasure and he feathered kisses along the sensitive skin of her neck. He stepped back and she felt bereft.

"Let's remove your nightdress."

She helped him gather it up and slip it over her head with fingers made clumsy by her need for him. The garment joined his banyan on the floor. He picked her up and laid her on the bed before joining her and throwing the covers over them.

"Your body is beautiful. It's a pity the room is so cold."

They lay on their sides and he explored her with his hands. He put his mouth near to her ear.

"Feel free to join in but please only touch me above the waist."

"Why?"

Max laughed. "Trust me and I'll explain later."

She ran a hand over the strong muscles of his back. His fingers found the soft flesh of her thighs and she put her head on his chest. There was that lovely smell of warm male again. She must ask him what cologne he wore. She forgot all about cologne as a finger slipped inside her followed by another. He removed them and she whimpered.

"You're ready, sweetheart."

He raised himself on his arms and moved over her. Keeping most of his weight off her he kissed her. Instinctively she opened her legs and gasped when she felt him gently nudging at her entrance. There was a sharp stab of pain and then she relaxed. She tingled from head to toe and wanted something but wasn't quite sure what. Her body seemed to be moving of its own accord in time with his. She felt Max reach a hand down between them and something inside her exploded in ecstatic release. She cried out and lifted her hips up. Max shuddered and fell onto her briefly before lifting off and rolling to the side, still with an arm around her.

Georgie curled up as close to him as she could get. She couldn't remember the last time she had felt so relaxed. From the rhythmical sound of his breathing Max had fallen asleep. Perhaps this strange marriage might work out. The more aroused she had become the more he seemed to like it. He must think her dreadfully unsophisticated to worry about appearing unchaste with her new husband. Well now she knew he wanted her to be passionate she could enjoy that side of things. Then perhaps he wouldn't be tempted to take a mistress when they were in London.

She pushed the thought to the back of her mind. She was safe and her new husband appeared kind, if a bit irritable at times. He had every excuse for that with the frustration of having his family around, even though he clearly adored them. Perhaps in time he would come to adore her too. At the very least he would try and treat her well from what she had seen of him so far. Even girls whose family should have known better were married off to awful men sometimes. She was lucky and must count her blessings. It would be silly to let fear of Max losing interest in her hold her back from learning to love him. She held a hand to her cheek. Did she perhaps love him a little bit already?

Georgie felt the covers move off her. She opened her eyes to see Max climbing out of bed and donning his robe. The room felt pleasantly warm and sunlight was slanting around the edge of the drapes making patterns of little flecks of dust. She must have joined Max in sleep. He smiled at her and walked back towards the bed, with the light from the window behind him. She caught her breath. He had a magnificent physique.

"Georgie, sweetheart, I suspect it will soon be time for us to go to church. As much as I would like to give you a repeat performance," he grinned at her and her insides fluttered, "I think I had better send for some food."

Her stomach growled and she laughed. "I am rather hungry."

He bent over her and kissed her forehead. "I'll have a hot bath prepared for you as well. You may find you are a little uncomfortable after your first time."

She felt heat flood her cheeks. Oh dear how long would it take before she felt at ease with being a wife. She didn't want to bore him with her naiveté.

"Thank you, Max."

"I won't be long." He disappeared through the connecting door.

* * *

Jepson was laying out his clothes in his dressing room when Max put his head around the door. He dispatched him to order a breakfast tray for them to be sent up to Georgie's room followed by a hot bath at a suitable interval. Their first time had gone better than he had expected, with Georgie throwing off her maidenly modesty to a large extent. It was unnerving to find out that his London reputation was quite so widely bandied about. He had always taken such care to behave with

121

circumspection when he was at Hargreaves. If truth were told he wouldn't have gone to that wretched pre-Christmas house party if he hadn't had an eye to Lydia Winters, who had been throwing out lures to him in London. If he had known it was a ring she was after he would have kept well clear.

He breathed deeply. It was a relief to get their first time over. Now he could relax and ignore his nephews' childish pranks. Lord how had he thought Georgie a woman of easy virtue in the inn? He must have been as drunk as a wheelbarrow. Pleck kept a respectable house and he should have realised he wouldn't have any woman in who wasn't a lady. He slapped his forehead. He'd thrown guineas at her. Could that be why she was so worried about seeming wanton with him? She had grown up with a clerical family; perhaps they had been particularly strict with her on matters of sexuality.

He would like to think that was all it was and yet he had the feeling something was bothering her. He didn't want her to be worried about anything. She had definitely enjoyed her first experience with him and showed every sign of having a passionate nature. With luck all would be well. He couldn't wait to show her off in London. A few weeks quietly at Hargreaves first would be best. It would give her time to settle down and become comfortable with her role. She needed feeding up as well. He went back to join her.

She was seated on the sofa near to the fire wrapped in her robe. It looked several sizes too big. Eliza must have given it to her. He could give her the fancy set he'd bought but at this time of year she needed a warm robe. As soon as the weather eased he would have to take her into Canterbury to buy some things. They might even be able to find word of her friends at the same time. She looked up and smiled at him. His heart skipped a beat. She was such a sweet girl.

"Jepson said some of the footmen have been sent up into the attics to find the sledges for this afternoon. Would you like me to ask them to save one for us?"

"That sounds like fun." Her face clouded over. "I suppose I had better talk to Mrs Powell about the Christmas meal before we go to church."

"No don't worry about that. I don't think you'll have time. I expect everything is in hand and we can ask Eliza to check."

"If you are sure she won't mind. I've been working her hard teaching me what to do in running a house like this."

"No, of course, she won't. I'll ask her to talk to Mrs Powell while you have your bath."

There was a knock at the door and two footman entered at Max's command. They carried a tray each. One was laden with dishes covered with silver lids and the other chocolate and coffee pots together with plates and cutlery. The footmen placed them on a side table and pulled up two chairs. Max thanked them as they withdrew.

"Hmm. This looks wonderful. Mrs Powell must have anticipated our order." To his surprise Georgie's face turned a vivid red. She blushed easily but even so. He caught her hand. "What's wrong, sweetheart?"

She avoided his glance and stared at the floor. He waited but she said nothing. "Georgie, darling, what have I said to upset you?"

She gulped and looked up at him. "It's nothing. It's just...."

He squeezed her hand. "If something is troubling you it troubles me. I'm truly famished but I'm not going to eat this wonderful breakfast until you tell me what is wrong."

She took a deep breath. "The thing is I'm still not comfortable with Mrs Powell after what ....."

He ransacked his memory to recall what she had said about Mrs Powell before. Good Lord did the woman have the audacity to say something to her that first day?

"Mrs Powell didn't actually voice her suspicions of you being a woman of easy virtue when I brought you back to the house did she?"

Georgie nodded. Her shoulders drooped and she looked wretched.

Anger gripped him and he raised his voice a notch. "She had no right to question my motives like that, particularly when it meant insulting my guest. You should have told me the whole story before. Eat your breakfast before it goes cold and we will work out the best way to remove her without causing comment."

"That doesn't seem fair. She was probably being loyal to you at the time. Eliza told me how many women have set traps for you over the years."

He handed her a plate. "Perhaps. Don't worry about her now it's time for breakfast."

What had Eliza told her? She wouldn't have mentioned Lavinia, would she? No even Eliza would hesitate to bring that episode up. He applied himself to the food. Georgie had a point about fairness but if she had been insulted like that the relationship with her housekeeper was never going to heal if it hadn't by now. He would have to help Mrs Powell find a similar job and give her a suitable payment in recompense.

He chomped away at his breakfast. This was good, Mrs Powell had been an exemplary, if cold, housekeeper but he was damned if he was going to have Georgie embarrassed on a daily basis. The pleasant interlude at the Hall he had been looking forward to, with only the two of them, would have to go. They could go to London straight after Christmas if the roads were passable. London was thin of company so early in the season and he could introduce Georgie to some of the finer things the capital had to offer without falling over people he knew all the time.

Mrs Mills would have Hargreaves House in good order, although it needed refurbishment. Georgie might enjoy supervising that. Mrs Mills was a far gentler soul than Mrs Powell. Now there was an idea. He'd enlist her help. He couldn't think why Cook had recommended Mrs Powell. He had never taken to her himself.

Chapter Twelve

Max smiled and Georgie breathed a sigh of relief. He was so angry about Mrs Powell she wished she hadn't told him what had happened. The more she thought about it the more she realised she would have to make her peace with the woman somehow. If she asked Max to replace her, as Eliza had suggested, she might be angry enough to spread rumours wherever she moved to.

The truth itself was scandalous enough to have them ostracised if it got out, whatever Max said. Especially as someone had seen them together in that room at the inn. She frowned and looked out of the window with unseeing eyes. Max caught her hand and ran his thumb over her palm. She shivered and yet heat surged through her body.

"That's better. You look more relaxed now. Don't let Mrs Powell worry you, sweetheart. I have an idea."

Georgie shifted in her seat. How she desired this man and he had been so gentle with her. The problem with Mrs Powell didn't seem important at that moment. She smiled up at him and an answering gleam flared in his eyes. He moved towards her and she closed her eyes waiting for his kiss. There was a knock at the door and he shot upright, leaving her feeling bereft.

"Come in."

There was that cross but controlled note in his voice that she was coming to recognise. Two footmen entered and deposited a tin bath in front of the fire. One of them put more logs on the fire before they left.

"We are destined to be thwarted, aren't we?" Max smiled at her. "It's probably for the best though. I don't want to wear you out."

"I'm sure I would manage." Georgie rested a hand on his arm and captured his gaze.

Max shook his head and laughed. "Unless I'm hearing things your hot water is about to start arriving. We can rectify matters later. I'll see you downstairs in an hour or so. Wear your warmest clothes. We may have to walk to church."

She watched his retreating back. She still didn't know him but what she had seen of him so far was promising. There was no denying the spark of attraction between them. There again not many women would be able to resist Max's charm and he was known as a womaniser. It would be wise not to read too much into that.

She thanked the footmen as they emptied their cans of hot water into her bath. More arrived, closely followed by Martha bearing an armful of towels. The last can was emptied and the door shut behind the footmen. Martha added a generous sprinkling of lavender to the water. She climbed into the tub and sat back with a sigh of pleasure.

"Thank you, Martha, I love the smell of lavender."

"There's a whole garden full of lavender, my lady. It's next to the rose garden. The old Marchioness loved the gardens. They're beautiful in the summer."

"That sounds exciting. There's so much I don't know about

this place."

She leaned forward so Martha could help her wash her hair. An hour Max had said. She couldn't afford to stay in the bath too long.

"I had better get out Martha or my hair won't be dry in time to go to church."

Martha put her head on one side and chewed her bottom lip.

"What is it, Martha?"

"Why not wear it shorter? It will be easier to manage. It's so heavy at the moment it's a wonder you don't get a headache when you put it up."

Martha held out a towel and she stepped out of the bath into it, drawing it around her shoulders.

"I've got some scissors, my lady. I always cut everyone's hair at home."

Georgie hesitated.

"I wouldn't cut too much off. You would still be able to wear it up."

Georgie studied her thick chestnut brown hair that hung down to her waist in a silky cloud. It would be a wrench but so much easier to manage.

"Alright, I'll have it cut."

Martha's eyes lit up. "Thank you. I love cutting hair. I'll fetch my scissors."

She skipped out of the room. Georgie watched her go. Oh dear. What if Martha messed it up? Well if she did she would have to have it cropped by a professional next time she was in Canterbury or even London. She shivered, London was a scary prospect but sooner or later Max would take her there. She didn't want to have to face Cousin Mary, or Max's friends come to that. Surely, he would want to wait for the season to be well established? She could relax for a while yet. She dried herself and slipped on the robe Martha had laid out for her.

Martha returned and set to on her hair. Georgie's heart beat faster as long locks started hitting the floor around her. What if Max didn't approve? She squared her shoulders, it was important to hang on to her own identity. Max couldn't expect to dictate things like that. Eventually Martha gave a grunt that sounded like approval and stood back for a moment.

"There that looks lovely. Have a look and see what you think, my lady."

She stood in front of a large looking glass. Released from most of the weight holding them back her waves became more like large curls. They bounced just above her shoulders.

"Are you sure it's long enough to put up?"

"Oh yes. The curls make it look shorter. Sit on that chair in front of the fire and I'll help you rub it dry."

Martha pulled up a footstool to perch on and between them her hair was soon nearly dry to the touch.

"Leave it like that until it's time for you to go and then I'll put it up in a knot on top, my lady. It should be dry when you go out."

Half an hour later Georgie felt ready to face the world. She allowed herself another glance in the looking glass. True to her word, Martha had wound her hair in a topknot high on her head and teased little tendrils into mini ringlets on either side of her head. The girl on the edge of womanhood had been replaced by a lady of fashion. Martha helped her into the warm pelisse and hat Eliza had given her. She almost skipped down the stairs to meet Max.

Maybe she would be able to fill the shoes of a marchioness successfully. She must do so to fulfil her side of the bargain.

At last she had the feeling it could all work out. If she could captivate Max, perhaps he wouldn't feel the need to carry on with his previous lifestyle. They were cut off from the outside world so she could forget about Cousin Mary for a while. Whatever happened she intended to enjoy herself today.

Max was chatting to Eliza and Nat at the foot of the stairs. He turned towards her and his eyes opened wide.

"Georgie, you've changed your hair. It looks lovely."

He smiled at her and Nat and Eliza receded into the background.

"It was Martha's idea. She's cut quite a bit off so it's easier to manage."

"It suits you. We're in luck. The coachman is confident he can get us as far as the church. As long as the service isn't over long, we should have time to try out the sledges this afternoon."

They went outside to see three carriages lined up. Max helped her into the first of them and they were joined by Nat and Eliza. The Fordhams climbed in to the second carriage. They moved off at a sedate pace. Everywhere was covered in a glistening white coat which muffled the sound of the horses' hooves. The lines of trees on either side of the drive seemed to have kept some of the snow off. Their branches groaned under the weight of snow. They reached the big gatehouse and the road outside looked to have been cleared and ashes spread. They turned onto the road without incident.

Georgie smiled at Eliza. "No Peter this morning?"

"No, he's so excited he wouldn't be able to sit through the service. I left him in the nursery with Judith. Only the promise of some sledging later pacified him."

Max laughed. "He hates being left with a baby, doesn't he?

The servants who can be spared and want to attend are in the third coach. Are you happy with that, Georgie? It's something I should have consulted you on."

"Of course, I am. Don't forget I grew up in a vicarage. Everywhere looks beautiful today, like something from a fairy tale. I hope it won't be too dangerous for the horses."

"My head coachman is happy. There are no real slopes on the way to the church and he thinks the horses will be better for a run. This is the smallest coach so I expect we will arrive well in front of the others."

"Oh, that reminds me," Eliza said, "we usually invite the Armstrongs to our Christmas dinner as well as the Wrights. Do you want to carry on the tradition, Georgie?"

Georgie caught her breath. "I do but I'm worried they will disapprove if they guess I ran away."

"I hinted at some problems with your cousins." Eliza blushed. "I also let them believe that there had already been an understanding between Max and you. As soon as your period of mourning was over Max suggested you bring forward your wedding."

Georgie was appalled. "Cousin Mary will tell everyone the truth."

"If the Armstrongs are happy to receive you I don't think anyone will listen to her. They said that your Aunt had a poor opinion of Mrs Hutton and they were surprised when she was named as your guardian."

"It was a case of there being no one else. I wanted to go and stay with my old governess but Cousin Mary went to court."

Max squeezed her hand. "Don't worry I'll deal with Cousin Mary and her son." He pushed his jaw out. "They have far more to lose than us. With my ring on your finger no one will dare cut us."

Georgie was unconvinced but there was no point running away from an obligation. "If it's normal custom to invite the Armstrongs it would look strange if we didn't."

Eliza looked stricken. "I agree with you but I'm sorry if I got carried away and said too much. Try not to worry. I'm sure we will brush through any difficulties."

"You were only trying to help. I'm determined to enjoy Christmas."

"That's the best way to think about it. We'll have a message sent to them as soon as we are back. They may not be able to make it through the snow, of course."

Lord Overton looked up. "I've had one of my grooms have a scout around this morning. The road to Canterbury is pretty much blocked but this area isn't as bad."

Max squeezed Georgie's hand. "We'll try and get them to Hargreaves if we can. My head groom can take the message. He'll know if it's going to be possible. You'll feel better once you've spoken to them."

"I think you're right, but I don't want them taking any risks. Do we need to inform to the Wrights?"

"Yes. Mrs Wright will probably be in the congregation if you want to mention it to her."

The coach turned a corner and Georgie was thrown onto Max. The feel of his body pressed against her set her pulse racing. She longed for time alone with him. At least she found him attractive. Being obliged to be intimate with someone like Algernon would have been horrific. The coach arrived at the church and Max jumped out and lifted her down. She accepted his arm and they made their way inside with Eliza and Nat immediately behind.

Mrs Wright greeted them warmly. Georgie saw her opportunity.

"We would appreciate it if you would join us for Christmas Dinner this evening." She laughed. "I'm afraid I didn't think of it yesterday."

"Indeed not. It would have been wonderful if you had. We would be delighted to accept."

"We'll send a carriage for you," Max said. He turned towards Georgie. "What time my love?"

Georgie dredged her memory. "I think we said seven o'clock." She looked to Eliza for confirmation.

"Yes, we did. We'll send the carriage to pick you up a little before that."

Mrs Wright nodded. "That would be perfect. Thank you."

A group of people arrived behind them and they left Mrs Wright to greet them. Max and Eliza introduced her to several families, mostly tenants of the estate, before showing her to their pew. It would be hard memorising all the people Max was connected to but she had managed with her uncle's parishioners. All the same the high sides of the pew gave her a welcome reprieve.

Georgie enjoyed the service and steeled herself for more introductions on the way out. Max kept these to a minimum, promising to throw a party in the summer to introduce his bride to the neighbourhood. Hargreaves Hall provided a lot of work and the villagers seemed happy with that. They left Eliza and Nat talking to a couple near to the church. Max handed her into the coach and climbed in beside her.

He put an arm around her. "This is cosy. When we're travelling alone think of all the fun we can have."

Georgie laughed. "Don't make me blush. The others will be

here soon."

Max kissed her on the cheek and released her. "You're going to find me an unfashionably attentive husband, sweetheart."

The others arrived and Georgie sat back against the squabs. What did he mean by that? A bubble of happiness welled up inside her. She tamped it down. It wouldn't do to hope for too much.

"I hope no one minded us rushing off," Max said. "The best slopes for sledging are a good walk and we haven't a great deal of time to spare before the light starts fading."

Eliza burst out laughing. "They're used to you, Max. The summer party was an inspired idea. It would be lovely to revive the tradition now you have a hostess."

Max looked down at the floor before meeting Georgie's eyes. "Yet again that is something I should have consulted you on. I blame the lack of time to prepare. I'll take on a second secretary and they can help you with this sort of thing."

"That might be helpful but they won't know any more of your people than me."

"True but I could always lend you my secretary, Charles."

They arrived back at the Hall and Barton announced that a second breakfast awaited them. Max rubbed his hands together. "Excellent. Cold weather always makes me hungry. I suggest the sledging party meets by the stables in one hour."

They caught up with Eliza, Nat and Peter on the way to the stables. Peter ran around amongst them until his mother called him to order.

"Peter, where are your manners. Say hello to Aunt Georgie if you please."

Peter stood still long enough to address Georgie. "Can I come on your sledge Aunt Georgie? Uncle Max always goes the fastest."

Max laughed and swung him up onto his shoulders as Georgie had seen him do from the window. He loved the little boy. Her stomach muscles tightened for a moment. She mustn't think about the possibility of not bearing him a son. She concentrated on the general merriment and her discomfort quickly passed. They heard the Fordham boys talking to the grooms holding the ropes of the sledges.

Rollo's clear tones rang out. "I want this one."

Max broke into a trot, which had Peter laughing so much Georgie was afraid he would fall off. She saw Max tighten his grip on the youngster's legs. He would never let him fall.

"Oh no you don't, young sir," Max said. "If you turn that sledge over you will see it has my name on the bottom."

Rollo gave up the sledge with a forced looking smile. She exchanged a glance with Max who grinned. He walked back towards her and bent close so only she could hear.

"I'm afraid young Rollo takes after his mother. Wakeley will have some fun with him before too long."

They claimed their sledges and the group set off along a path to the hills beyond the home farm. Max led the way pulling the sledge seemingly effortlessly with one hand. He gripped one of Peter's legs with his other arm. Georgie smiled. He was so strong he had managed to carry her more than a mile in loose snow so the light frame of Peter was no problem. She looked around at the fairytale landscape in awe. The white blanket covering everything glistened brightly every time the sun popped out from behind the clouds. The snow scrunched under their feet as they walked along.

"We must have had a hard frost after the snow settled," Max said. "We should have great conditions for sledging."

He smiled at her and looked almost as excited as Peter, who was waving his arm behind Max's back.

She smiled back and nodded at Peter. "He's wielding an imaginary whip."

Max turned to look at him. "It's no good whipping me, young man. I can't go any faster on this snow. We're in front of your parents as it is."

"Aww, Uncle Max. I can't wait to fly down that hill. We'll beat Rollo won't we?"

"I think we can manage that."

Georgie threw her head up to feel the wind on her cheeks better and laughed.

"I haven't been on a sledge since I was a little girl, with my father. It must have been shortly before he died."

"Oh, I'm sorry."

"Don't worry. It's so long ago I can hardly remember him. I do remember the fun we had that day though."

Max speeded up. "Are you alright at this pace? I don't have a free hand to help you."

"I'll have you know I'm used to walking miles in all weathers."

She had forgotten how much fitness she had lost with her cousins and was soon breathing heavily. She pressed on, determined to keep pace with Max. They were the first to reach the top but Nat and Eliza were right behind them.

"We claimed the privilege of age and insisted on passing the others," Nat said.

Georgie gasped at the vista below them. White fields punctuated by humps where hedges and trees must be. "This is a breath-taking place."

Max rested the sledge against a bush and squeezed her hand.

"It will be even more breath-taking when we go down again."

Nat came up to them and lifted Peter down. "Come on, young man, let's leave your uncle in peace."

"I want to go with Uncle Max so we can beat Rollo."

"Come with us and we'll go first so you'll be bound to beat Rollo." He led a still protesting Peter off to join his mother on their sledge.

Max put an arm around Georgie's shoulders. "We'll give them a few minutes start. I don't think the Fordham boys are far behind. We'll hold Rollo off to make sure Peter is down before him."

"I love this part of Kent with the hills all around. It looks even prettier with its snow blanket."

"Yes, it is lovely. I have several other properties, even one near the sea, but I always prefer Hargreaves. Right, Nat has got them going well. Come on."

Max settled her on the sledge and climbed on in front of her. "Tie your scarf around your mouth before we set off. Now the trick is to stay balanced. Hold on to my waist and follow every movement I make."

Georgie did as she was bid and copied the way Max fixed his scarf. She wrapped her arms tightly around his waist.

"Ready?"

"Yes, ready."

Her voice sounded muffled even to her own ears but Max must have heard. He moved them into position and she gave herself up to the warm sensations sweeping through her at the feel of his body wedged up against hers. The sledge gathered speed and even with the scarf she realised what he meant by breath-taking. She ducked so her face was sheltered by him.

Max seemed to anticipate every contour. He must know

137

these hills well. She rolled with him when he veered from one side to another. She peeped out from behind him and could see they were gaining on Nat and Eliza. With Peter sandwiched between them they were less able to sway into the contours. She seemed to have gained a second wind and tried to look around but they were moving so fast everything was a blur of white and silver with the occasional splash of green, where a bush rose above the snowy wasteland. It was nearly as exciting as last night.

Thank goodness Max couldn't read her thoughts, or heaven knew what he would have made of that. He seemed to take his prowess as a lover very seriously. A chuckle escaped her. Being married was rather liberating in some ways. She loved the way he had told her to enjoy it and forget all the strictures about how a young lady should behave. Perhaps he was right and it was all a hum to hide how wonderful being with a man could be.

Max glanced over his shoulder and she smiled at him. His answering smile froze.

"What the devil. Hold tight." He swung the sledge sharply right.

Georgie could see Rollo careering towards them. He seemed to have taken a short cut down a steeper face of the hill. His sledge missed them by little more than a foot or two. She shouted a warning at Nat and Eliza as loudly as she could. She hung on to Max and copied his every move. They had avoided a collision but couldn't keep on an even keel. Max slowed them down by continuing to steer across the slope and used his legs to try and slow them further. They came to a shuddering halt and toppled off the sledge into a snowdrift. She had somehow rolled a few feet away from Max.

She ignored the snow trickling down the back of her neck and struggled to pull herself to her knees. "Are they alright?"

Max was already staggering up. "Yes. Thank the Lord. Nat somehow pulled them aside out of the way like us, even though he had less notice. It was fortunate I looked around when I did. I hope Peter didn't get squashed."

She managed to stand and grabbed his hand.

"They don't seem to be getting up. Come on."

Chapter Thirteen

Max needed no second bidding and they scrambled and skidded downwards. Peter's head poked out from a snowdrift. He reached him first and quickly loosened the rest of the snow around him and lifted him up. The little boy was crying loudly. Eliza and Nat were lying nearby. All the breath seemed to be forced out of Max's lungs. He handed Peter to Georgie and bent down to them. Nat groaned and turned onto his back.

Nat tried to sit up. "Is Eliza breathing, Max?"

Max threw himself to the ground next to his sister. Her face was partially buried by snow. He let out a deep breath when he saw her hand move and quickly scraped the snow from her face.

"Eliza, speak to me."

He was rewarded by a groan and Nat scrambled up to them.

"I'm still with you." Eliza's breath was coming in painful gasps. "Just winded."

"Thank God for that." Max left Nat to look after her and turned to Georgie who was trying to console Peter. "Peter, there's no need to cry. Your Mama and Papa are safe."

Georgie caught his eye and surprised him by grinning. "He's not worried about them."

Peter wriggled in Georgie's arms and Max lifted him from her.

"It's n-n-not fair, Uncle Max." Peter ran his sleeve across his tearstained face. "Rollo cheated, we should have won."

Max daren't look at Georgie, whose shoulders were heaving. "Rollo will be disqualified. Now don't you think you ought to go and look after your parents?"

They joined Nat and a still panting Eliza.

"We managed to throw Peter free but didn't have time to land properly," Nat said. He was white-faced and a muscle twitched in one cheek. "When I get my hands on Rollo he won't sit down for a week."

Max put a hand on his shoulder. "It's worse than a boyish prank, Nat. Rollo is seventeen and he should have more sense. He's too wilful by half. I'll have it out with Wakeley. This sort of behaviour needs to be taken in hand." He ground his teeth. "If he doesn't place serious sanctions on Rollo I'll want to know the reason why. He could have killed all of us."

Max looked down at his hands and saw they were shaking. His heart was beating a furious tattoo in his chest. "Come on. Let's get back to the house." He stepped towards Georgie and pulled her close. It was good to see she was calm in a crisis. His heartbeat slowed down as he held her. "Are you alright?"

"Yes. I didn't have time to be worried for us but it was scary watching that sledge gaining on the others. I'm sorry I found Peter funny but at least he's not upset by it."

Max laughed. "The little scamp. I hope he doesn't turn out as reckless as his cousin."

"I don't suppose he realised how close they were to disaster."

He found Peter and hoisted him on to his shoulders. "We'll

take Peter, Nat."

Eliza nodded her thanks and Nat put an arm around her shoulders.

"Thanks, Max. If you help me get Eliza onto the sledge I'll take her straight back to the house."

Max glanced up the hill. The younger two Fordham boys had stopped and were walking their sledge down the slope with great care. They had more sense than Rollo. He called out to the boys.

"Tim, your Aunt Eliza is badly winded and Nat is taking her straight back. Once they are down on the flatter ground can you follow and give him a hand."

"Leave it to us, Uncle Max," Tim called back.

Max waved in acknowledgement and turned to Georgie who had retrieved their sledge. "We'll walk until the boys are down."

He led the way down the slope, cutting across to reduce the angle of descent. He held on to Peter, who was singing to himself, with one arm and helped Georgie with the sledge with the other.

"I'm sorry my thoughtless nephew has spoiled your fun. I don't think we'll have time for another attempt today."

"Don't worry, Max. We might be able to have another go tomorrow. There's no sign of a thaw."

Georgie smiled at him and he nearly slipped. She had such a sweet smile. If they hadn't got Peter he would have been tempted to take her off to the shepherd's hut near the foot of the hill. He gave a sigh of pure pleasure. He was as reckless as Rollo in his way, asking an unknown to marry him like that. Still how many bridegrooms knew their brides well? He seemed to have done rather well for himself. Most young women of his acquaintance would have been a liability in a situation like this. Georgie had stayed her calm self.

He suppressed a grin. She had been anything but calm in bed and that was both a revelation and another blessing. He could hardly wait to get her to himself. Would there be time before she went off to oversee their Christmas dinner? It was a shame that task would be overshadowed by her discomfort with Mrs Powell. He owed it to her to sort that out as soon as he could.

He felt Peter wobble and stopped to lift him down. The little scamp snuggled in his arms and his head dropped onto his shoulder.

"We can sledge this last bit now by the look of it." He wedged the sledge against a bush with his foot. "Jump on and I'll hand Peter to you."

They settled the sleepy Peter in between Georgie's legs and Max climbed on to the sledge in front of them. He pushed off with his feet and they glided down the last section of the hill. He jumped off when they reached the bottom. "If you stay on the sledge with Peter I'll pull you along to the stables."

* * *

Georgie gathered Peter to her and watched Max's broad back as he dragged them across a bumpy patch. A shiver of awareness went through her as she imagined his shoulder muscles bunching to take the strain. She did her best to shield Peter from the worst of the motion. They reached the smoother surface of the path that wound along the base of the hill. She glanced down at Peter and his dark lashes were brushing his cheeks. With the resilience of childhood, he was still fast asleep. He was a darling. Would she ever hold a son of Max's in her arms?

She must stop worrying about that and concentrate on trying to make this marriage work. Max seemed a controlled sort of man. It was hard to know what he was thinking. He had done well calming Nat down when he must have been angry himself. He gave every appearance of a man who stuck to his word and Rollo was in for an uncomfortable time that was for sure. There did seem to be a reckless streak in the family. Cecilia had certainly learnt a hard lesson. Hadn't Max displayed that same impulsiveness when he offered her his hand?

They were skirting a section of woodland. Was that where they had interrupted their greenery collection to kiss? It had the same musty smell of damp foliage but perhaps all woodlands smelled like that in winter? She sighed. To forge a good relationship with a man like Max and become part of a lively family would be a dream come true. How often had she fantasised about how life would have been if her parents had survived to produce a brood of siblings, including a brother to inherit the family home.

They reached the stables. Max helped her off the sledge and pulled it into the stables, with Peter curled up on it still fast asleep. He came back with the boy in his arms.

"I've told them to keep all the sledges there ready. We'll try again tomorrow." The muscles around Max's lips tightened. "Without young Rollo."

Barton opened the door himself when they reached the house.

"Lady Eliza is in the drawing room, my lord."

They left their outdoor wear with Barton and hurried to see her. Nat was on his knees unlacing Eliza's half boots.

"How is she, Nat?" Max asked.

"She's got her breath back but her ankle is swelling up."

"I can answer for myself, thank you. I might have a sore ankle but my other senses are working."

Nat laughed. "I'm almost sorry you're able to talk again."

Georgie watched Eliza bat him on the arm. They were a well-matched couple and Eliza insisted on being taken seriously. Would an example like that encourage Max to want the same or would he naturally be more autocratic than Nat?

When Nat tried to remove the boot from her damaged foot Eliza let out a squeal.

"Ouch. That's painful."

Nat managed to remove the boot and a pale faced Eliza sat back.

"I hope Peter wasn't too much trouble," she said.

Max laid him on the sofa by Eliza. "He's been asleep since I took him off you. I'll send Jepson down. He'll know if it's broken or not."

He moved towards Georgie and put his arm around her waist.

"I don't believe it's broken. By all means send Jepson though," Eliza said. "I know he'll have some way of easing it."

Nat paced around the room. "I'd still like to flay Rollo alive."

"So would I but apart from relieving our feelings it wouldn't achieve anything." Max stroked his chin. "Punishment isn't enough. He needs a lesson in how to be responsible. Let's leave him to stew for a bit, expecting some sort of retribution. I'll give it some thought."

Max might look in control of his emotions but Georgie could feel the anger in him from the way he held himself. Even the arm around her tightened its hold. She couldn't suppress a shudder. He definitely had autocratic tendencies. How much freedom would she have with him?

"What's the matter, Georgie?"

"I was thinking I wouldn't like to be Rollo at this moment."

"I'm glad you're not." Max grinned at her and she felt his arm relax. "Don't worry I don't think you're capable of ever acting as stupidly as he did today. Let's go and find Jepson."

She allowed Max to lead her up to his bedroom. Her insides were quivering. She would have to deal with Mrs Powell on her own. Eliza wouldn't be able to help with her ankle injured. Eliza had been wonderful but it was time she faced up to the task of ordering the household. The sooner she got used to Mrs Powell the better but her disapproval was so obvious it was difficult to put it out of her mind.

* * *

They found Jepson in Max's bedroom, laying out clothes.

"Lady Eliza has need of your ministrations, Jepson. She hurt her ankle in a fall off their sledge. She doesn't think it's broken but she's in considerable pain."

"Ah. I expect that was what Viscount Summerton was on about. He was the cause of the accident I imagine?"

"I'm afraid so. He came to my room, did he?"

"Yes, my lord. He said to tell you that Viscount Summerton wanted a word with you and was most insistent that I have a message sent to him as soon as you came up to change."

Max felt his temper rising again. "He was, was he? Well the young whippersnapper can cool his heels a bit longer. Have a footman tell him I send my regards and will be available to meet him in the library at, what shall we say?"

He shrugged out of his greatcoat and dropped it on the bed. He grinned at Jepson's pained expression. He extracted his pocket watch and raised his eyebrows at Georgie.

"What time did you say our Christmas dinner would be ready?"

"Seven o'clock but Eliza tells me the tradition is to exchange family presents before the Christmas day dinner rather than St Nicholas's day. I thought half past six would be a good time for everyone to gather."

"That gives us four hours. Jepson, tell Viscount Summerton," he placed extra emphasis on the title, another mark against Rollo - trying to intimidate Jepson with it, "I'll meet him in the library at half past four. In the meantime, I won't take kindly to being disturbed."

Jepson grinned. "Yes, my lord."

Max's own lips twitched. Rollo was far out if he thought that sort of tactic would hold any sway with Jepson. He sobered up rapidly. Rollo appeared to be harbouring a greatly inflated opinion of his own importance. The door closed behind Jepson. He glanced at Georgie to see a vivid blush colouring her cheeks.

He took both her hands in his. "There is no need to be embarrassed. Jepson is far too well-mannered to be laughing at what he must know are my reasons for not wishing to be disturbed. We were both amused at Rollo's attempt to influence Jepson by bandying his title around."

She nodded but her cheeks stayed a dull red colour. Oh Lord, she wasn't going to turn missish on him was she after such a promising start? "What is it Georgie?"

"Rollo is still a boy." She paused.

He felt a stab of impatience. They had better things to do than discuss Rollo but he sensed it was important for Georgie to have her say. He smiled at her and waited. At least it wasn't their marital relations bothering her.

"You have every right to be angry with him but I don't think that attempting to impose your will on him has any chance of success with a boy like that."

"You're correct. I assure you I have no intention of trying to do that. It would set a bad example if I did. Any sanctions need to be agreed with his father in any case."

"Had you considered that he may have been trying to apologise and used his title to boost his confidence?"

He laughed. "I can see you are going to act as my conscience. I will bear that possibility in mind."

"Are you sure you will? You can be quite intimidating you know."

Ah perhaps this was about their relationship? "I hope I don't intimidate you, Georgie."

"No, but Rollo is young enough to attempt to brazen it out and make you even angrier."

She blushed again and he took her in his arms. "Sweetheart, I've known Rollo since he was a few days old and I've worried about how his character is developing. I hope I'm not the overbearing sort of man that I don't want him to turn into. He must have a care to the rights of others."

She stared at the ground. "I'm sorry, Max."

He kissed her forehead. "You have nothing to be sorry for, my darling. I want you to be my conscience. With the sort of power that I wield it would be easy to step over the line of acceptable behaviour. Please feel free to bring me to account at any time."

She nodded but looked far from convinced. Did she find him intimidating? They still hardly knew each other and she was in a vulnerable position. He would do well to remember that in his dealings with her. Her happiness was important to him.

"I'll remember what you said when I talk to him."

"Thank you, Max."

"You still look worried, Georgie. I don't expect you to agree with me all the time." He smiled at her. "How could I with sisters like mine?"

Her expression relaxed and she laughed up at him. Excitement surged through him and wrought the inevitable consequence. He stood back to gather his composure for a moment.

"How would you feel if I was to lock the door and we turned our minds to something else?"

"I think that's a wonderful idea. Standing next to you like this does terrible things to my insides."

He shivered with desire and ran across to lock the outside door of his room. Georgie was waiting for him.

"Your room?"

Georgie threw her arms around his neck. "Kiss me first before I explode with longing."

He compromised by kissing her and pulling her into her room at the same time. He locked her door and manoeuvred her over to the bed wrapped in his arms. He broke the kiss to throw off his jacket and waistcoat.

He whispered in her ear. "Would you like to remove the rest of my clothes?"

She shivered and he laughed out loud. "I can see that you do. Take your time."

Her eyes opened wide. She reached up and lifted his shirt. He raised his arms and between them the shirt soon joined the pile of clothes.

"Do you need help with the buttons on my breeches?"

She nodded. He loved the way she blushed that delicate

shade of pink. Carefully he undid all the buttons on the front of his breeches. Then he waited. She appeared to take a deep breath then helped him step out of them. He grinned when she gasped.

"I've never been one to wear smallclothes with tight breeches. It spoils the line of them."

Georgie's eyes shot to his face. "You remind me of a Greek statue except..."

Max burst out laughing. "If you mean what I think you mean, thank you for the compliment. However, you never see a male statue when he is being tormented by the nearness of a beautiful woman. It's my turn to undress you. Unless you would rather I didn't?"

"Yes please."

She smiled at him and his resolve to take things slowly wavered for a moment. He gritted his teeth, every nerve a quiver. He stripped her clothes off item by item, lingering long enough to kiss each new part of her uncovered. Desire pulsed through him but he kept his passion in check. Gently, he led her to the bed and lay down with her.

"Now, my adorable nymph, I am yours to command, for a while at least."

She stroked his chest and he felt his torso quiver. Her hands travelled to his waist and stopped.

"Max you said you would explain why I shouldn't touch you down there."

He nibbled her earlobe and grinned as she arched her back. "Because it might spoil our fun. Today I think you can but only for a moment."

He kissed her and trembled when her fingers closed around him. He let her explore for a few moments before calling a halt.

He put his lips close to her ear.

"Are you ready for me, sweetheart?"

In answer she rolled on to her back and pulled him with her. He kept himself in check, ignoring the frantic rhythm of his heart. His kiss was gentle at first but when she responded he deepened it. She sighed when he entered her. He kissed her again, holding still with an effort of will to allow her to set the pace. He didn't want to rush her. As soon as she moved beneath him his control broke. He managed to make sure she was satisfied before he reached his own release. He lost himself completely in the moment then came to with a start when he realised she was silently sobbing.

"What is it, sweetheart?" His stomach took a sickening lurch. "I didn't hurt you, did I?"

He was rewarded with a watery laugh. "Oh no, I didn't know such pleasure existed."

He lay on his side and pulled her close. "Then why are you crying?"

She didn't answer. Something must be wrong. "If you don't tell me what's wrong then I can't help you?"

Oh Lord, that had come out far too sharply.

"I'm just happy, Max."

"That's good, my darling." He hugged her to him. Was there something she wasn't telling him? He was too tired to work it out.

* * *

Max hauled himself out from sleep. He grabbed his pocket watch. Good, half an hour should be enough time to change for his interview with Rollo. Georgie sat up next to him. Her hair was hanging loose and she looked as sleepy as he felt.

"We're going to have to get up, my love. First though I have a present for you."

He climbed out of bed and went into his room. He hadn't meant to give Georgie the silk nightwear and undergarments for a while yet but the time seemed right and he couldn't wait to see her in them. He shuddered; it was cold without clothes. Once he had found the package he was looking for he threw his banyan on and returned to Georgie.

"I'll give you these now." He grinned and watched her open the parcel.

"Oh they're lovely." She held up a flimsy silk nightgown and laughed. "I can see why you wouldn't want to give me these in front of everyone else. I wish I had known about presents, I would have asked you to buy some in Canterbury."

"Don't worry. The archbishop's staff had me kicking my heels for so long I had time for a lot of shopping. I got you something suitable for public viewing and things for everyone I thought might be here. They can be from both of us."

"That's good. I'm looking forward to this evening."

"We'd better ring for Jepson and Martha. I have to talk to Rollo in half an hour." He kissed the tip of her nose. "You're cold."

"Martha will soon have the fire roaring. I'm going to offer her the position as my maid unless you have any objection."

"None at all. She seems a quick learner and she works miracles with your hair.

He rang his bell and helped Georgie into one of the silk robes he had given her. He studied her face. For someone who had been so happy a few minutes ago she looked decidedly dejected. What on earth was the matter? Something was bothering her.

"What's wrong, nymph? Is it Rollo? I give you my word I will be careful with him."

Georgie sighed. "It's not that. I'll have to deal with Mrs Powell on my own with Eliza injured."

"I promise we'll resolve that situation as soon as possible but for now you'll have to face it."

"I know and I can manage on the household side. I'm worried about," she hesitated, "oh I don't know." She blushed a fiery red.

"About what?"

"She'll take one look at me and realise what we've been doing." She studied the floor and refused to meet his gaze.

He winced. He had to take some blame here. It was a bit of a blur but he could remember mistaking her for a whore. If she hadn't been unsettled by that Mrs Powell's attitude might not have upset her quite so much.

"Georgie, you haven't had much experience in dealing with the superior sorts of servants found in a big household. It will become easier I promise. Besides which the woman should have kept her opinions to herself. She was badly at fault there, so we're justified in moving her on."

There was a knock on the connecting door. He went across and opened it. "Jepson wait for me in the dressing room for a moment if you will."

He ran his hands through his hair and walked back towards her. "I'll turn her off today if you want me to."

"No, I'm being silly. I know it's none of her business. I don't think we can get rid of her, for a while at least. Come on we'll both run out of time."

She shooed him into his own room and he heard her bell ring. What was he thinking of getting married at Christmas?

He ought to be helping his new bride to settle in to her responsibilities not entertaining his family. With Jepson's help he was ready in twenty minutes. He ran down the stairs and found Wakeley waiting for him in the library.

The earl jumped up when he saw him. "I'm sorry, Hargreaves. I was put out by Rollo's behaviour the other night but he has gone too far this time."

"He has and at this moment I'm wishing him to the devil. I don't know what's to be done with him. Excuse me a moment."

He put his head around the library door and called to a passing footman. "Stay by this door. When Viscount Summerton arrives knock hard before he reaches it."

"Yes, my lord."

Max went back into the library and shut the door behind him. "Take a seat, Wakeley. I suggest we sample some of this fine port I've been saving for Christmas. I very much doubt that we'll see Rollo until at least a quarter of an hour after half past four."

He filled two glasses and gave one to Wakeley before taking the seat next to him.

"Do you have anything planned for my illustrious nephew? He was bandying his title around in an attempt to gain entrance to my bedchamber. Of course, Jepson was having none of it."

"It will have to be something demanding to bring him up short."

"That's what I said but Georgie suggested he might have been no more than heedless and facing up to his actions by trying to find me as soon as possible."

"Too kind by half. She's a sweet girl, Hargreaves. I'm not sure how you found her but you've done very well there." His eyes twinkled. "Saved yourself a deal of aggravation from the womenfolk into the bargain."

Max burst out laughing. "That was a serious consideration in my decision."

Wakeley raised his eyebrows at him and waited.

"I felt obliged to offer her my hand because I might have compromised her if you must know." He grinned. "She wasn't at all sure she should accept and I used that argument about saving me from my sisters on her."

"From what I've seen of her, I think you've had a good bargain."

Max jumped up and took a turn around the room. He pointed at their glasses. "Would you like another?"

"Yes please."

Max refilled them and handed one to Wakeley before sitting down. "Georgie is quite lovely and has a generous spirit. After Lavinia I never thought I would find a lady capable of loving me for myself. Now I think I have and I can't believe my luck."

Wakeley beamed at him. "I'm so pleased, my boy."

Max nodded. "Thank you. I wonder if she is on to something with Rollo."

"I would like to think so but he has become quite wild of late. I never thanked you properly for rescuing Cecilia. The truth is I was haring off to Cambridge to sort out the debts he had run up, amongst other things, at the time. If I had been at home I would have been able to protect her."

"I don't think you can blame him for that. I remember my own father doing something similar for me."

"Perhaps, but it's his lack of consideration for other people that bothers me. I should never have let him go up to university a year early. He wasn't ready for that much freedom. He must make amends to his Aunt Eliza and Aunt Georgie, if I may call her that?"

"I'm sure she won't mind. Have you had him helping with your estate?"

"Good Lord no. There's plenty of time for that when he's older."

Max thought for a moment. "I wonder if that's the problem. My own father included me in estate matters when I was younger than he is. I enjoyed it and felt flattered by his attention. At last I was part of the adult world."

"It's worth a try. My agent is going on a tour of my northern estates at Easter. I could send him along. I'll wrap it up as a suitable punishment if you think that is sufficient?"

"Do that but tell him if he does well you will give him something he wants. We don't want to give him a distaste for estate duties."

Wakeley sat back in his chair and tossed back the last of his port. "That's easy. I'll let him buy a new hunter. Thank you, Hargreaves. That might work."

"Talking about hunters, my stud has a promising batch for next year. I'll give Rollo first pick if he mends his ways." That should please Georgie.

There was a sharp rap at the door. Max gathered himself. They needed to get the tone of this interview with Rollo exactly right if it was going to work. He didn't want Georgie thinking he was too autocratic.

Chapter Fourteen

Georgie watched Max's retreating back. He was every girl's dream and the perfect lover, so kind and generous. Would he always be so? She was in love with him already. How would she bear it if he lost interest in her?

Martha patted the last curl into place and led her to the looking glass. "You look lovely, my lady."

Georgie laughed. "Largely thanks to your ministrations. I hope you will accept the position of my maid permanently."

Martha clasped her hands together. Her eyes shone. "That's the best Christmas present anyone could give me. Ma will be so pleased. It's one less mouth to feed."

She did a little jig around the room. "Thank you so much. It serves old Ma Powell right. She said I would never amount to anything, the nasty...."

"Martha that's enough, you shouldn't talk like that about the upper servants to me."

Martha stuck out her chin. "I'm sorry but she's no friend of yours, my lady."

She didn't sound sorry and seemed poised to say more but Georgie resisted the temptation to let her. For now, she must find a way to work with Mrs Powell.

"Thank you, Martha. I'm going down to consult with Mrs Powell about the evening celebrations. You may take the rest of the evening off."

"You haven't changed your mind about me, have you?" Martha twisted a hand in her apron.

"Of course not. You're very young but it's time you learned to be careful what you say, that's all." Georgie smiled at her. "Where else would I find a maid as good with hair as you? Off you go now."

"Thank you, my lady." Martha bobbed a curtsey and ran out.

Georgie sighed. It was time to get it over with. Then she could relax. She strode down the stairs and found Barton in the hallway.

"Do you know where Mrs Powell is, Barton?"

"I believe she is in the dining room supervising the maids, my lady."

"Thank you."

Georgie strolled into the dining room and hoped she looked more confident than she felt. Mrs Powell, lips pursed, was standing over a maid who was polishing a sideboard.

"Is that the best you can do?" She spoke sharply. "I can see smudges all over it. Put some effort into it, girl."

Georgie frowned. There was nothing wrong with the girl's work. No wonder Martha hated Mrs Powell. She definitely had to go as soon as it could be arranged without comment.

"Ah, Mrs Powell. Do you have everything you need for this evening?"

Mrs Powell jumped and swung around to face her. "I didn't see you there, my lady. We'll soon have everything ready." She glanced up at Georgie from the corner of her eyes. "Lady Overton agreed the menu with Cook earlier."

Georgie's eyes narrowed. "Thank you, Mrs Powell. It seems everything is under control."

"I'll get on then." Mrs Powell bobbed the sketchiest of curtseys and walked out.

Georgie thanked the maid for her hard work and made her way to the drawing room. Eliza was sitting close to the fire with her leg propped up on a footstool. She smiled up at her and Georgie sat beside her.

"Thank you for dealing with the menu."

"I was so bored I had Barton fetch Cook in here for something to do. You don't mind, do you? You seem bothered about something."

"Martha was being disparaging about Mrs Powell and I told her off. She said something about her not being a friend of mine and I'm wishing now I had let her tell me what she meant."

"Mrs Powell is really bothering you, isn't she?"

"I've agreed with Max we will have to replace her at some point but I don't think we can do that straight away and avoid comment. She walked off so rudely it was almost asking to be discharged from her employment. I wonder if she is hoping to be paid off."

Eliza stared into the fire for a moment. "Are you afraid she is going to cause mischief, Georgie?"

"I suppose I am. My worry is that if she overplays her hand and tries to extract money from Max before he has offered any I can't see him agreeing."

Eliza burst out laughing. "I'm sorry, Georgie. I can't believe how quickly you are coming to understand Max's temperament. Don't let her spoil Christmas for you."

"I won't. As long as I stay civil and pretend not to notice any rudeness she can't force anything. My uncle used to say the only way to survive cathedral politics was to keep watch on your enemies. I think that advice applies to country houses too."

"I'm sure you're right. At least until your sudden marriage ceases to be news."

"True. For tonight I intend to enjoy myself. We were very quiet last Christmas without my uncle." A tear slipped down her cheek. She turned away from Eliza and sat down next to her.

Eliza took her hand. "Oh, you lost your uncle last year then? You have had a difficult time. I hope it's a comfort to you to have a new family now?"

"It is, believe me. You've been so kind." She forced a smile. "I'm afraid I haven't had a chance to buy any presents for you all but Max bought some in Canterbury from both of us."

"That sounds intriguing."

Georgie laughed. It's been so hectic I have no idea what he's found. I hope they're all suitable."

"He's good at finding things for children. It will be interesting to see what he's come up with for the rest of us."

A vision of the beautiful silk things Max had given her sent a wave of heat through Georgie. No one had ever given her anything half so fine. They put even the wedding gift of pearls into the shade. She snuggled into the sofa.

"The furniture is all so comfortable here."

Eliza laughed. "My mother insisted on it. Close your eyes for a few moments and relax. It will be chaotic once everyone is here."

Georgie did as she was bid. The heat of the fire and the smell of beeswax mixed with hints of spicy pine were so relaxing.

She came to with a start when she heard Peter's voice.

"Mama, you will let me stay until Uncle Max comes won't you."

"I will but I shouldn't. Look you've woken Aunt Georgie up."

Georgie sat up and stretched her back. She smiled at Peter. "It's a good thing you did wake me, Peter. I wouldn't want to miss all the fun."

Peter rested a hand on her knee. "Aunt Georgie, do you know what Uncle Max has got for me?"

"No, she doesn't, but I do."

Georgie jumped at the sound of Max's voice. His deep melodious tones had their usual effect on her senses. Hot shivers ran through her and she couldn't meet his eyes. For all she was enjoying being part of a family, what she wouldn't give for a few days completely alone with him, without even servants. She glanced up and the look Max shot at her suggested he was feeling the same. She studied the floor and hoped anyone noticing her pink cheeks would put it down to her proximity to the fire.

Peter jumped up and down in excitement. "Where is it, Uncle Max?"

"I'll have some footmen bring it in when everyone is here."

Sally and her family all entered together, shortly after Max.

"I'm glad everyone is here so promptly." Max pointed at Peter running around. "I was afraid I would have to buy a new carpet."

Nat laughed and scooped up his son. "Whose presents shall we have first Max?"

Georgie saw Max signal to a hovering Barton.

"Perhaps we should start with the ladies." Max exchanged glances with Nat.

Nat smiled down at Peter who stopped wriggling in his arms. "That would be the polite thing now wouldn't it, Peter?"

Peter hung his head. "Yes sir."

The door opened and two footmen staggered in carrying a large parcel wrapped in brown paper. Max pointed to a spot well away from the fire.

"I'm afraid they wouldn't want this present, Nat. Come on young man let's see you open it."

Peter squealed with delight and ran to the parcel as soon as his father deposited him on the floor. He tore off the paper to reveal a wooden castle with groups of toy soldiers inside the keep. Peter took a step back and gazed at it open mouthed.

"Thank you, Uncle Max, it's wonderful."

"I'm glad you approve, Peter. Perhaps you ought to count how many soldiers you've got."

Peter grinned at him and plopped down on his knees next to the castle.

Georgie was pleased to have everyone's attention attracted away from her but when Max took her hand and led her to a pile of parcels the footmen had left on a side table she felt heat flood her cheeks again. No wonder he had given her the silk items in private with everyone gathered around so closely. Max picked up three identical looking parcels and handed the first one to her, followed by one to each of his sisters.

Georgie peeled back the tissue paper covering to reveal a beautifully painted fan. Eliza and Sally had similar ones. She opened out the fan and smothered a gasp. The painting was intricately done but there was no mistaking the couple at the heart of the picture. They were miniature versions of Max and her wrapped in each other's arms. There was so much detail that their embrace was only obvious if you looked closely. Had

Max noticed? Her breath hitched for a moment.

She couldn't meet his eyes. "Thank you, Max. It's lovely."

He put an arm around her and bent towards her ear. "I thought it was rather appropriate."

Her legs trembled as if he had kissed her in public. He must have felt it as he tightened his hold on her briefly before pressing a kiss to her forehead and letting her go. Eliza and Sally added their thanks.

"I'm glad you like them." He walked across to the diminishing pile and selected a long slim parcel.

"This is for Cecilia in honour of her come out this season."

Cecilia tore off the tissue paper and turned her back on her brothers, who were grinning at her. She opened a red velvet covered box and gasped.

"Uncle Max! They're beautiful." She held out a shimmering string of pearls towards her mother.

"Those are absolutely perfect, Cecilia. That's a generous present Max."

Max laughed. "They were sold to me as suitable for a young lady at her first ball by the jewellers Eliza recommended. I'm sure I was their best customer this Christmas."

Georgie noticed his cheeks take on a tinge of red as he said it.

Sally fastened the pearls around her daughter's neck. Cecilia ran to the nearest looking glass to study her reflection.

She turned to Max, eyes shining. "Thank you so much."

Max bowed. "My pleasure." He moved towards the boys.

"I was completely stumped by what to get you three and your father." He pulled an envelope out of his pocket and handed it to Timothy.

Timothy opened it and swivelled around to face Rollo. "Oh!

It's an invitation for us to join Uncle Max at his hunting box at Easter, including Papa."

Rollo stood rooted to the spot. "I'm afraid I shall be otherwise engaged my lord." He bowed towards Max, his face wooden.

Max flicked a glance at Wakeley who nodded. "I realise that. I have agreed with your father that, if he is happy with your progress on estate matters, I'll invite you to my Irish stud farm in the summer."

Rollo's face relaxed. "Now that I would enjoy."

Harmony restored the family carried on opening presents. Georgie found herself the recipient of various trifles including a beautiful shawl from the Overtons that she was sure had originally been intended as a present from Nat to Eliza. She should have been thrilled. She smiled and thanked people in all the right places but all the time her thoughts were on Max's words. If he was going on hunting trips and visits to Ireland how much time was he intending to spend with her? Was she to be a convenience, available when required but discarded when he had better things to do?

A leaden weight settled in her stomach. She was a fool to dream of a love match. Max was considerate to his staff and tenants. He would be casually kind to her when she was with him. She remembered some of the smouldering looks he had given her. Didn't they mean something? Perhaps that was part of his seduction technique? She knew he had been a confirmed rake for years, although there had never been any talk of him seducing innocents. More fool her for hoping for more. She noticed Eliza watching her and forced a smile to her lips. It was a relief when Barton announced Mr and Mrs Armstrong and Mr and Mrs Wright.

After general greetings had been made and seats found for them, Georgie moved across to join the Armstrongs. Strange to think that if she had managed to reach them, the night she arrived, she would probably be attending this dinner as a guest.

Mr Armstrong stood and bowed. "Thank you for inviting us, Lady Hargreaves."

"Please be seated." Georgie sat next to Mrs Armstrong and smiled. "Our families are such old friends I hope you will still call me Georgie." She laughed. "It will be a long time before I become used to being called Lady Hargreaves."

Mrs Armstrong took one of her hands in both of hers. "Hmm. Something's troubling you, Georgie. What is it?"

She had known these people for years and couldn't deceive them. She decided to stick to the most general worry she could think of. "To be honest with you, my relationship with Lord Hargreaves didn't start exactly as Lady Overton told you."

Mrs Armstrong's eyes danced. "Don't tell us. If we don't know we can't lie. The important thing is he rescued you. It's obvious he already dotes on you and why shouldn't he?"

Georgie's heart skipped a beat. Could Mrs Armstrong be right? Was she worrying for nothing? She dragged her attention back to the conversation.

"Why not indeed, my love," Mr Armstrong said. "His Lordship is a lucky man." He smiled at Georgie.

"I can't tell you how happy everyone in the area is about your wedding," Mrs Amstrong said. "There has been a lot of speculation about who Lord Hargreaves might wed. Everyone is relieved he picked a sensible, caring young woman like you."

She squeezed Georgie's hand and let it go. "Lady Overton knows the ways of the polite world. My advice is to leave it all to her and say nothing."

Georgie nodded. "Thank you. I'm sure you're right. She's helped me enormously already. If you will excuse me I ought to go and speak to Mr and Mrs Wright."

Georgie spent a few minutes in greeting the Wrights until Barton announced dinner. Eliza signalled to her to lead the way to the dining room. They were a merry group. Georgie soaked up the happy atmosphere as if it was a concrete thing, forgetting her worries. For too long her life had been unremitting grief and gloom. It was lovely to enjoy cheerful company.

Max was telling some sort of tale at the opposite end of the table. His listeners burst out laughing. She tried to drag her gaze away from him. As if realising he was observed, Max glanced up at her and smiled. Her heart skipped a beat and she smiled back. She must hope and pray that Max wouldn't break her heart. At the very worst she had gained a congenial family.

It was a fabulous meal, with traditional favourites like roast beef, Christmas goose and plum pudding all featuring. Georgie felt as if she wouldn't be able to eat another thing for days by the end of it. The Hargreaves cook was excellent and all the dishes had been so tempting. Was it time for the ladies to retire to the drawing room? She glanced across at Eliza who gave her a small nod. She could do with spending months with Eliza, there was so much to learn.

"Shall we leave the gentlemen to their port, ladies?" Georgie smiled around the table.

Mrs Armstrong gave her an encouraging nod but she caught a speculative glance from Mrs Wright. She suppressed a sigh. They would have to get used to being the object of conjecture for some time, which wouldn't be helped by Mrs Powell's attitude. Would Max weary of it and wish he hadn't offered her marriage?

Chapter Fifteen

Max watched the ladies troop out. Was it his imagination or did Georgie seem edgy? She wasn't still worrying about Mrs Powell was she? Barton came in with a decanter of port and placed it on the table in front of him.

"Thank you, Barton. Perhaps you would send us another decanter of this and a decanter of brandy? Then tell the staff they may leave their duties for the rest of the evening. You may take what wine and spirits you think suitable down to the servants' quarters to help the celebrations."

Barton bowed. "Thank you, my lord. The staff will be grateful." He was smiling as he left the room.

Now that was a rare occurrence seeing Barton smile. Perhaps he ought to consult with him over Mrs Powell? It might be wise but not until after Christmas when the roads were clear and they could make their escape to London. He didn't want Georgie suffering any more than she already was.

A footman arrived with two decanters. "There is another full decanter of each in the library my lord."

"Excellent."

The door closed behind him. Max poured a generous measure of the port into his glass before passing the decanter around the table. He leaned back in his chair and raised the glass to the light of the candelabra in the middle of the table.

"Wakeley and I have already sampled this. I came across it in the cellar a few weeks ago. It must be one my father laid down."

There were general murmurs of appreciation as they sipped their drinks.

Rollo caught his eye. "Did you mean that about taking me to Ireland?"

"I certainly mean you to have the opportunity to go to Ireland and spend some time on the stud farm. Whether I'm with you depends on whether Georgie wants to go. If she doesn't, I'll send my agent over and leave him to show you around."

Rollo's face fell momentarily. Perhaps the lad would be fine after all. He was obviously desperate to be considered an adult and to mix with the men of the family.

"I expect Georgie will want to see Ireland. I hope so because I would enjoy showing you around the stud. There will be a batch of hunters ready for sale by the summer. If your father has approved it beforehand, you may select one. Your father wanted to pay me for it but consider it a coming of age present"

Rollo smiled slightly. "Thank you."

Good Lord, the lad was a cold one. He didn't seem particularly excited. "I've been told this year's crop is particularly good. You may have first choice."

"That will be interesting." Rollo had himself well in check but his eyes were glowing before he looked away from Max.

Timothy and Neil stared at their brother with mouths open. Max smiled at them.

"I'll do the same for both of you when you're Rollo's age."

Wakeley laughed. "Are you sure about this? If you have many more nephews it could prove very expensive."

"I'm more worried about the cost of pearls for my nieces. Come we are neglecting our guests. I understand you have known my wife for some time, Mr Armstrong."

"We've known her since she was born. Her uncle and I were at university together. Our paths led us in different directions but we kept in touch. When Mr Weston died, she and her aunt moved near to us and we saw a lot more of Georgie until Mrs Weston died."

"She's been through a difficult period then." Nat turned in his chair to look at him. "I'm sure Max will look after her well now."

Max grinned at him. "I most certainly will, Nat. I have every hope that we will be as happy as you and Eliza."

"I'm extremely glad to hear it, my lord," Mr Armstrong said. "She is a lovely young woman and will be a great support to you I'm sure."

Max nodded and passed the port around. It seemed such a long time since Georgie had fallen into his life and yet it was only a few days. He considered his next words carefully.

"It might have been better to wait until after Christmas and have a big family wedding but Georgie was scared of what those awful cousins she's had problems with would do. As my wife she is quite safe from them."

Mr Wright nodded. "I was so pleased to conduct the service. I'm sure you were right to secure her peace of mind."

The conversation turned general. Once they had finished their port Max led them towards the drawing room. He studied his eldest nephew. Was Rollo using him as a model of gentlemanly behaviour and was that what Georgie had hinted at? She seemed astute. He had to admit that he adopted an aloof manner sometimes and could be dictatorial. It was a front he had developed to help him deal with a huge enterprise, controlling hundreds of staff, at a very young age.

He hadn't realised the strength of the link between Georgie's family and the Armstrongs. Why hadn't she gone straight to them? The Armstrongs clearly had considerable affection for her and Mr Armstrong seemed entirely genuine in his responses. Surely, they would have taken her in and she would have known them well enough to realise that? An awful suspicion hit him.

Was she about to order transport to them when hunger drove her to eat some of an abandoned meal? Had she recognised him and set out to trap him? He shook his head in an effort to dispel the thought. How would hiding in the hay barn overnight have helped her to snare him? She couldn't have known she would be found by him. But then if she had another option why had she accepted his offer of marriage when all she knew of him was that he was a rake who drank too much? He shook his head trying to dispel his sudden doubts. She was so lovely he was worrying about nothing. Lavinia had seemed lovely too until he realised it was his friend who she wanted in her bed but his ring on her finger. All she wanted from him was his title and riches. He was a green boy then. He had far better judgement now.

His eyes met Georgie's as soon as he entered the drawing room. He broke into a spontaneous smile and she responded in kind. The tight knot his insides had wrapped themselves into dissolved. He'd lay a considerable amount of blunt that Georgie was a kind-hearted girl. She was sitting next to Cecilia who blushed and jumped up as he approached. She bobbed a curtsey and gave him a pretty thank you for her pearls before running off to sit by Eliza.

He sank into the vacated seat. "I'm glad to see at least one of my siblings' children is showing signs of tact."

Georgie gave that musical laugh that always made him want to whisk her off somewhere private.

"I think she is a little in awe of you, besides being horribly embarrassed by the trouble she put you through."

"The whole incident has dented her confidence. I told her not to worry about that. I was badly taken in once when I was two or three years older than her."

Georgie raised her eyebrows in enquiry.

He shrugged. "It was a long time ago. I was only a boy at the time. I'm not sure Sally wouldn't have done better to keep her at home for another year until she regains some of her confidence."

"She'll be alright once she's established. I think she's worried the story will have leaked." Georgie hung her head for a moment before squaring her shoulders and meeting his gaze. "She's not the only one to be nervous."

Max took one of her hands and ran his thumb around the palm. She shuddered and closed her eyes. Her immediate response to him drew an answering surge of excitement. It was fortunate their corner was in one of the gloomier parts of the room. He leant towards her.

"I had better stop touching you or I'll be forced to carry you up to bed."

Georgie's eyes flew open and she smiled at him. "You're having the same effect on me."

Max placed her hand by her side and sat back. "There's no need for either of you to worry." His expression hardened. "No one will dare to challenge us openly. Besides I'm confident my sister, Augusta, Duchess of Cathlay, will be able to squash any rumours. The whole of the Ton is terrified of her."

Georgie giggled. "Augusta is your oldest sister, isn't she? If she's that scary should I be worried about her?"

"Very possibly, she still terrifies me. Yes, she's the eldest. Her husband is formidable too. The Cathlay family are spending Christmas with relatives of Cathlay in Berkshire this year. They will leave for London as soon as the weather is suitable, which is lucky for us."

Georgie laughed out loud and he grinned back at her.

"It will take me a long time to get used to the idea of being part of a large family. I don't even know all the names yet but I've heard Eliza and Sally mention Augusta with awe."

"It was much quieter when she left home but I think we're all secretly proud of her. She has the ear of most of the government. Of course, being married to the Duke of Cathlay is a big help in that."

"You will have to make me a list of all the names of children and spouses."

"I'll try. When my parents were alive we used to have a big gathering here in the summer. Once you're settled it's something we might reintroduce."

"I would like that. It would be easier if I met a least a few more of them first though."

People seemed to have moved into groups. A quick glance around showed no one looking in their direction. Max edged up closer to Georgie until he could feel the heat of her thigh pressed against his. He put an arm around her and drew her close. She closed her eyes and rested her head on his shoulder. His thoughts turned to quiet evenings in the future, spent together with no family intruding. Once he had introduced Georgie to the Ton, he planned on staying put in the country for at least a year.

* * *

Georgie gave a sigh of contentment. She felt so safe with Max's arm around her. The events of the past couple of years, which had dragged her down so much, seemed so far away it felt like they were from a different country. In a way they were. She was living in a completely different world now. No matter how reliable or otherwise Max proved to be, she was sure that he would protect her from people like Cousin Mary. The sounds of people chatting receded until all she could hear was the sound of Max's heart beating steadily against the ear that was resting on his chest.

The next thing she knew she was being carried up the grand staircase, in Max's arms. She tried to sit up.

"Keep still, Georgie. I don't want to drop you."

She lay back, eyes closed. The smell of the wonderful cologne that haunted her dreams tickled her nose. Max ran up the rest of the stairs as if she weighed no more than a powder puff. This time he didn't have mounds of snow slowing him down, or a sore head. She heard him kick a door open and opened her eyes. Max laid her down on her bed.

She stretched. "How long was I asleep? So rude of me."

Max perched on the edge of the bed next to her. "Well over an hour but don't worry. I don't think anyone noticed for some time. For once my family were giving us some privacy. The Armstrongs said they were glad you were so relaxed. I saw them to the carriage when they were ready."

"Thank you, Max. They're such good people."

"It seems you know them well, much better than I realised. Why didn't you see Mr Pleck and hire a carriage to take you to them?"

Georgie finished waking up with a jolt. Why was he thinking about that? A hand flew to her cheek. "I was afraid you might return and tell everyone I was a whore." It sounded rather lame said like that but it was the truth, or at least part of the truth.

Her eyes found his. He didn't look convinced. "I didn't plan to go to them because Cousin Mary had a legal hold on me until my birthday. She has a friend who is a rather sinister lawyer."

Max cradled her hand and some of the tension ebbed out of her.

"Yet you were trying to get to them later?"

"I had no choice then. I didn't feel safe at the inn even if Mr Pleck would agree to give me a room." She glanced at Max who had the grace to blush. "I was confident they would take me in, but I didn't want to put them in the position of aiding a criminal act by arriving before reaching my majority. The church might have disciplined Mr Armstrong if it had come out. It would have been difficult to keep my presence secret at the vicarage."

"Perhaps, but you would have been more likely to be discovered at a public place like the Golden Cross."

She must try and make him understand. Her head was aching but she ploughed on. "No one takes much notice of comings and goings at an inn. If Mrs Pleck had been there, I could have stayed hidden until Christmas Eve quite easily."

"You look exhausted. I don't know why I'm making such a fuss. I was just surprised to see how fond of you the

175

Armstrongs are." He bent over and kissed her forehead. "You need some sleep. I'll send Jepson to fetch Martha to help you undress."

Georgie forced herself into a sitting position. "Don't have them dragged away from the staff party, Max."

He laughed. "No matter what I say to Jepson he won't join the party until he has put my clothes away. Martha will want to attend you."

He kissed her again and strolled to the connecting door. Fatigue and disappointment overwhelmed her. Didn't he trust her? She threw a corner of the bedcover over her head as sobs racked her body and the tears flowed. So many tears she thought they would never cease. Eventually her breathing slowed and the tears stopped. If only Max would come back and put his arms around her.

There was a soft tap at the door. "Come in."

Martha entered. "His Lordship sent Jepson for me, my lady. He said you were exhausted and needed my help."

"I don't want you to miss your party."

"It's no matter." She pulled a face. "Old Ma Powell sent me to bed early anyway."

Georgie noticed Martha's rumpled clothing and the cap clinging to her head at an odd angle. "I'm sorry if you were woken up."

"I wasn't asleep."

Martha helped her up and out of her clothes. Georgie selected one of the warm nightgowns Eliza had given her. She didn't feel like wearing one from Max's present. She squeezed her eyes and mouth tightly shut. She didn't want to cry in front of Martha. She had had such different plans, ones which included Max undressing her. Martha offered to fetch a warming pan but she sent the by now sleepy girl back to her own bed. She curled up under the covers but sleep eluded her.

Why was Max suddenly suspicious of her actions? Did he think she was more experienced than she was? She couldn't help herself responding enthusiastically to his lovemaking. Surely that wouldn't be enough for him to think she had tricked him? He had told her to enjoy herself and she had taken him at his word. A flash of heat surged through her. Perhaps most innocent girls took longer to feel comfortable with that side of things.

Even so he had seemed happy that she was enjoying herself in the marital bed. There must be something more. She had to find out. She felt safe from the world with Max to protect her but if he didn't trust her, she would never find love with him. Eliza had hinted at the problems he'd had with girls trying to trap him into marriage. What was it he'd said earlier? Something about telling Cecilia he had been a bigger fool than she had and at two or three years older. What was the name he had mentioned? Lavinia, that was it, wanting to marry him for material gain but loving someone else. She would have to try and get Eliza to tell her the whole story.

She'd laughed at other girls declaring instant love when a young man took their fancy. Now she knew it could happen. She couldn't think of any other reason she had allowed herself to be railroaded into this sham of a marriage. Yes, Max could be forceful, arrogant even, but she could have withstood him. What a fool she had been. Max was a rake. He would always be able to respond to an attractive girl and he'd shown he found her attractive. That didn't mean he loved her. All the people she had loved in life had gone. Marrying a man who, deep down, she thought could replace them had been foolhardy.

She had to try and protect what was left of her heart.

Chapter Sixteen

Max woke up with a start. Had he left Georgie sobbing? It sounded like it before she threw the covers over her face. He never had known what to do with a crying girl. She must be exhausted with all that had happened to her. Conscience pricked at him. She was too intelligent not to realise he had suddenly been assailed by doubts about her. Those doubts seemed ridiculous with daylight streaming in through the windows. He must have been overtired himself. She'd told him before that her instinct was to hide until she reached her twenty first birthday. Hiring a coach at the inn would have been far too public an action.

He jumped out of bed and threw on his banyan. The view from the window showed that the snow was starting to melt. Big chunks were hanging to the edges of branches leaving splashes of brown behind. He wandered around unable to move his thoughts away from Georgie. Where was Jepson? Perhaps it had been an extremely good party in the servant's hall. No matter how many times he told Jepson to rest downstairs until hearing the bell, he was always waiting in the dressing room when he awoke. Was he too stern an employer?

There was a knock at the main bedroom door and Jepson entered with a tray containing a coffee pot, two cups and plates of fresh smelling bread with a mixture of preserves.

"Martha tells me Her Ladyship is still in her room, my lord. I took the liberty of bringing up a breakfast tray for you."

Max suppressed a grin. Trust Jepson to know what was best to do. Martha must have told him her mistress seemed upset last night.

"Thank you, Jepson. You may have some time off. I'll ring the bell when I have need of you."

Jepson placed the tray on a side table and bowed his way out.

Max picked up the tray. He was across the room to the connecting door in a few swift strides. There was no answer to his knock. He hesitated for a moment before pushing the door open. He held his breath until he saw Georgie still asleep in the big four poster bed that looked far too big for her small frame. He was about to tiptoe out when she opened her eyes and smiled at him. Relief ran through him with a jolt. If he had upset her last night she didn't look as if she was going to hold it against him.

He set the tray down on a side table and pulled it near to the bed.

"Jepson thought we might like to breakfast alone this morning." He held his breath until Georgie smiled at him again. Perhaps he had imagined those sobs?

"I'm famished. Jepson is a treasure. How long has he been with you?"

"His family were tenants of the estate. He wanted to go into the army but there is something wrong with his feet. He can't do too a great deal of walking so he had to find other employment. My father had him trained as a valet."

Max sat on the bed and picked up the coffee pot. The bread was still warm from the oven. They demolished all of it. He shot a glance at Georgie from under his brows. She seemed quite composed this morning. He moved the table away from the bed and sat beside her. She seemed inclined to ignore what had been said the night before and he was happy to follow her lead. He took her hand and ran a thumb around her palm, remembering the effect it usually had on her. She shuddered and leaned backwards exposing the white flesh above her nightgown. The overlarge gown had slipped off the shoulder nearest to him.

He ran a series of light kisses from her shoulder and up her neck to her ear. He heard a soft moan but she didn't move towards him as she usually did. Perhaps she was tired and didn't want intimacy this morning? With an effort he held himself in check.

"Georgie, would you like me to join you in bed? I'll understand if you're too tired."

She looked away from him and for a moment he thought she was going to refuse him. Then she caught his gaze. He could lose himself in those shimmering grey eyes.

"Of course, I would, Max."

Was he imagining it or had she hesitated? He ached with passion but should he ask her again? She ran her tongue around her lips and he was lost. His banyan landed in a heap on the floor and he slipped under the covers into the space she made for him. His mouth found hers and after a brief hesitation she responded to his kisses. Their coupling was a welcome release for him and yet even as he collapsed by her side, sleepy with spent passion, he knew something was missing.

It was almost as if she was holding herself in check. Her exuberant enjoyment, which had delighted him so much, was gone. Perhaps she had a headache or something of that nature? She had her back turned to him. He rolled so that he was cradling her with his body and put his arm around her waist. She gave a little sigh that he wanted to believe was contentment. Then he remembered that her nightgown, which had ended up on top of his banyan on the floor, wasn't one of the ones he had given her. Was the shimmering effect in her heavenly, grey eyes he'd been entranced by caused by unshed tears? Oh Lord, he had upset her. What could he do to make it up to her?

He woke up an hour later when Georgie climbed out of bed. She smiled at him and seemed perfectly happy. He reclaimed his banyan and saw that she was wearing one of the dressing gowns he had bought her. Perhaps he was imagining things. She might have simply been sleepy. He offered to have Jepson order a hot bath for her and she accepted.

For once Jepson wasn't in his rooms so he rang his bell. Jepson came in a few minutes later together with a footman carrying his hot water for shaving. Max sent the footman back downstairs with orders to organise hot water for a bath for Georgie. Jepson seemed quieter than usual.

"Was it a good party last night, Jepson?"

"Tolerable, my lord."

Max eyed him carefully. "Are you feeling quite the thing?"

"I'm very well, thank you. I had no more than a glass of port."

Max nodded and allowed Jepson to shave him. He was certainly a lot quieter than normal. Perhaps he'd drunk more than he liked to admit to. Jepson laid out an outfit for him and he dressed quickly. He ran lightly down the stairs and into the breakfast room, in search of something more substantial than bread and coffee.

Eliza and Nat were the only people in there, which was a relief. "Where is everybody?"

The boys have all gone sledging before the snow disappears. I think the whole family breakfasted early with them," Eliza said.

Max piled his plate with ham and eggs and sat down opposite to them. Nat handed him a still warm coffee pot.

"Thank you. It's a relief to have a quiet breakfast."

Nat and Eliza exchanged glances.

"Sally was saying that the boys would like to go back home after today if the roads are passable," Eliza said. "The idea was to come back for twelfth night if you agreed."

Max laughed out loud. "Don't tell me my family are developing some tact after all these years."

Nat and Eliza joined in. "Surprising isn't it. I think it was largely down to Rollo wanting to go back to Canterbury to meet up with his friends but Sally did say it would be better if we all went to give you two some peace."

Max raised an eyebrow at her. "Does that mean you're leaving as well?"

"That's the plan." Eliza looked around the room but they were alone. "The only thing is will Georgie be alright managing Mrs Powell on her own?"

The door was slightly ajar. Max walked across and checked the hallway but there was no sign of any servants about. He shut the door before sitting down again.

"That is something of a problem but it will only be for a few days. I can't for the life of me think why Cook recommended Mrs Powell to me. But it does mean I'll have to be tactful about how I go about turning Mrs Powell off. I would hate to lose

Cook as well."

Eliza grimaced. "That's true, although Mrs James has been at Hargreaves Hall since she was first in service. I don't think she's likely to leave over it. Georgie was worried about dismissing Mrs Powell straight away. She's probably right about it being best left for a bit."

Max nodded. "She said that did she? If the thaw holds, I mean to take Georgie straight up to London after Twelfth Night. I'm sure she'll enjoy putting Hargreaves House to rights." He hesitated and Eliza finished for him.

"You're thinking to take Mrs Mills into your confidence?"

"Yes. She wrote to me before Christmas to say she thought the time was coming for her to retire fully."

"Ah. She can help you find a new housekeeper without causing comment. You're becoming amazingly good at plotting, dear brother."

Max gave her a mock bow, largely to cover his confusion. Was Georgie worried about causing unfavourable comment or was she keen not to upset Mrs Powell for some reason? She had been wary of her right from the start and he only had her word for the reason for that. Suddenly the opportunity he had yearned for to spend time alone with Georgie didn't seem so appealing. If there was something that she wasn't telling him he wasn't sure he wanted to know. Eliza was watching him closely and he caught himself up.

"If we can get Hargreaves House into shape quickly enough, I might offer Sally the chance to combine Cecilia's come out ball with a ball to introduce Georgie to the ton. What do you think?"

Eliza screwed up her nose in thought. "It hasn't been used for a long time but Mrs Mills will have kept it in reasonable shape. It's got one of the best ballrooms in London. Sally's is nowhere near as big. See what she thinks but it could be a good idea."

Max nodded. "That just leaves the worry of that disturbance at the church before the wedding. Now the snow is melting it won't be so easy to keep a look out for strangers entering the grounds."

"Ah, I've had a message from the groom who is tracking those two." Nat said. "They've set off in the direction of London. My man will follow them and see what he can find out. He'll report to Bright as soon as he's back at our London house. We'll go to London as soon as we can."

"That's reassuring, but could there be more men about?"

"He's confident there were only two. They were quite well dressed, perhaps they were sent to try and stop the ceremony. Let's hope he doesn't lose them and we might find out."

"If Selina was prepared to go to that sort of length then she's more of a threat than I realised." Max stroked his chin.

"I think you're safe for now, but take sensible precautions. Don't go out without protection and when you go to London make sure you take an armed guard with you."

Eliza's hands flew to her face. "Surely Selina isn't a danger. I mean half the time she's just been after money to bail Bertie out."

"It's amazing what people are prepared to do for money and position." Max's shoulders slumped. "Let's hope it was a false alarm."

* * *

Georgie watched as Martha sprinkled lavender into the tub.

185

She stepped out of her robe and climbed into the soothing water. Martha stoked up the fire and went into the dressing room to select a gown. Not that there was much choice yet. Georgie lay back and let the heat of the water soak into her. She still had a headache but the smell of the lavender helped to relax her and she could feel it lifting.

Max could be so thoughtful. He seemed more like his normal self this morning. Perhaps things would be alright between them once they got to know each other better. It would break her heart if they weren't. She stretched trying to release the sudden tension in her body. Max was becoming far too important to her sense of wellbeing. She was already a little in love but it would be safer to keep her distance until she was sure of him. She laughed. She may as well try and hold back the tides.

When she arrived downstairs the adults were all gathered in the drawing room. The men stood up as she entered. Max came forward to greet her. Was it her imagination or did he look a bit strained?

"How do you feel now, Georgie?" He sounded concerned.

"Much better thank you. The headache that has been bothering me since yesterday has disappeared."

Max seemed to relax. "Good. It's time to distribute the Christmas boxes amongst the staff."

She greeted the others and set off with Max for the servants' hall. The staircase down to the servants' quarters was a good width and well lit, quite a contrast with the one in Cousin Mary's house. All the servants were lined up waiting for them. Martha gave her a shy smile, quickly suppressed when Mrs Powell's gaze alighted on them.

A footman followed them down with a large money box.

Georgie watched, intrigued, as Max opened it to reveal tidy rows of envelopes. She leaned closer and noticed each one had a name on it. It must have taken ages for someone to make all those. Max greeted the staff and asked Georgie to be ready to hand each envelope out. He worked methodically through each name. Some of the younger staff looked desperate to open theirs. Georgie smiled at each one as she handed the envelope over. She was gratified at the number of servants who gave her an answering smile.

Eventually Max dismissed all the servants apart from Barton and Mrs Powell. He took out the last two envelopes, which were larger than the rest. Georgie took a deep breath and handed Mrs Powell hers. She managed to produce a smile but was rewarded with an insolent glare. She kept her features firmly fixed. Barton came forward and her smile became sincere. He bowed and smiled back at her.

"Thank you, my lady. May I say how good it is to have the old tradition of the mistress of the house handing out the Christmas boxes revived?"

Georgie inclined her head. "Thank you."

"I agree with you, Barton," Max said. "I'm sure the whole household is glad to have a mistress again. Thank you both for all your hard work, over Christmas and throughout the year. Now we had better get back to our guests."

Georgie accepted the arm Max held out to her. She glimpsed a disgusted expression cross Mrs Powell's face. It was so fleeting, she almost wondered if she had imagined it, but she knew she hadn't. Max led her back up the stairs. When they reached the hall he drew her towards a sofa near to the fire burning in the hearth. There was a spicy tang in the air from the thin branches of pine wrapped around the oak yule log at its heart.

"I own several properties but Hargreaves Hall has always been my favourite, perhaps because my mother loved it too. It's the place I always think of as home and I expect we will spend a bigger part of the year here than anywhere else."

Max leaned back and stretched an arm along the sofa behind her. There was no one about and Georgie wondered why he didn't put it around her shoulders. She turned so that she could see his face. He looked relaxed enough, if a little stern.

"It is lovely here. This part of the building must be quite old."

"Yes, it is. Various Hargreaves have added to the original Hall over the centuries but I think that's part of its charm. My mother loved the history but she was a kinder mistress than many from previous generations." He lowered his voice. "The previous housekeeper, Mrs Mills, was here from before I was born. She's a more congenial soul than Mrs Powell."

Georgie laughed. "That wouldn't be difficult."

Max's answering smile seemed strained. "No indeed. Mrs Powell certainly doesn't seem to like you."

Georgie felt a blush flood her cheeks. She lowered her head and stared into the fire. "I suppose the manner of my arrival was rather unconventional but she shows no sign of warming to me."

Max sighed. "No. At times, her manner to you just now seemed insolent. Mrs Mills is in semi-retirement at Hargreaves House in London. It hasn't been used by the family in years."

Georgie glanced at him in surprise. "I thought you were in London quite often?"

"I am but I have a smaller property my father bought for

me when I came of age. I propose we move to London straight after Christmas. Do you have any objection?"

"No, of course not, if that's what you wish." Would it make any difference if she did?

He stared at her for a moment and then seemed satisfied. "Good. I propose we enlist Mrs Mill's help in finding a new housekeeper suitable for here."

Georgie nodded. "Is Mrs Mills thinking of retiring completely?"

"Yes, she is. I see you've worked out my reasoning. People will think Mrs Mills is looking for someone to replace her. Whoever you select with her help can spend some time in tandem with Mrs Mills and if you're still happy with her we'll offer her the position here."

Peter came running down the stairs with a panting maid trying to catch up with him. Max's face lit up.

"Peter, apologise to your nursemaid for running away from her."

"But, Uncle Max, I don't need a nursemaid now I'm wearing breeches."

"Apologise, Peter." Max's voice deepened a little.

Peter hung his head. "I'm sorry."

"That's better." Max addressed the nursemaid. "Don't worry. I'll look after this young scamp until his parents claim him."

She smiled and bobbed a curtsey. "Thank you, my lord. I'll go and see to Miss Judith."

He moved away from Georgie and lifted Peter to sit between them. Georgie felt her insides knot together. The fear of not providing Max with an heir she had forgotten about briefly hit her anew. She heard a trill of laughter and Eliza hobbled into view. Nat had an arm around her waist helping her to walk. They looked so happy with each other that Georgie felt the knot in her insides twist tighter. Would she and Max ever achieve such a comfortable rapport?

"There you are, Peter," Eliza said. "Nurse said you don't want to leave Hargreaves Hall, but we'll be coming back for the Twelfth Night party."

"Want to stay here."

Nat bent down and scooped up his son. "I'm sorry, old man, we have to go home for a few days."

"Why can't I stay without you?"

Nat and Eliza exchanged grins. "We need you with us," Nat said.

Max stood up. "If you're a good boy I'll take you somewhere special when you come to London."

Peter looked from Max to his parents with his mouth hanging open. "We're going to London?"

Nat set him back on his feet. "We are if we can get everything done at home that we need to in time."

Georgie tried not to smile as she watched the emotions on Peter's face before he capitulated.

"I'll help you then. When can we go to London?"

"Once Twelfth Night is over, we'll go as soon as the roads are clear. Come on. Let's leave your uncle in peace."

The Overtons had no sooner disappeared when Cecilia came out of the drawing room. She walked across to them and Max stood up.

"Oh, Uncle Max. You're the best of uncles. I do hope Hargreaves House can be ready in time." She dropped down next to Georgie. "It'll be famous if I can share my debut with you, Georgie. I'll feel so much happier with two of us sharing the attention."

Georgie's heart lurched. It seemed Max had discussed his plans with everyone except her. She forced a smile for Cecilia's sake and glanced up at a still standing Max. "Am I correct in thinking that Hargreaves House has a magnificent ballroom?"

Max nodded. "Yes, it does. I hope you like the idea. I need to go and speak to Wakeley, if you'll excuse me?"

She inclined her head. "Of course."

Max gave her a curt bow and was gone. Where was the happy bridegroom who had consulted her on everything? Mrs Powell's attitude to her seemed to have unsettled him further. Or was there another reason for his distancing himself? She forced her attention to the happily chattering Cecilia.

Chapter Seventeen

Max's head was beginning to ache. The notion that Georgie was afraid of Mrs Powell in some way kept intruding on his thoughts. Did the woman have a hold over her? If she did it could only mean one thing. How would he bear it if Georgie proved to have schemed to trap him? He could try questioning Mrs Powell but he didn't want her guessing he intended to move her on. Besides, if Georgie had lied to him he wanted to hear it from her own lips. At least she had the excuse of being in danger from her cousin. Could he even be sure of that though?

The library was unoccupied when he reached it. He closed the door and strode over to the window. He had been so hopeful that he had found love. It would be too cruel if Georgie turned out to be as heartless as Lavinia. The snow-clad view failed to hold his attention. He poured himself a brandy and sat down in an armchair in front of the fire. It might be melting outside but it didn't feel much warmer. Strange how he could think about mundane matters like that when his world was falling down around him. He could only hope they would be able to forge a reasonable relationship whatever the truth of it.

He sipped his brandy and savoured its heat as it slipped down. A small part of him refused to believe that Georgie was the same as all the other women who had tried to trick their way into marriage. She hadn't even accepted him straight away, although that could have been a ruse to deflect suspicion. She was by far the most intelligent of the candidates for his hand, the legitimate ones provided by his sisters included. As unlikely as it seemed could she have engineered that meeting?

He put his drink down and rested his chin in his hands with his elbows on his knees. He had drunk so much the day before he must still have been in his cups when he carried her home. What had possessed him to think that marrying Georgie on impulse like that would give him the best chance of happiness? She was lovely and it was no surprise that he desired her. What he hadn't bargained for was falling in love with her so quickly. He had to try and guard what was left of his heart until he could find out the truth about their meeting.

The door opened to admit Wakeley. "Sally has been telling me about your plan to open up Hargreaves House and hold a joint ball. Mighty generous of you. It applies in reverse if it can't be done in time."

"Thank you. I'm confident Mrs Mills will have the house in reasonable shape. It should be possible." He waved a hand towards the decanters on a side table. "Will you join me in a drink?"

Wakeley beamed at him. "Don't mind if I do." He poured out a brandy and sat opposite to Max. "Cecilia has taken to Georgie. It's put some backbone into her. I can't believe how upset she got over that worthless lump."

Max's stomach contracted at a memory of the mocking face of Lavinia when he caught her in bed with one of his rivals. "I can. It's a terrible thing to find out someone you thought loved you is playing you for a fool. I'm not sure which is worse, the lost love or the feeling of being cheated."

A dull flush coloured Wakeley's cheeks. "Ah, of course, I had forgotten about that episode with Lavinia Fellowes."

Max gave a harsh laugh. "I don't suppose the Ton has. If you remember I ignored all the rules of gentlemanly conduct and broke off my engagement. I would understand if you'd rather not have your daughter linked with me in any way."

"I'm proud to have you as a brother-in-law, Hargreaves. I can't speak for the ladies but most of the men I know were glad you did. I'm sorry, but Miss Fellowes was a minx and a nasty one at that. I'm so glad you've found Georgie."

Max nodded to hide his expression. "We need to be prepared to face down more than one scandal."

"Yours is old news. There might have been a few whisperings but, with your prompt actions, I don't think Cecilia's story ever got out. I was worried she might struggle in London but with Georgie to support her I think all will be well."

"There is also the problem of our rather hasty marriage which might cause talk." Max looked away and rubbed at his chin.

"I shouldn't worry about that. Sally and Eliza have had their heads together." Wakeley stretched his legs out and smiled. "They're confident your marriage can be passed off as a longstanding arrangement, delayed because Georgie was in mourning. Don't forget Sally knew Mrs Weston quite well at one time from their work with local charities."

"I hope you're right but it may not be that easy."

Wakeley gripped his shoulder. "You're worrying too much. Hardly surprising after the humiliation Lavinia caused you."

"Perhaps." Max got up and fetched another drink. "Would Cecilia be better to wait until next year when Augusta's eldest girl will be ready to join her."

"Sally thinks it would be worse if Cecilia has too much time to dwell on her lucky escape. And Cathlay isn't keen on girls coming out into society too young. It might be two years before they present Fiona." Wakeley beamed at him. "Cecilia's looking forward to her season now she has Georgie to share it with. Such a warm young lady."

Max cursed inwardly. He couldn't say more without exposing his fears about Georgie.

"I intend to set off for London straight after Twelfth Night. The sooner we start on Hargreaves House the better. I'll have a message sent to Augusta when the roads are passable. She will know how to face down any scandals."

"Sally had the same thought. You'll be in hot water with Augusta for not waiting for her to attend the wedding."

Max nodded. "Don't I know it."

If he could bear it, he would be best to tell Augusta the whole. Including his fears about Georgie. Perhaps he was seeing problems where there were none, but Mrs Powell's attitude towards Georgie was strange.

* * *

Max went off to play billiards with Nat and Wakeley after dinner. Georgie chattered with the ladies in the drawing room before pleading fatigue. The strain of trying not to appear as if she was waiting for Max to return had brought on a repeat of her headache. When she reached her room an excited Martha, asking questions about London, made her nerves jangle even more. It was a relief when she was finally alone.

She climbed into bed and waited for Max to appear. Her

candle burned low and still she waited. She reached over and snuffed it out completely. The large bed felt so empty without Max lying beside her. She took herself to task. There would be plenty of time for her and Max to be together when their guests had left. He was being a good host. It was a long time before she fell asleep.

She didn't see Max the following day until they waved off the Fordhams midway through the morning. He offered her his arm but seemed preoccupied. They ate an early luncheon with the Overtons before they too left for home. Georgie had only known Eliza for a few days but she felt bereft without her support. They made their way back up the steps to the front door. Barton greeted them.

"A messenger has arrived, my lord. I believe he's from your secretary." Barton picked up a letter from a table inside the door and handed it to Max.

Max studied the envelope. "Looking at this writing I'm sure you're correct Barton. Excellent."

He led her into the drawing room but didn't seem inclined to talk. Georgie sat down and watched as he opened the letter.

"Now I know why I pay my secretary a handsome wage. Have I mentioned Charles Breakwell to you before?"

Georgie nodded. "Yes, I'm sure you have."

"He's staying with his uncle in Porchester and is ready to come back whenever I have need of him." Max laughed. "Since that's half way to London I'll have him bespeak rooms in Porchester for us on the seventh of January. I'll go and write a note for the messenger to take back with him."

Georgie watched his retreating back. He seemed a lot more cheerful now he was organising their removal to London. He had seemed so pleased with her at first. Was that merely a show for his relatives? What was she going to do with herself? She could look for a book in the library but Max was probably in there writing his letter. She didn't want to pester him. If she was on better terms with Mrs Powell, she could busy herself with household matters. Eliza had said to deal directly with the cook on menus.

She fought down her reluctance and jumped to her feet. It was time she got to know the cook better. She remembered the way down to the housekeeper's room. Her breathing quickened when she reached it. Pinning a smile on her face, she knocked on the door.

"Come in."

Georgie gulped in a big breath and pushed open the door. "I would like to consult with Cook if you would be so good as to direct me to her."

Mrs Powell was sitting at her desk. She didn't stand up and Georgie felt a spurt of anger. She resisted an impulse to turn tail and run. "The cook if you please."

Georgie locked gazes with Mrs Powell and waited. This was a battle she was determined to win. Mrs Powell lowered her eyes and pulled herself to her feet.

"My joints are aching today," she said, head bowed. "I'll take you to her myself."

She waved Georgie out into the corridor. "The kitchens are through the second door along, my lady."

Georgie sailed through the door indicated, head held high. The delicious smell of a joint of beef roasting on a spit over a modern looking range was the first thing she noticed. It was a bigger kitchen than she was used to, with three scrubbed pine tables in the centre. An impressive array of dried herbs hanging along one wall caught her eye as she walked in. The place was a hive of activity, with people scurrying here and there, but Cook was obvious from her uniform. She wiped floury hands on her apron and bobbed a curtsey. The other staff shot wary looks at Mrs Powell and retreated to the farthest corners of the cavernous kitchen.

Georgie blessed her excellent memory for names and faces, honed helping her Aunt and Uncle with their parishioners. "Mrs James is it not?"

Mrs James bobbed another curtsey. "Bless you, my lady. Fancy you remembering my name."

She relaxed a little. Cook seemed disposed to be friendly. She turned to dismiss Mrs Powell. Her smile nearly wavered as she glimpsed the glare covering Mrs's Powell's face. It was fleeting but so venomous Martha's words ran through her brain. 'She's no friend of yours.'

"Thank you, Mrs Powell."

Mrs Powell sketched a curtsey and stumped out. Georgie watched her leave. She needed a moment to compose herself. Mrs James regarded her with a rather wary expression. Her hands fluttered at her side. Strange that she should be so nervous. Perhaps Mrs Powell had that effect on her.

"I have a lot to thank you for, Mrs James."

She went bright red and stared at Georgie. Was Barton the only normal one amongst the upper servants?

Georgie tried again. "Your cooking is excellent. Our wedding breakfast and then the Christmas dinner were triumphs. I'm afraid we will need to prevail on you and your staff for the Twelfth Night Dinner as well."

Mrs James's arms stilled and her facial expression became more relaxed. "It's no bother, my lady. We love a challenge. I'll put together a suggested menu for you to consider."

"I would like to see it but I will rely on you. I don't have much experience of this sort of event."

Mrs James smiled at her. "I'm always open to suggestions. Now I understand dinner is only for two this evening. Do you have any favourite dishes you'd like me to prepare?"

Georgie fell into a conversation about food. She was used to ordering menus for small groups. Mrs James was as amenable as Mrs Powell was surly. She felt so comfortable she could have stopped in the kitchen all afternoon. Eventually she called a halt and slipped back up the stairs. She felt like a criminal in what was now her own house and couldn't resist glancing behind her to see if Mrs Powell was about.

She caught a glimpse of a black gown disappearing around the corner below her. It looked like the woman had been spying on her. What had Max been thinking of employing someone like that in the first place? She shook her head to try and dispel images of Max that jostled for space in her mind. The object of her thoughts came into view.

"Ah there you are. How did you find Mrs Powell today?"

"I only saw her briefly. I went to speak to Cook."

Max gave her a hard look but she couldn't face talking about Mrs Powell and her rudeness.

"I see. I've sent the letter to Charles together with another note for Augusta. I've asked him to arrange a courier to deliver it to Augusta. I can't say I'm looking forward to the dressing down she'll give me."

Georgie studied his face. "Oh dear, will she be very angry?"

"She'll calm down eventually and I have a feeling we'll need her diplomatic skills."

Georgie hung her head. That was all she needed, an irascible sister-in-law to add to a belligerent housekeeper. Fatigue hit her. She had always longed for adventure and yet now she had it she longed for a quiet life.

"Some people are never satisfied." She looked up to find Max staring at her.

"What was that you said?"

Oh heavens, she must have spoken her thoughts aloud. "Nothing, Max. I'm sorry for all the trouble I've caused you." She swayed slightly and tears formed in her eyes.

"I wish my aunt was still alive."

Tears threatened in earnest and she ran past Max and up the stairs. When she reached the privacy of her rooms she locked the external door and the one to Max's suite. She threw herself on the bed, stopping only to kick off her shoes. He seemed so cross. Their marriage was never going to work. Sobs racked her body until she slumped into an exhausted sleep.

* * *

Jepson wasn't waiting for him when Max entered his bedroom. He reached for the bell but dropped his hand. He could bear it no longer. If Georgie was being blackmailed by Mrs Powell for her part in a plot to ensnare him, he needed to know. He marched to the connecting door and tried to open it. What the devil. He tried it again and shook it until it rattled but the solid oak door and brass fittings wouldn't budge. Georgie must have locked it on him. He strode about the room, running a hand through his hair until it stood on end.

Some people are never satisfied. Had he heard her correctly? If so, it could only mean one thing. Hell and damnation. It felt like a tight fist gripped his chest. Why had he been fool enough to think he might find love at last? Georgie had seemed upset when she came up. If she had locked her door it was unlikely that he would get anything out of her. No, he would have to accept the situation and make the best of the marriage that he could. He had been half way to falling in love with the chit. At least now he could spare himself that.

He moved over to the window. The last of the day was disintegrating into what looked like being a stormy night. The thaw had brought rain with it in abundance. If it stayed this mild there should be nothing to stop them travelling to London straight after Twelfth Night. He slapped a hand down onto the window sill so hard that it stung. He gave it a shake and stared at the scudding clouds rushing to cover up the last of the evening light. It was as if they mocked him for ever believing Georgie had lit up his life with joy.

What nonsense was this? He shook his head in an effort to dispel such fanciful thoughts. It was a pity he had promised Sally and Eliza a party. He would have been glad to set off for London at first light. At least there he would have plenty of distractions to take his mind off his ills. The best he could do was to send another message to Charles to remind him to have everything organised for travel on the seventh of the month. He had no idea how he was going to face his bride in the meantime.

Jepson appeared quickly once he rang the bell. Max stayed in the shadows so he wouldn't see his face clearly.

"I have a fancy for a hot bath, Jepson. I believe there is plenty of time before dinner."

"Very good, my lord. I'll have one brought up to you straight away."

Max lounged on a chair at the side of the room and watched Jepson put his head around the door. Footsteps receded along the landing but Jepson returned with a footman. He must have had two stationed there.

"It will be with you shortly." Jepson directed the footman to stoke up the fire and then go and help carry up hot water.

Max sighed. He heard the sounds of Jepson moving around in his dressing room selecting clothes. Life went on whatever setbacks it threw at you. He felt worse than he had that night he'd discovered Lavinia in bed with another man. Lavinia had been a dream which deep down he'd realised wasn't real.

Dammit, he had been glad he'd caught them as it gave him the excuse he'd needed to end the engagement. Any lingering doubts were put to the rightabout when Lavinia hadn't even had the decency to give her name to the withdrawal. The scandal had been huge but it had been worth it to avoid her scheming talons. Georgie had seemed a different sort of woman altogether, kind and unassuming. Perhaps she was. Her situation had been desperate and he had to hope she'd decided to trap him only after recognising him at the inn.

Then again, didn't Mrs Powell have friends nearby? One of them could have been the man who had seen them together. It would be unbearable if Mrs Powell was known to Georgie and had helped her plan the whole thing. Whatever had happened Mrs Powell had to go sooner rather than later. He couldn't bear to witness Georgie prevaricating about the woman now he had worked out the truth. He didn't want a blackmailer in his house in any case.

Why hadn't Georgie denounced him when he stole that kiss? Had she reckoned on avoiding a scandal by finding him at the hall? She wouldn't be the first person to underestimate the effect of cold. If so that suggested a degree of cunning that was worrisome. Mrs James had recommended Mrs Powell. He would get Charles to make discrete enquiries into the woman's background to see if Georgie could have known her.

Jepson's voice telling him his bath was ready sounded far away. He took a deep breath. He was going round in circles and he had to stop. Maybe it was better not to enquire too deeply. Then he could believe the best of Georgie possible. He had to make this marriage work on some level. She might already be carrying his child. He hauled himself to his feet and threw off his clothes.

He climbed into the tub and rubbed his hair, with a ruinous amount of soap, as if trying to wash away his worries. He would run mad if he didn't stop thinking about it. Eliza was too taken with Georgie to be impartial but he needed someone to talk to. For once in his life he prayed that he would see Augusta soon. She might be a dragon but if anyone could help him make sense of all this it was her.

He dipped his head under the water to rinse his hair and opened his eyes as he surfaced. Traces of soap stung at them. The ever-reliable Jepson handed him a jug of cold water and a towel. He dried his face and accepted another towel from Jepson to douse his eyes with cold water until the stinging eased. He threw the last of the cold water over his head. That might put some sense into him. Despite the roaring fire a shudder ran through him.

Jepson disappeared into the dressing room. He climbed out of the bath tub and reached for another towel. A few minutes of vigorous rubbing had him dry and feeling calmer. He was the Marquess of Hargreaves. His world might have collapsed around his ears but he was damned if he was going to let it show.

Chapter Eighteen

Georgie made her way down to the drawing room, as they had done when they had company. It seemed the logical thing to do and she didn't feel ready to deal with Max in anything less than a formal setting. She had to face the truth. His attitude to her had changed completely as soon as his sisters had departed. Her brown velvet gown, topped with the shawl Eliza had given her, wasn't enough to keep the chill of the evening at bay. She shivered, unable to believe Martha's assertion that it was a lot warmer now the thaw had set in.

The room was empty and she found a chair near the fire. There was a sofa closer still but she didn't want to share it with Max if he came in. She lay back with her eyes closed. It was such a short time since they had sat on that sofa seemingly in tune with one another. She closed her eyes tighter. She absolutely wasn't going to cry. Her hands curled into such tight fists that her nails dug into her palms. Eventually the hot stinging sensation of unshed tears eased and she dared to open her eyes.

She was in time to see Max sweep into the room. He halted in front of her and performed the sketchiest of bows. His features were concentrated into a tight mask and his eyes had deepened to the colour of a stormy sea. It was impossible to tell what he was thinking. He smiled at her but there was no sign of the usual laughter lines, at the corners of his eyes, to soften his expression. Pride helped her to rise and drop a curtsey. She lifted her eyes to his as she rose. He was the first to break the contact.

He held out his arm to her. "Barton tells me dinner is ready."

She placed her fingers lightly on his sleeve and allowed him to lead her into the dining room. In other circumstances she would have enjoyed the beautifully prepared meal. As it was, she barely tasted what she ate. One course merged into another. She allowed Barton to refill her wine and then realised it was for the third time. All the same she tossed back the fine burgundy as if it was water. Max was talking about estate matters and she forced herself to concentrate.

"I imagine you must be used to dealing with parishioners?"

"Yes, I helped my aunt a lot with visits. I missed that when we moved to Canterbury for uncle to take up his position in the cathedral."

"Good. You'll be comfortable with the duties of looking after our estate workers and tenants. That was something my mother took very seriously."

Despite her worries Georgie found herself speculating about his mother. "Were you close to her?"

"I suppose I was, in the indolent manner of sons. I went away to school quite young but I always enjoyed our summer holidays at Hargreaves. That was when I spent the most time with her."

Georgie sighed. "I can barely remember my mother. My aunt was a wonderful substitute, although she was many years older."

Max gave her a genuine smile. Some of the knot of tension in between her shoulders eased. She smiled back but the moment was lost when Barton entered with the port decanter.

Max's brow creased into a frown. "I would prefer to take my port in the library, Barton."

* * *

Georgie drank a solitary cup of tea in the drawing room and made her way up to bed. With Max ensconced in the library even the solace of a book was denied her. She had been so pleased when she found the section with novels that must have belonged to Max's sisters. Some of the older ones had perhaps belonged to his mother. How stupid not to take at least one there and then. Tomorrow she would select a few and leave them in her bedroom.

Martha was waiting for her with one of the diaphanous nightgowns Max had given her. She would have loved to rip it into shreds. Instead she smiled as well as she could and allowed Martha to help her into it. Even with the roaring fire in the hearth, the room felt chilly. Martha, bless her, had put the usual flannel covered hot brick into her bed. She climbed in gratefully and drew the covers up to her chin.

"It's cold tonight, Martha. You get a hot brick for yourself and get off to bed."

Martha shuddered. "I daresn't do that, my lady." Her face drained of colour.

Georgie studied her. "Because of Mrs Powell?"

"Yes, my lady."

A spurt of anger ran through Georgie. "If she tries to stop you ask her to come and see me, Martha. I want you to be warm and that's all there is to it."

Martha bobbed a curtsey. "Yes, my lady."

"Good." Georgie watched her rush out of the room.

She doubted if she would follow her order. The girl was frightened of Mrs Powell for sure. That alone was enough reason to sack Mrs Powell in the circles she had been brought up. Max was right to want her gone. The thought of Max made her heart ache with longing. She sighed, what was she to do? He had every right to expect to share her bed. She wouldn't rebuff him but she wouldn't seek him out either. She had far too much pride for that.

She snuffed out her candle and rolled the covers around herself. Perhaps that would put him off tonight. It would be hard to face him straight after his desertion of her. She rolled onto her back, and studied the play of the light from the flames of the fire on the ceiling. It was going to be a long, sleepless night. Her prophecy proved wrong. The next thing she knew Martha was relaying the fire and the first streaks of watery, winter sun were creeping around the edges of the drapes.

In spite of her wish for a night without Max, she was infuriated by the empty place beside her. There wasn't so much as a dent in the pillow to suggest he had joined her in bed. Two nights without him and her treacherous body was protesting. She asked Martha to bring her breakfast up and stayed in her room until mid-morning. All was quiet upstairs and there was no sign of Max downstairs. Was she glad or sorry? It was hard to say. Barton appeared as she hesitated in the hallway, wondering where to go. She asked for tea to be served in the marchioness's sitting room. It was time she made an effort to fill her new role.

She strolled along the corridor and paused in the doorway to the room that was to be hers. It was far too large to be called a sitting room but there must be ways to make it seem cosier. The room was beautifully decorated, although the elaborate French style of furniture from the last century wasn't to her taste. When she was in London, she would have to think about how to stamp her mark on it. Refurbishing Hargreaves House would give her an opportunity to see what she liked and where it could be obtained. She selected a seat near to a window which allowed in some of the morning sun.

Barton delivered the tea tray himself. He beamed at her and lowered the tray onto a table by her side. "May I say, my lady, it's wonderful to have a marchioness in the house once more. His Lordship said to tell you he is in the library working on estate business."

Georgie smiled back at him. "Thank you, Barton."

She lingered over her tea but there was no sign of Max appearing from his library. Barton must surely have told him where she was. She wrapped up well and went on a stroll around the gardens, imagining the loving attention that had gone into designing them. The gardens near the house were softer than most she had seen on country house open days. Max's mother would have been the force behind them. What had she been like? Georgie found herself wishing she was still alive. She might have been able to help her understand Max better.

After her walk, Georgie had a lonely, late luncheon in the breakfast room and went back to her sitting room. It was well into the afternoon before Max left the library. She heard him send a footman to the stables to request his horse be saddled up. Once he had left, she entered his den to collect some books. She paused by his desk. The smell of his cologne lingered in the air and her heart contracted.

She selected a pile of books and asked a footman to carry them up to her bedroom. She ought to take them into the marchioness's sitting room. Somehow, she still couldn't see herself as a marchioness and had done enough pretending for one day. The little chair in front of the bedroom fire was a cosier option for reading. She picked the liveliest looking book. Even so her thoughts kept wandering to a pair of eyes whose colour had changed from deep blue to the angry, grey blue of a stormy sea the night before.

At last it was time to dress for dinner. She was about to ring for Martha when the maid entered with a pale blue, silk evening gown over her arm.

"I've finished altering this now, my lady."

Georgie smiled and silently thanked Cecilia for leaving a couple of dresses for her. It was lovely and might help to bolster her confidence when she joined Max. She had been so wrapped up in misery she had forgotten all about them. She tossed her head back. This would never do. She might be heartbroken but the last thing she wanted was for Max to notice. All she had left was her pride. That and the hope she might still be able to salvage something from this marriage.

For a start she could try and tempt Max back to her bed. Martha seemed to catch her mood. She spent a long time on her hair and produced a stunning result with the help of curling tongs. Georgie's lustrous chestnut hair was piled high on her head with little tendrils allowed to escape at the sides. When Martha was satisfied, she threaded a ribbon around the arrangement and added a tortoiseshell comb encrusted with tiny diamonds, a present from Sally.

Martha stood back and surveyed her handiwork. "There. I'm

right pleased with that, my lady. It's the first time I've used those tongs. The countess's maid showed me how to do it."

Georgie laughed. "I thought you looked rather nervous." She studied her reflection in the looking glass. "You've done a wonderful job, Martha."

Martha beamed at her and bobbed a curtsey.

"There is no need to curtsey to me, Martha."

"Ooh there is, my lady. You look so grand dressed like that."

"Thank you. If I do, it's down to your skill."

* * *

Max prowled around the drawing room. Would Georgie come here first, as she had last night? He'd thrown himself into dealing with the estate business Charles had sent, more to avoid her than because it was urgent. He was honest enough to admit that deep down he wanted to return to how they had been in the first couple of days of their marriage. His jaw clenched. He had to accept that was not going to happen. He had been a fool and he needed to protect himself from further pain. At the same time, he had to make the best of it and forge a working relationship with her. One where he could be comfortable.

It had been surprisingly easy to avoid her today. She had become wary of him it seemed. Was she pre-occupied with worries over Mrs Powell? Some distance had been what he wanted but heat rushed through him at memories of their lovemaking. Had she locked the door on him for a second time last night? His groin tightened and he wished he hadn't been too proud to put it to the test. Whatever else, he needed to find a way back into her bedroom.

She knew he wanted an heir and visiting her bedroom

wouldn't give away his feelings for her. Perhaps he should be a little more attentive tonight? The anger in her eyes when he had left her alone after dinner had been obvious. At the same time, he didn't want her to realise the power she had over him.

He smiled at himself as desire hit him so hard that he doubled over for a second. He had no choice but to be more attentive. The sound of footsteps had him straightening up and marching across to the window. It was too dark to see much outside but at least he had his back to Georgie when she entered the room. He turned his head and bit back a gasp. In a fashionable gown, with her hair dressed so becomingly, she looked truly magnificent. He walked towards her and bowed, before taking her arm and leading her into the dining room.

"You look delightful tonight, Georgie."

For a moment he could have sworn that she flinched. The moment passed so swiftly he wasn't sure if he had imagined it.

"Thank you. Cecilia left a couple of gowns for Martha to alter for me." She shivered. "It's not as warm as my brown velvet."

They reached the dining room and Barton opened the door for them. Max nodded his thanks and led Georgie to her chair.

"A thicker shawl might help. You must buy yourself a new wardrobe when we reach London. However, Hargreaves House is a more modern building than the Hall and a great deal warmer."

The first course arrived and they applied themselves to the food. Max finished first and sat back sipping his wine.

"I must say Mrs James is a wonderful cook. Various friends have tried to persuade me of the benefits of a French chef but I don't think she can be bettered."

Georgie caught his gaze. "I made some suggestions on the menu but I agree Mrs James is far too good to replace."

She looked nervous. Perhaps now was the time to discuss Mrs Powell? The door opened and several footmen entered. Max waited until the first course had been removed and they had helped themselves to some of the dishes of the next. The fish was beautifully done but it might as well have been sawdust as he struggled to find the right words. There was no easy way, he might as well be blunt.

"Talking about replacing people, I've decided we should remove Mrs Powell straight away."

Georgie jumped at his words and his spirits sank. He carried on.

"You have been consulting with the staff. Do you think they could manage without a housekeeper for a while?"

She hesitated for several moments. "What about organising the party for Twelfth Night?"

"That's the only stumbling block, which is why I'm asking what you think."

"I own I would be happier with Mrs Powell gone but it would be better to leave it until after we go to London, surely."

Max watched her through narrowed eyes. She looked decidedly uncomfortable. A sigh escaped him. "No, it wouldn't. I'm waiting for your opinion on how the staff might manage without her."

"Mrs James seems unflappable and Barton is so efficient I'm sure he would be able to help." She hesitated. "I still feel guilty about getting rid of Mrs Powell at all, even though I suspect she's not very kind to the staff, especially the younger ones. The fact is she couldn't be blamed for having doubts about me."

Max studied her through narrowed eyes. She twisted a loose tendril of hair around a finger and her gaze flitted around the room. Was she embarrassed or feeling guilty? A lead weight settled in his stomach.

"I don't agree. It seems an unlikely reason for her open dislike of you now. Why would a housekeeper risk one of the best positions in England?" His voice softened. "Is there anything more you can tell me which might explain her attitude?"

Georgie's cheeks flamed and she appeared near to tears. He waited to see if she would reply but she lowered her head and stayed silent. If she wasn't telling him the truth how could he hope to be loved for himself?

He sighed. "She has to go, Georgie. I'll write to Charles and have him come to pay her off and arrange transport to wherever she wants to go."

Georgie nodded, still without meeting his gaze. "As you wish." Her voice sounded dull and flat.

For a moment, he hoped she might say more but the entrance of Barton forestalled any chance of that.

He smiled at Barton. "I believe I will join Her Ladyship in the drawing room this evening, Barton. I'll take my port in there."

"Very good, my lord. Shall I arrange for a tea tray as well?"

Max looked towards Georgie, who again merely nodded.

"Yes, a tea tray for Her Ladyship." Max couldn't stop himself putting the emphasis on the last word. She had got what she wanted; she might as well enjoy the status of being his wife.

A subdued Georgie accepted his arm and he led the way to the drawing room. He regretted his harsh tone. The nearness of her sent shockwaves through him and he would surely explode if she denied him her bed again tonight. Whatever she might have done he wasn't the sort of brute who would force himself on an unwilling woman. He had some ground to recover if he wanted to keep lovemaking firmly established in their relationship.

As a start he led her to the sofa immediately in front of the fire. "You'll be a lot warmer here."

Her cheeks were red as she sat down. Whether from embarrassment or the heat of the fire he wasn't sure. For a man with seven sisters he was singularly inept at understanding women. The tea tray arrived, closely followed by his port. He settled back, glass in hand. He couldn't help but notice that Georgie had edged as far away from him as she could get. That didn't augur well.

The expanse of creamy white neck and bosom exposed when she lifted her head to drink had him writhing in his seat. Fortunately, she wasn't looking at him. He had never met a woman who aroused his passions so easily. He tossed back his port and reached for the decanter.

"This is a superb port, one of my father's. He was something of a connoisseur."

Georgie gave him a tentative smile. "I like tea, but I think you gentlemen have the best of it."

Without thinking, Max held out his glass to her. "Try it."

Georgie hesitated but accepted the glass and took a few sips. "This is very fine indeed."

Their fingers brushed as she returned the glass. A flash of energy shot through him. He jumped up and rang the bell. He had to move away from her before he gave away his current state of frustration by trying to kiss her. He needed her to make the first move. Would an innocent young woman do that? His experience was limited to willing widows. He asked the footman who entered for another glass.

Georgie appeared to relax as she sipped her port. She put her glass down and licked her lips. Max closed his eyes. It was better that they were a little way apart. Once they were in London there would be few opportunities to be together like this. If they were ever to reach a comfortable place he ought to try and get to know her. He glanced across at her. She seemed as disinclined for conversation as he. Estate business was as safe a topic as any.

"Charles is the best of good fellows but I wish he hadn't sent me quite so much estate business to deal with." He almost shuddered as he remembered all the time he had wasted before Christmas in pursuit of what he had thought of as his interested widow, including that disastrous house party. Now he could barely remember what Lydia Winters looked like. It had all been a game to him but having a wife was a serious matter. If he hadn't been looking for an easy way out, he wouldn't have ended up in the kind of deceitful arrangement he had dreaded.

Georgie turned her lovely grey eyes on him. Was there a hint of a smile in them?

"Is that why you have been closeted in the library so much?"

"I'm afraid so." His cheeks burned at the lie. "I've ploughed through the most urgent papers but it will keep me tied up until our move to London."

"I see."

She turned towards him with her lips parted. Her eyes seemed to be asking him a question. The urge to take her in his arms was almost overwhelming. No, he mustn't let her see how much he was in thrall to her.

She picked up her glass and downed the last of her port. "If you will excuse me, I think I'll retire now."

He dipped his head. "Of course."

He drank the last of his own port. Her polite declaration felt like a silent criticism of his boorish behaviour the evening before. He had sought sanctuary in the library without any finesse at all. It had been hard enough to sit through dinner after discovering her treachery. Even now he couldn't sort out his swirling thoughts. She replaced her glass and stood. He eased himself to his feet and walked with her. They parted company at the door of the library.

"I have a couple of more things to read but I won't be long."

He waited for her answer but she merely nodded. No invitation but she hadn't said anything to put him off joining her. Perhaps a glass of brandy would give him the courage to try his luck. Once they had an heir that excuse would be denied him but he would worry about that when it happened.

Chapter Nineteen

Georgie went into her bedroom to find Martha already waiting for her.

"It's beautifully warm in here. Thank you for keeping the fire so well-tended. This gown is lovely but thinner than my brown velvet. Remind me to buy some thicker shawls in London."

"Are we going soon, my lady?"

"It depends on the weather but I expect we'll leave shortly after the Twelfth Night party."

Martha bounced up and down with excitement. "I don't care what Mrs Powell says. I'm sure it will be wonderful."

Georgie was too tired to ask her to explain what she meant. "I would like to go straight to bed."

Martha was a quick worker. Within twenty minutes Georgie was in bed listening to the sound of the door shutting behind her. She rubbed at her temple with the heel of her hand. Could things get much worse? Max wasn't even giving her a meaningful say in household matters now. Why had he changed his mind about leaving Mrs Powell in place until after they had established themselves in London?

Mrs Mills sounded the sort of loyal retainer to give her good advice on whether the situation with Mrs Powell could be resolved without removing her. She felt so guilty about causing someone to lose their livelihood, no matter how much she told herself Mrs Powell was unkind to the other servants. Max had commented on Mrs Powell's insolent behaviour when they had given out the staff presents, so she wasn't imagining it. Even so, her embarrassment on that first evening might be colouring her judgement.

Tonight, it was almost as if Max was blaming her for Mrs Powell's attitude. It did seem strange that she would be so openly hostile. Eliza had agreed that she might simply be hoping to be paid off. Perhaps because she felt her position was untenable after her initial reaction to Georgie's arrival? Still something of an extreme reaction unless she had another position to go to and had seen an opportunity to extract a parting gift?

She banged a fist into the bed. Whatever, the solution to the problem should have been her decision. Max had no right to order her about like that. A sob escaped her. Legally he had every right to tell her what to do. She pulled a pile of pillows behind her and picked up the book from the table by the bed. It was an exciting tale but she kept stopping to listen for the sound of Max arriving. She had abandoned her book and was about to give up and snuff her candle out when the connecting door between their rooms opened. For a big man he moved stealthily. She hadn't heard him come upstairs.

She couldn't tear her eyes from the door. Max came through wearing his banyan and stopped with his hand still on the doorknob.

"Are you too tired tonight or would you like me to join you?"

Georgie's pulse leapt and heat pooled in the lower part of her stomach. "I'm not ready for sleep yet."

Max hesitated and then approached the bed. Georgie busied herself with tidying up the pillows.

"I've been reading. I found some novels your sisters must have left and brought them up here." She faltered as she noticed his rather forbidding expression. "I hope that was acceptable?"

"Of course. Everything that is mine is yours now." Max narrowed his eyes briefly and his expression was stern.

Why were men so hard to read? Was he irritated that she had even asked or angry that she had helped herself? He walked towards her. She threw back the covers and waited. That seemed to be all the invitation he needed. He dropped his banyan to reveal his naked body. Georgie gasped at his masculine beauty. Powerful thighs were topped by a fine torso, rippling with the muscles of an active man. Her eyes dropped lower. His desire for her was obvious.

She slipped out of her nightdress and watched him walk towards her. He climbed into bed beside her and pulled the covers over them. To her surprise he propped himself up on an elbow and put a finger her under chin to lift her face to his. Their eyes met.

"Are you sure you want this tonight? You only have to say if you would prefer to go straight to sleep." He gave a bark of laughter. "I've done this in the wrong order haven't I? I should have asked you before I undressed."

She felt as if he was trying to look into her soul, his gaze was so intense. "Yes, I do. Want this, I mean."

"You don't have to lock your door if you want me to stay out at any time. A word will be enough."

He released her chin and she lay back on her pillows.

"I'm sorry if I angered you by locking my door the other day.

It wasn't you. I didn't want anyone to come in. I still miss my aunt dreadfully. Sometimes it washes over me and I need to be alone for a while."

"Why would I be angry? What I was trying to say was that I would never expect to exercise my conjugal rights if it wasn't what you wanted too."

He moved closer and put an arm around her shoulders. "If you're quite sure you're happy could we proceed?"

His breath against her ear made her shiver. For her answer she raised her lips to his and kissed him. He responded and they were soon entwined.

"Let's try something different." He rolled on to his back and pulled her on top.

Confusion gave way to excitement as she followed his instructions. It felt good to be controlling their tempo. When he reached between them to caress her sensitive spot she was lost. Ecstasy crashed over her and she was relieved when Max followed her immediately to his own climax. She hadn't the energy to move for a while. He rested for a few moments and then left her with nothing more than a kiss on the forehead. The bed felt empty without him.

* * *

Max went back to his room, his thoughts in turmoil. When he was with Georgie it was hard to imagine she was anything other than the sweet girl she seemed. On the other hand, he was sure she had been as aroused as him even before they started. Perhaps a lot of virgins enjoyed marital bliss very quickly? That was one question he had no intention of asking his sisters. Taken on its own it was no reason to be suspicious either. He would interview Mrs Powell with Charles. If she confirmed his suspicions at least he would know.

* * *

Georgie had gone out for one of her solitary walks when Charles arrived the following morning. Max watched her retreating back from the window of the library. She looked so vulnerable with her shoulders hunched against the wind. He was gripped with a powerful surge of regret at what might have been and it was a moment before he could greet his secretary.

"Ah, Charles, I'm glad you managed to make it through."

Charles grinned at him. "The roads are completely clear now. I see things are going well with your marriage."

Max frowned at him. "What makes you say that?"

"It was obvious from the way you were watching Lady Hargreaves set off on her walk. Sorry, I shouldn't pry, but I'm so happy for you. My uncle knew the family. He said she's a delightful girl."

Max grunted. "Hmph! If you hadn't sent me so much estate work, she wouldn't have to go out walking on her own." The lie felt awkward on his tongue but he had to keep up appearances.

"Have you managed to find a mount for her?"

Max sat at his desk and gestured to Charles to take the other seat. "I haven't thought to ask her if she rides."

Charles raised an eyebrow at him. "I suppose it did all happen rather suddenly."

Max sighed. "It did. All sorts of lurid rumours were flying about. I hope they've died down now."

"All we heard in Porchester was that you'd married Miss Sherborne as soon as she was out of mourning for her aunt. A longstanding engagement I understand."

Max burst out laughing. "Charles, if you weren't the nephew of one of my father's dearest friends I swear I'd dismiss you on the spot. As you very well know, I had no thoughts of marriage in my head when I sent you off to Porchester early. How is your uncle by the way?"

Charles pulled a face. "Not in good shape I'm afraid. Although the doctor assures me it will be a while yet. Once your affairs are up to date and I've seen you off to London, I'd like to take unpaid leave of absence if I may."

"Of course, and I insist on paying you. I've cleared most of the outstanding things."

Charles gave him a hard look. "On your honeymoon? Things are not going as smoothly as I thought then. She's not a secret bluestocking, is she?"

"I've no idea. She's been reading a lot but I think they've all been novels."

Max jumped up so abruptly his chair teetered on the brink of falling. He walked around the room and stood at the window with his back to Charles. Eventually he marched back to the desk and slumped into his seat.

"It's a sorry tale and I don't know the truth of it. I need your help so I'm going to have to tell you my suspicions." Max felt his cheeks heat up. Charles was more of a friend than an employee but even so this was awkward. "Would you like a glass of brandy first?"

"No thanks, it's far too early for me. I wouldn't say no to some coffee though."

Max thought for a moment. He had been too on edge to eat much breakfast. "Let's go into the breakfast room. I'll have Barton send for coffee and more food."

"Now that's the best offer I've had all day. I started out so early I'm famished."

It was easier to fill Charles in on the circumstances of his marriage and his suspicions as they ate. That way he could avoid eye contact. He downed a cup of coffee and watched Charles start on a large plate of food. He gave Charles a summary of the events leading up to his marriage.

"The thing is, Charles, the strange attitude of Mrs Powell has unsettled me. I've never known an upper servant be openly insolent as she is to Georgie."

Charles stopped eating and flushed. "That may simply mean that Mrs Powell was so scandalised by Lady Hargreaves travelling around the country unchaperoned that she can't hide it. Not that Lady Hargreaves had a great deal of choice by the sound of it."

"I convinced myself I was overreacting and then something even odder happened." Max sighed. "It was the day your letter arrived. I saw Georgie coming up from the servants' quarters and caught a glimpse of Mrs Powell disappearing. I asked Georgie how she got on with her but she said she only saw her briefly as she had gone to talk to Cook. Georgie seemed distant as if she was worried about something."

"There's nothing in that."

"Except I overheard her say, 'Some people are never satisfied.' I asked her to repeat it and she looked horrified. I'm sure she was so lost in her thoughts she hadn't realised she had spoken that aloud. I'm afraid Mrs Powell has some sort of hold over her."

"She could have been referring to anything." Charles put down his cup and patted his stomach. "I couldn't manage another thing. Are you sure you aren't reading too much into this Max and letting your bad experience with Lavinia Fellowes colour your judgement? Uncle was thrilled when he heard the news. Said she was the sort of kind, sensible girl you needed to help you look after estates like this."

"That's what I thought at first. Her story sounded so plausible and I admired her for having the courage to escape an awful situation. Now I even wonder about that. I only have her word for it that the abuse from her relatives actually happened."

Charles put his head on one side. "Let's take it one thing at a time. Whichever version of Lady Hargreaves's interaction with Mrs Powell is correct, the housekeeper has to go."

Chapter Twenty

G eorgie stared at the strange horse being led into the stables. Her heart missed a beat. What if Cousin Mary had sent someone after her? Whoever it was they must be in the house for the groom to take the horse. She should be safe enough and Max would see them on their way in no time at all. At least she felt secure now. All the same she wouldn't stray far from the house.

She wandered down to the rose garden. For some reason she always felt at peace here. There was a brisk breeze and, even in the shelter of the brick walls enclosing each formal garden, it felt cold. She decided to cut short her walk. Inside the house she made a detour to the library in the hope of finding out who had arrived. The door stood ajar and there was no sign of anyone.

She ran up the stairs and found Martha in her room. The maid's face glowed with excitement and she broke into a big smile when she saw Georgie.

"You'll never guess, my lady." Martha jumped up and down.

"Guess what, Martha? Take a deep breath and tell me."

"I had it from the parlour maid who is walking out with the second footman."

Georgie threw her cloak on the bed and waited. There was

no hurrying the girl.

"Mrs Powell has been taken to the breakfast room and Mr Breakwell is talking to her along with His Lordship. It looks like they're going to send her away from what the second footman managed to hear at the door."

"When was this?"

"Just this minute."

Max must have sent a messenger direct to Mr Breakwell, unless he had turned up on some other matter. They should have consulted her before they made a final decision. She didn't like the woman but she ought to have a fair hearing. She could hear her aunt's voice deploring the way servants were often dismissed on a whim without a chance to defend themselves. She marched into the breakfast room without knocking. Mrs Powell was standing with her back to her, facing Max across his desk.

A sandy haired man of medium height, presumably Mr Breakwell, moved between Mrs Powell and Max. He thrust an arm out in the direction of the door.

"I have a carriage at your disposal, Mrs Powell," he said in a firm voice. "I suggest you take His Lordship's generous offer."

Georgie stood and watched, no one had noticed her and it sounded too late for her to intervene.

"Pah! A year's pay against what I know." Mrs Powell's voice rose. "It'll do as a down payment. I'll be ready in ten minutes." She lifted her chin and snatched up an envelope from the corner of the desk.

Mrs Powell turned around and stared when she saw her. "Here she is, the wanton, scheming hussy. You'll rue the day you married her and no mistake."

Georgie gasped at the venomous look Mrs Powell gave her

as she stalked out. Why had she wasted any sympathy on the woman? The room seemed to spin around her before settling back down. She looked at Max and the naked fury on his face took her breath away. He nodded at the other man who followed Mrs Powell out of the room. The door closed and she risked another glance at Max. His deep blue eyes had taken on that darker, stormy hue and his features appeared harsher than normal.

She squared her shoulders and walked to the desk. Max was still sitting so she dropped into the chair opposite. She forced herself to breathe steadily. His hands were on the desk and both knuckles showed white. After what seemed like hours he sat back and joined his hands behind his head.

Max's lip curled. "How long have you known her?"

Georgie was bemused. What was he on about? "Who do you mean?"

Max jumped out of his chair and circled around towards her. Georgie felt a frisson of fear and then he pulled up short.

"Don't trifle with me, madam."

He sounded so angry. Heavens above, had she married a madman? Her mouth dropped open as realisation dawned. She licked lips that felt shorn of all moisture.

"Are you saying you think I knew Mrs Powell before I came here? That I tricked you in some way?" She jumped to her feet. "Well, if that's your attitude, why don't you divorce me and have done with it. You're rich enough."

She ran out of the room, determined not to let him see her cry. Was Mr Breakwell still around? Perhaps he could arrange transport for her to Yorkshire? She ran through the main rooms but could find no sign of him. If only she could ride she'd steal a horse and disappear. How could he believe that of her? Her legs felt heavy and she had to force them to carry her upstairs. Once in her room she locked every door and gave vent to a crying fit that dwarfed her tears the last time she had locked herself in.

Mrs Powell had looked so vindictive she must have made something up to extract more money. How could Max take the word of a servant over her? Didn't he know her well enough to realise she had been brought up to be honourable? She pummelled the bed with her fists and howled. She hadn't expected to hold the interest of a man like Max for long but she had expected to be treated with respect. How could he?

Thinking her a liar was worse than spending time with a mistress in some ways. If he didn't trust her it was hard to see how they could forge any sort of working relationship to bring up children in. She'd run from one bad situation to another. She would be better off if he did divorce her but he wouldn't want the scandal. Would his sisters help her to persuade him if she told them how things were? Somehow, she doubted it. These old families had a lot of pride.

* * *

Max ran a hand through his hair as Georgie stormed out. She looked angry but distraught. He thought about running after her but it wasn't going to help with them both being agitated. She was playing a dangerous game suggesting divorce. It would serve her right if he took her up on it. His anger abated slightly when he realised she could already be carrying his child. He was not so selfish as to risk a child of his being born out of wedlock, even if it was a girl.

When he felt calmer, he would go and find Charles. If he

hadn't heard the comment Georgie had made to herself that day he could almost believe she was innocent. Yet all the evidence pointed to Mrs Powell changing from one blackmail victim to another. She would come unstuck at that. The look of fury she had given Georgie on the way out squashed any hope he had that Georgie was an innocent party.

He slapped a hand against his thigh. How could one man be so unlucky in love? He dropped into his chair and laid his head on the desk. Oh Lord, he was well and truly in love with her despite what she had done. He could have forgiven her, fool that he was, if she had confessed it all to him. This was far worse than Lavinia's betrayal. She had been a youthful fancy but his love for Georgie was deep and abiding. He couldn't imagine ever loving anyone else. How could that have happened in such a short time?

He ran Charles to earth down by the stables. The look of sympathy in Charles's eyes was almost his undoing.

"Georgie trapped me into marriage with Mrs Powell's help, didn't she? What other explanation can there be?"

Charles shook his head. "It certainly looks bad."

Max sighed. "My cook, Mrs James, recommended Mrs Powell to me. I believe Mrs Powell has relatives in Hargreaves village."

"I'll make some discreet enquiries."

"Thank you. I know I don't need to ask you to keep all this to yourself."

Charles slapped him on the back. "Of course not, Max. Lord, it always used to be the other way around, with you helping me out of scrapes. I'll do everything I can."

Max nodded. "Is that a trunk coming out? Mrs Powell packed up her things quickly."

"She did. Perhaps she expected to be dismissed. I wouldn't give up hope Max. Georgie might not have set out to trap you."

"I have to face facts, Charles. I hope something can be salvaged from this disaster of a marriage."

He turned away from Charles and trudged back to the house. Barton was hovering in the hall and he asked for a decanter of brandy to be sent to the library. When it arrived, he felt too lethargic to pour himself a glass. He pushed it away and went to the window. A post chaise bowled past, with Charles following on a fresh horse.

He jumped to his feet. Brandy was no answer. He ought to check with Hadley that none of his blasted cattle had taken harm, something he had forgotten to do. Then he could ride out to the farm cottages at the edge of the estate to see if the renovations of last summer had done their job. He didn't want to think about how he would face Georgie at dinner later.

He felt better when he was out and about. He let his horse have its head on the way home and a short but fierce gallop helped to loosen the tension in him. All too soon he was back at home. He dropped his horse off at the stables. His head groom was able to tell him that Mrs Powell had set off for London. She ought to have been put on the common stage but he wanted her as far away as possible as quickly as possible. He also wanted to know that she had indeed arrived at her destination.

London was it? That didn't tell him anything. A dismissed servant with a grudging reference had far more chance of finding a new position in the anonymity of London. The wretch would probably land a new job straight away and be a year's wages to the good. All he asked was that it was with someone who didn't know them, which wasn't that likely. He was beginning to regret his decision to make straight for London.

It would cause too much comment if he changed his mind now. There was no way to mend things between them quickly and it would be difficult to put much distance between him and Georgie at the Hall. In Town they would regularly dine out with other people and not always together. He could disappear to his club whenever he wanted company or simply to get away. It would be easier for him.

Georgie didn't even have estate business to occupy her at the Hall. In Town he could give her a free hand to redecorate Hargreaves House. Why was he sure she would have excellent taste? Eliza would help and Sally too after the kindness she had shown Cecilia. They would help her renew her wardrobe as well. Yes, his sisters would keep her amused in town, which would make it even easier to keep his distance.

Then there was Augusta to reckon with. A change of plan would have her arriving at the Hall before the ink had dried on the letter. He shuddered at the thought. It was going to be bad enough explaining why he had foregone a proper family wedding. Now things had gone so spectacularly wrong she would give him hell. At the same time, she would rally round and if anyone could make it right with the Ton it was Augusta. For her to do so she needed them to be in London.

He had a few more days to survive at the Hall. Tonight's dinner would be an ordeal. Barton seemed subdued when he joined him in the library to check if Charles would be coming back for dinner.

"No, he has to get back to his uncle as quickly as possible." That was true in the strictest sense and he didn't want it being made common knowledge that Charles was charged with making sure Mrs Powell reached her destination before he returned to Porchester.

Barton nodded and withdrew. Max watched his retreating back. He hadn't even asked if he wanted anything else as he usually did. He must be imagining things but he could swear his normally decorous butler sniffed as he went out. He sighed and made his way upstairs. Jepson was laying out his clothes for dinner. This time there could be no mistake. His valet's face was rigid with disapproval. From what he had heard about Mrs Powell he didn't think they were sorry to see her go. One of the servants must have heard his quarrel with Georgie. It appeared his staff had fallen under her spell nearly as strongly as he had.

He went down to dinner with a heavy heart. He entered the drawing room, half expecting Georgie not to be there, but she was sitting on a chair by the fire. Her back was ramrod straight. The only signs that she was feeling less than serene were her swollen eyelids and dark smudges under her eyes. He would love to think she was upset because she felt something for him, not worried about losing the position she had won.

Dinner felt interminable. The conversation never strayed from safe subjects like estate management and even their taste in books. That line was started by Georgie. He had to hand it to her she had courage. Not once did she mention the quarrel or her suggestion of divorce. The icy distance she maintained suggested he would not be welcomed in her bed after dinner.

In a way that was a relief. His anger was still simmering under the surface. He could feel it in the ache at each temple and the tension in his back. Other parts of his body were still clamouring for her attention. They would have to wait until he was ready to forgive her or had at least learned to forget her deception.

Chapter Twenty One

The following days fell into a similar pattern. Max rode out a lot and stayed in the library the rest of the time. Georgie spent her time reading and taking solitary walks. She didn't see him until he joined her for dinner each evening. The first night she was relieved when he didn't visit her bedroom. She still lay awake for hours listening in case he changed his mind.

She was heartbroken when he continued to ignore her. The warmth, joy even, of their early encounters had helped to give her hope that the marriage might work. Besides which, she was young and healthy and Max was a skilful and considerate lover. Her body craved for the attention. Relief swept over her when the fifth of January eventually arrived. The day was taken up with welcoming the Overtons and the Fordhams. The weather looked like staying mild enough to travel the day after the Twelfth Night party, unless Max changed his plans, of course. At least in London there would be more to distract her.

With his family there, Max fell into a better seeming frame of mind. He was more attentive towards her and she would have been hopeful of a thaw in his attitude if she hadn't seen Eliza give him a searching look more than once. He was determined to put on a show for his sisters it seemed. Pride stiffened her back and she played her part to the best of her ability. By the end of the day she almost believed her own acting.

Max sat on the sofa next to her when the gentlemen rejoined the ladies after their port. "Eliza and Sally sounded happy to help you find what you need for the refurbishment of Hargreaves House."

"Yes and they're taking Cecilia and me to their modiste for a new wardrobe apiece as soon as we arrive." She watched his face. "It sounds ruinously expensive. Have you done anything about sorting out my inheritance?"

Max clapped a hand to his brow. "No, I haven't. Charles's uncle took a turn for the worse and I didn't think to give the task to anyone else. I'll have my London man of business sort it out for you when we're there."

"I would be grateful." She glanced away from him as she felt heat flood her cheeks but it had to be said. "I've no idea how much there is but it should be more than sufficient to pay my dressmaker's bills."

She glanced back at him and was surprised to see that his cheeks looked red, unless it was a reflection from the fire.

"There is no need for my wife to pay for her own clothes."

Georgie sighed and said nothing. He sounded angry but it would appear he had decided to ignore her suggestion of divorce. She was glad. If nothing else she loved being a part of his family. Many people survived on less.

Everyone was tired after travelling and went to bed early, leaving them alone in the drawing room. Max took her hand as they walked towards the door. She glanced up at him in surprise at their first physical contact for days.

"Is there anything you want to tell me, Georgie?" He kept his voice soft but a muscle twitched at the corner of one of his eyes.

Georgie shrugged. "There is nothing I can tell you but I wish you would tell me what I am supposed to have done."

"Mrs Powell didn't give me much detail. I was hoping you would tell me the truth of exactly what happened."

"You know exactly what happened." Georgie shuddered. "I was running away from a forced marriage. You frightened me at the Golden Cross and I decided to walk to Benfort across the fields. I took refuge in the barns when my strength faded and you found me in the morning. There is nothing else to tell." She glared at him.

He flinched away from her. "Oh Georgie, if you would tell me the truth I could forgive you."

"There is nothing to forgive. I have told you the truth and if you don't believe me you don't know me very well. Why do you believe a surly servant rather than me? There was something sinister about that woman."

Georgie clenched her hands into fists and stormed out.

* * *

With no housekeeper Mrs James had stepped into the breach. With her help Georgie had the preparations for the party well in hand. Eliza and Sally sought her out in the morning to offer their assistance. Between them they checked all the furniture was being moved into the best positions.

"How many people have you invited?" Eliza asked.

"Apart from the family, the Armstrongs, the Wrights and about six or seven families in the area that Max suggested." Georgie turned towards Sally. "Max said you're an excellent pianist and we might have some dancing if you don't mind

235

playing."

"Not at all. Which room do you suggest? It doesn't sound as if there will be enough couples to make it worth opening up the ballroom."

"I thought the Marchioness's sitting room would be adequate for a few couples and there's already a piano in there. Max suggested I have it redecorated so any furniture and carpets we remove can stay out afterwards. Georgie bit her lip at their expressions. "I was forgetting, it was your mother's room."

Eliza smiled at her. "Yes, it will be sad for us to see it changed but we'll get used to it and it's your room now."

"I'm so sorry to drop it on you like that. I simply hadn't thought about it before. I don't have to change it if you would rather it was left."

Sally laughed. "Mama called it her folly. She hired someone to oversee the redecoration, including new furniture, while she went on a trip up north. It was much too elaborate for her but she was too frugal to redo it. I'm sure she'd want you to change it but keep a better watch on the project than she did."

"Very true," Eliza said. "We had dancing in there quite often, dancing lessons too. Mama said that being light to move around was the one advantage of the fancy furniture."

"That's something to remember. If there's anything in there either of you would like as a keepsake please say. I'm sure Max won't mind." Her hand flew to her mouth. "That applies to your other sisters too. I can't believe I still have five to meet."

Eliza put an arm around her shoulders. "Don't worry, Georgie, I'm sure they will all love you."

Georgie grimaced. "Max says Augusta will be furious about there being no big family wedding. He's not looking forward to seeing her in London."

Both sisters doubled up with laughter.

"No indeed," Eliza said. "She will ring a peel over him for sure.

"How is Mrs James coping with being in charge of all the arrangements?" Sally asked.

"She has it well in hand. It will only be the family for dinner. We're going to have it early and there will be a light supper later for everyone. Max thought it best."

That was one suggestion Georgie had been happy to comply with since it meant less time to interact with the Armstrongs. It would be awful if they guessed how things stood between her and Max. She was kept busy all afternoon but everything was ready in good time for her to change for dinner. She found Martha had finished altering the second dress. This one was a peach colour with long, lace trimmed, sleeves and a lacy bodice. Georgie loved it on sight, it brought out the highlights in her chestnut hair.

Dinner was a riotous affair with young Peter allowed to attend. The Fordham boys were lively company, although Cecilia seemed a little subdued. After dinner Cecilia joined her and Max in the drawing room.

"Is Charles coming later, Uncle Max?"

"I'm afraid not. His uncle is seriously ill and he is staying with him for the moment."

"Oh dear. I hope his uncle is better soon."

Max rested a hand lightly on her arm. "I'm afraid there's little likelihood of that Cecilia."

"That's sad. Poor Charles, he hasn't had a great deal of time with him, has he?"

Max agreed then leaned across to Georgie. "We'll need to be

in the hall in a few minutes ready to receive our guests."

Barton was already waiting near to the main door.

"You must be tired," Max said, "I don't mind if you give a footman the door opening duty tonight."

Barton drew himself up to his full height. "This is a momentous evening, my lord. I wouldn't dream of deserting my post."

"If you insist, Barton. Thank you."

Max tucked her arm in his and drew her towards the door of the sitting room. The sound of music filtered out to them. They found Sally practising on the piano.

"That piano has a lovely sound, Max."

"My mother loved her music. My father had it shipped over from somewhere on the continent, I forget where, at enormous expense."

A wave of regret washed over Georgie. It would be lovely if Max thought enough of her to go to that sort of trouble for something which he knew she would enjoy. At least he was acting as if their argument of the night before hadn't happened. Perhaps because his family were there but it made the atmosphere between them more bearable. She changed the subject.

"You all call Mr Breakwell, Charles. Is he a relative?"

"No, but my father and his uncle were great friends. I first met him at school. I was in my last year when he arrived. There was some sort of family feud between his father and uncle. I took him on as my secretary straight from university. His father had died by then and I persuaded his uncle to receive him. They've been the best of friends ever since."

They heard the sound of a carriage drawing up and took up their position between the door and the sitting room. Georgie sighed. Max was so kind and considerate to other people and yet he was ready to believe the worst of her. She was distracted by the sound of laughter on the steps outside. Barton announced the first family.

Georgie knew a moment of terror. How would they receive her? She had been so busy with the arrangements she hadn't stopped to think about the people she would have to meet. She needn't have worried. All the families seemed cheerful sorts and disposed to like her. Max was subjected to several congratulatory slaps on the back and she received some fulsome compliments from the local squire but she was satisfied she had made a good impression.

Inside the sitting room Max drew her into the quietest corner. It was still a struggle to hear him with the noise of greetings amongst people who hadn't met for a while.

"Georgie, I forgot to ask you if you can dance."

"I certainly can." She felt rather affronted. "I had lessons with some friends when I was young and I told you we spent over two years in Canterbury."

"Good. Sally wants us to open the dancing."

He walked up to the piano and raised a hand. He was a good half a head taller than most of the men there and people quietened down quickly.

"Lady Wakeley has agreed to play for us so we can have some dancing. Tables are set up in the library for those who prefer cards."

Several of the older people present disappeared towards the library and the rest found chairs around the periphery of the room. Sally was walking around organising dance partners. Georgie tried to hide a smile as she half dragged Rollo over to a very young lady who appeared completely tongue-tied.

Max joined her. "Sally has strong views about making sure young people, especially the girls, are comfortable with dancing before they arrive in London."

"Are these families likely to go to London for the season?"

"Yes, in the main. The young lady Sally has bestowed on Rollo is a friend of Cecilia. The poor girl is dreadfully shy."

Sally made her way back to the piano and announced that Lord and Lady Hargreaves would start off the dancing.

Georgie had always loved dancing and tapped her toe in time to the introductory bit of music. Max took her hand and she caught her breath at the feelings that shot through her. Dancing had never been as intoxicating as this. Other couples joined in and she gave herself up to enjoying the music. When the dance finished Max led her over to Eliza, sitting at the edge of the floor.

Eliza pulled her into the vacant seat next to her. "I could shoot Rollo. My ankle isn't quite ready to stand up to dancing and that looked such fun."

Georgie forced a smile. "Max says some of these families will be going to town for the season."

"I'm sure he's right. He's chosen well. They're all good-natured souls and some are friends of the Fordhams." Eliza lowered her voice. "Don't worry about London, Georgie. I'm sure it will all work out."

She nodded. "As long as you're there I shall cope. I had better go and attend to my hostess duties. Should I circulate amongst the older guests?"

"That would be well received." Eliza gave her hand a squeeze. "You're a natural at this."

"I hope so. I'm terrified."

She spotted the Armstrongs talking to the squire and his wife.

That would be a good place to start. She stayed chatting to them for a while. With the noise of the dancing it was impossible to talk about anything intimate so she didn't have to worry about them noticing her unhappiness. The next group were easy to talk to as well. Before she could join anyone else, she heard Sally say that this would be the last dance before supper.

Max came alongside her and pulled her into a set that was forming. When they finally came to a breathless halt she realised she was actually enjoying herself. She glanced at Max but his expression was too inscrutable to read. Was he enjoying dancing with her?

Max tucked her hand in his arm. "We need to lead everyone into supper."

Georgie nodded and they made their way to the dining room. Oh. So that was why he had danced with her again. Her happy mood evaporated. It was no good thinking Max was thawing towards her. He was simply doing his duty as a host. She concentrated hard on maintaining a cheerful front. She thought she had succeeded until Eliza caught up with her and led her to a chair.

"Come and sit. You will be worn out. That forced gaiety doesn't fool me. You two have had a setback, haven't you? I said as much to Nat yesterday but he wouldn't have it."

Georgie felt like crying. What if everyone had noticed?

As if she could read her mind, Eliza leant towards her. "Don't worry no one else will notice. We can't talk here but, if you need some advice on how to handle my pig-headed brother, I'll be happy to help as soon as we meet up in London."

The rest of the evening passed in a daze for Georgie. She stood with Max to see their guests off. He released her arm as soon as the last one had left.

"I've challenged Nat to a game of billiards." He nodded to her and walked off.

She had been right not to read too much into his show of unity. At least she had survived the party and tomorrow they would be on their way to London.

Chapter Twenty Two

N at was already in the billiards room, playing against Rollo. Max flopped onto a seat with a good view of the game, glad of an opportunity to relax. The evening had gone off better than he could have hoped for but the effort of appearing part of a loving couple had taken it out of him. Young Rollo was a promising player but Nat was still too good for him. They shook hands and Max watched a disgruntled Rollo slide out of the room.

Nat strolled across to him and grinned. "Rollo doesn't like losing. He reminds me of you when I first knew you."

"Good Lord. I hope I've never been so petulant in defeat?"

Nat raised an eyebrow at him and smiled.

"I'll take that as a challenge. Come on it's time for our game."

They were well matched normally and a tired Max put up a valiant fight, not wanting to appear too jaded. Nat eventually won by a small margin.

"Well done, Nat. It's bed for me now." He ignored Nat's sly smile. "I need some sleep ready for tomorrow. Don't think you can lie in too late in the morning, will you? I want to have all visitors gone in time to set out by midday."

"You're keen to get away. Is everything alright? I thought

Georgie seemed exhausted tonight when she thought no one was looking."

"Everything is fine. She's upset by the episode with the Powell woman." Max rolled his shoulders back to try and ease the tension in them. "Once she meets Mrs Mills, I'm sure it will ease her worries about running a large household."

"What happened then?"

"Charles agreed with me that it was better to move Mrs Powell on now. Georgie happened to come into the breakfast room as we were talking to the wretched woman, who caused quite a scene." It was near enough to the truth to be hard to refute and he didn't feel like confiding in anyone, not even Nat.

"I see. As long as the dry weather holds, we'll be in London two or three days after you. We're breaking the journey with friends." Nat narrowed his eyes at him. "I'll be happy to help if you want any advice."

Max stalked out of the room. He didn't want to hear any more. He ran up to his room and slammed the door behind him. Fortunately, Jepson had obeyed instructions for once and taken himself off to bed. Should he visit Georgie tonight? He rubbed a hand over his temple to ease his throbbing head. It was all too much and despite his cravings for her he needed a good night's sleep before they set off for London. He threw his clothes over a chair and clambered into bed.

Thoughts of Georgie kept intruding as he tossed and turned. A vision of Lavinia telling him she wasn't looking forward to sleeping with him, when she was still warm from another man's bed, hit him like a physical pain. At least Georgie had adhered to her side of their bargain, uncomplainingly, when it came to the bedroom. Although did her willingness in that area suggest she hadn't been the complete innocent she professed to be? Damn Nat for setting him thinking about it all over again when he had managed to find a measure of calm. He was as bad as the servants in taking Georgie's part. They were all a bunch of fools. Weren't they?

Max awoke the next morning feeling as if he hadn't been to bed. He did a series of stretches to loosen tense muscles. If he felt like this now what would a few hours in a coach do to him? Why not ride? He had opted to split the journey over two days and a quick glance out of the window showed the weather to be dry. He rang for Jepson and dressed in riding clothes. There was no sign of Georgie down at breakfast. A message from the stable did nothing to lighten his mood.

"Bad news?" Nat asked.

"Nothing serious. My horse has a swollen leg so will have to stay here for a while. My spare had to be retired a few weeks ago. I'm hoping something in the new batch of Irish horses will suit me later in the year. I'll look for something in London to tide me over. I must ask Georgie if she can ride."

Nat gave him a hard look. "You never were much good at choosing horseflesh. You'd better wait for me before you select anything."

Max laughed. "I admit you have a particularly good eye for horses but I'm not that bad. I'm taking my deputy head groom to London with me too."

"Do you mean Larkin?"

"Yes. If he settles in London, I'm planning to make him my head groom there."

"Excellent choice and if I'm not available you won't go too far wrong if you take him with you."

Max relaxed as Nat fell into a discussion about horses as he'd hoped. Nat was too perceptive for comfort. Perhaps he was right and he had been too hard on Georgie. It was something he would give some thought to, but in private.

Nat and Eliza left with their entourage straight after breakfast. The Fordhams followed shortly after but not until Sally had annoyed him by taking him apart for a little chat. Even Sally had fallen under Georgie's spell it seemed. Perhaps not surprising given how kind Georgie had been to Cecilia. Could they all be wrong?

His headache of the night before started niggling at him as he waved them off. Georgie was nowhere to be seen but Sally told him she had already said her goodbyes. Could she be avoiding him? She had appeared a lot quieter lately. He kicked at the edging of a flowerbed, dislodging a stone. He bent down to replace it. Lord, he was so confused. The coach rumbled out of hearing and he went down to the stables. An excited Larkin was checking on the horses while the family coachman did the same for the travelling coaches. He called Larkin across.

"How's Indigo faring?"

"It's nothing that won't mend with rest."

"That's good. I don't suppose there is another horse I could ride for the first stage to London is there?"

Larkin bit his lip. "I don't think we have anything else up to your weight, my lord."

"I was afraid you'd say that. We'll have to see about buying some more horses in London."

Larkin's face lit up. "My uncle works on a stud in Oxford-shire. Their horses are the best and they have a batch ready to sell."

"Will those be young horses?"

"Yes, my lord. They will be well trained though."

"That might do for me but I expect Lady Hargreaves will want an experienced mount. I'll think about it. Would they mind if we posted up to Oxford from London and had a look if we can find time?"

"I'm sure they will be happy to see us, my lord. They like to know their horses have gone to good homes."

"Excellent." He nodded at Larkin who touched his cap and carried on with his work.

He walked back to the house whistling. He had forgotten about Larkin's uncle. Horses from that source were always sought after. This might be a chance to steal a march on Nat. If he was allowed to, he might buy some more carriages horses as well. Nat would be green. It would also be a good excuse to get away for a couple of days if he needed to. His mood sobered. When he had first married Georgie, he would never have envisioned wanting to find excuses to get away from her.

At last they were on the road. Georgie looked startled when he joined her in the coach.

"Are you not riding at least the first section? My uncle always liked to."

"I'm afraid my horse has a sore leg and I haven't got around to finding a replacement for the one we had to retire a while ago." He glanced down at his long frame and smiled ruefully. "None of the horses the grooms use to take messages and so on are able to carry a large fellow like me."

Georgie gave him a brief but genuine smile. "Being tall does have its advantages. You found it easy to get everyone's attention when we were dancing last night."

"True, but I must purchase a spare horse. That reminds me, you need at least one mount too."

"I've never learned to ride. I drove a gig around my uncle's

247

parishes from when I was quite young."

"We'll have to arrange some lessons for you. That will be best left for when we're back at the Hall. What about driving? Is it something you enjoy?"

"Oh yes. I'm held to be an excellent whip." A blush rose up in her cheeks. "Oh dear, that sounds boastful."

"Not if it's accurate."

They took a sharp bend and he was thrown against her. His whole body came to life at the touch of her soft body against his. Why had he shunned her bed last night? Hours spent in close company with her were going to be agony.

He said the first thing that came into his head to distract himself. "Perhaps we could get you a phaeton to drive in London."

Her face lit up. "I should like that. Could I have one drawn by two horses? I've always wanted to drive a pair."

"It's harder than a single horse but I could teach you." What had he done now? There was no going back on it. Her face was glowing with excitement.

"That would be lovely." A cloud passed over her face. "I don't want to be a nuisance if you're too busy."

Max considered her carefully. Had she just skilfully manoeuvred him or was she genuinely that self-effacing. She was waiting for his answer.

"Why should I find teaching my wife to drive a nuisance? It will be a few weeks before we can have a lady's phaeton made for you and find horses. I'll start the lessons as soon as we have."

"Thank you. I shall look forward to that."

He nodded. "My pleasure."

He lowered his head as if trying to rest. He had better pray she was the woman all his relatives thought her to be, or his heart would break into little pieces. The only way to find out for sure was to get to know her better. If they were wrong how would he bear it?

His coachman was a cautious soul in winter conditions and they trundled along at a slow pace. He smiled at the thought of the younger driver in charge of the coach travelling behind them, which carried their luggage and servants. His patience would be sorely tried by the time they got to London. He was woken by the lurch of the coach as it turned into the yard of an inn.

He was leaning into Georgie and threatening to squash her. He pulled himself up straight and looked out of the window.

"Good Lord. Sorry, I shouldn't have said that but this is our first stop. I must have been asleep for hours." Georgie smiled at him and his heart missed a beat.

"Around two hours I would say."

They were back in the coach and on their way within a few minutes. The sky was clear and it was near to full moon. Max gave permission for the second coachman to set off in front. They were little more than an hour away from their destination for the night. He couldn't help smiling at the stolid resistance of their driver to reaching any pace much above a trot. Jepson would have everything organised by the time they arrived.

He could feel the heat of Georgie next to him and passion shot through him. If only they had been in better accord, he would have risked seducing her in the coach with the other coach bowling along in front. He stole a glance at his wife. This time she was the one with her eyes closed. He almost wished he had never found out about her links to Mrs Powell. They could have had so much fun. As it was, his only contact with her was when she nestled against his shoulder.

She didn't wake up until they reached their destination. The inn looked surprisingly full for the time of year. People were taking the opportunity to travel whilst they could. With the clear sky temperatures were already dropping. They would have to take care on the last leg tomorrow. He shook Georgie gently awake. She turned startled eyes towards him.

"This is where we're stopping for the night. It looks busy. I'm glad I had the forethought to ask Charles to book rooms for us."

He jumped down and lifted her to the ground.

"Thank you. This is where Mr Breakwell is staying, isn't it? Will he come here tonight?"

"That was the original plan but his uncle is so ill I don't expect to see him."

He guided Georgie through the press of people and carriages. There was more than one curious stare sent in their direction. He kept his head down and avoided eye contact with anyone. The last thing he wanted was to have to chat to acquaintances with things so uncomfortable between him and Georgie.

Jepson was waiting for them inside the hallway and led them straight upstairs. He opened a door for Georgie and Max could see her maid waiting for her. His room was next door. It was the best room in the inn but his heart sank when he saw the truckle bed in the attached dressing room. He glanced around at Jepson.

"I'm afraid there's a prize fight on tomorrow, my lord. The landlord insisted Mr Breakwell had only bespoken these two rooms."

Max looked at Jepson's sceptical expression. "You don't believe him but don't see what we can do about it. I fear you are correct, Jepson." He grimaced. "This is not the sort of situation I like my wife being put in."

"Quite so, my lord, I've persuaded the landlord to provide dinner for her ladyship and her maid in their room."

"Thank you, Jepson. That's the best we can do. I hope we all manage to get some sleep tonight."

"We're above the kitchens here so we won't hear the worst of the noise and the inn has thick walls." Jepson moved over to the bed to finish laying out clean clothes.

Max walked to the window and looked out. Jepson was right; they were in the quietest part of the inn. He wanted to thump the windowsill. Georgie seemed a little less forbidding today but there would be no opportunity to talk here.

He stalked across to the door. "I'm going down to stretch my legs, Jepson. They're far too long to be cooped up in a coach for hours. I plan to buy more horses soon. Lady Hargreaves doesn't ride but she does drive. I'm going to have a phaeton made for her and look for a quiet pair of carriage horses."

He ran lightly down the stairs. Why had he given Jepson so much information? It was almost as if he was seeking approval by boasting of his intended present for Georgie. It was certainly uncomfortable when his servants were finding it difficult to meet his eyes at times. Could someone who had won them over so completely be a schemer? He knew Porchester quite well and set off down a quiet route to gain some solitude. Hopefully the cold air would serve to dampen the ardour he had been struggling with for hours. There would be no way he could share her bed with her maid in the dressing room nearby. Despite a brisk pace the cold seeped through his clothes and he retraced his steps.

Jepson had laid out a plain outfit for him. He changed quickly and went down to take his dinner in the coffee room. The benches were of different sizes and he found a low slung one in a quiet corner, so his height wasn't too obvious. He kept his back to the room, hoping no one would recognise him. His strategy worked so well he was jerked out of his thoughts by hearing his name mentioned.

"That's a rum do with old Hargreaves. I was told he ravished a young woman waiting to be picked up by friends for Christmas. It was at the Golden Cross, near to Hargreaves Hall."

"You haven't heard the best of it. It turned out the girl had connections to the Archbishop of Canterbury, no less. The blighter was forced to marry her. Always thought there was bad blood there after the way he jilted the Fellowes chit."

"Did he really? Who's the girl he's married?"

"Some nonentity from a church family."

There was a commotion and another man pushed his way into the group discussing him. Max risked a look and groaned inwardly as he recognised an acquaintance.

"Now that's enough of that nonsense. I know Lord Hargreaves and he's a decent sort."

At least he had one defender. He couldn't bear to hear anymore. He drank the last of his ale and negotiated his way around the edges of the room, keeping to the shadows. He needed to warn Jepson to try and hide their identity. There was a set of back stairs near to the coffee room. He ran up them and managed to navigate his way to his room. He quickly explained the situation to Jepson.

"I've already thought of that, my lord. I've told the drivers and grooms not to use your name. Mrs Powell was a thoroughly unpleasant person. I expected her to make trouble." He gave

Max an accusing look. "I never understood why you let Lady Lovell foist her onto you in the first place."

"What had Mrs Powell got to do with Lady Lovell? Mrs James recommended her."

"Mrs Powell worked for Lady Lovell, who was supposed to have dismissed her on a whim of her son's." Jepson sniffed. "Which I didn't believe for a minute. Sent to spy on you I'll be bound. Lady Lovell only took Mrs Powell on in the first place to find out more about your family."

Max felt lightheaded and flopped down on the bed. "Why on earth did Cook recommend her to me then?"

"I expect she felt sorry for her. Mrs Powell and Mrs James started work as maids at Hargreaves Hall at the same time. We all assumed you agreed to annoy Master Cuthbert."

Max threw a punch at the mattress and wrenched his shoulder. Charles had been called to his uncle's sick bed and he had been so pleased to find a replacement housekeeper he hadn't even bothered to read Mrs Powell's reference."

"Why didn't you tell me that before?"

"It never occurred to me that you didn't know, my lord."

Max lowered his head into his hands. If he was on his own he would have cried like a baby. It wasn't guilt that had made Georgie so subdued and distant. She must be furious with him for doubting her. Why had he been such a fool to think all women were untrustworthy like Lavinia? He would love to go back downstairs and drink himself insensible.

The risk of being recognised was too great. His priority had to be shielding Georgie as much as he could. With Jepson's quick thinking they might get away in the morning without her finding out what was being said. The man was a treasure. This was worse than anything he could have imagined. There was enough truth in it for it to be dangerous.

Even Augusta was going to find it hard to help him extricate them from this mess. Jepson was almost certainly correct in thinking Mrs Powell had been stirring things up. He groaned as he remembered Georgie saying it would be safer to become established as a couple in London before they dismissed the woman. She had got her measure. How could he have been so stupid? He longed for another walk but he couldn't rule out running into someone who knew him.

He sent Jepson down for a decanter of brandy. As soon as Jepson was gone he threw off his coat and punched the bed with both fists a few times. That did little to relieve his feelings. He jumped up and strode around the room feeling like a caged tiger. He ought to at least give Georgie some inkling of the problem and warn her to stay hidden but he couldn't face her. He didn't know how he was going to face her tomorrow. Jepson came back with a decanter barely a quarter full. He went to remonstrate but looked at Jepson's wooden countenance and thought better of it. It would have to do.

"Could you get a message to Lady Hargreaves asking her to stay hidden until we leave tomorrow Jepson?"

"I've already impressed that on her maid, my lord. I used the excuse of the probability of hordes of drunken men roaming around. Martha's a good girl. I'm sure they'll stay put until they hear from us."

Chapter Twenty Three

Georgie picked at her supper. The meat pie and vegetables were overcooked but reasonably edible. She ought to eat as much as she could to keep her strength up. The closer they got to London the more nervous she felt. She could only hope things would improve between her and Max before she had to face the formidable Augusta. Even Sally and Eliza sounded in awe of her. Was Max thawing towards her? He had seemed a little less forbidding in the coach yesterday.

She was still furious with him but they couldn't go on like this. She would find it difficult at any rate now she had tasted the delights of the marriage bed. He could always take a mistress in London, if he didn't already have one. The only way she could see her life being fulfilling would be having children and if she couldn't tempt him into her bed that wasn't going to happen. She sighed; the arrangements here made it impossible for him to visit her tonight, even if he wanted to.

By the time she climbed into the carriage the following morning Georgie felt thoroughly jaded. She had lain awake for much of the night and her nerves were on edge. Max would either accept her or he wouldn't. She had done nothing wrong and it was up to him to heal the breach. If Augusta took against her perhaps she would urge Max to divorce her.

It should be possible in a rich and powerful family like theirs. In many ways that would be easier than loving him and suffering the daily pain of his rejection. Away from him she would eventually heal. Max landed on the seat beside her and the coach pulled away. She closed her eyes and hoped for sleep to speed up the journey. The coach lurched and curses rained down from the driver's box. She opened her eyes to see Max with his head out of the window. He came away from the window abruptly.

"It's merely the press of traffic holding us up. I believe there's a prize fight in the area today. If Charles hadn't been so pre-occupied, he would have realised and booked us rooms in another town."

"Martha said there was a prize fight." Georgie shuddered. "Nasty things."

Max laughed and her spirits lifted. "I enjoy a bout with Gentleman Jackson when I'm in London. There's a great deal of science to it. I agree with you about prize fights though. It would be better if they were stopped before someone was seriously hurt. Often they're not."

The coach picked up speed and they left Porchester behind. Georgie dropped into a genuine sleep and woke up at their first stop. Max seemed to have withdrawn into himself and she was relieved when they set off on the last leg of the journey. They pulled up in front of an imposing mansion midway through the afternoon. Max stayed long enough to introduce her to Mrs Mills, who seemed genuinely delighted to meet her, before he disappeared.

Georgie turned to the housekeeper and pinned a smile to her face. She would concentrate on making a good impression on the staff and try not to imagine that Max was rushing off to visit a mistress.

"I'll have warm water sent up to your room for you to freshen up, my lady. Ring the bell when you're ready and I'll fetch you down to meet the staff. Would you like a tea tray to be sent up too?"

Georgie gave her a genuine smile. "That sounds wonderful, Mrs Mills. I shall look forward to meeting the staff."

She followed a maid up the stairs. Apart from Mrs Powell, the staff at Hargreaves Hall had been lovely to her and she was curious to meet the London ones. Martha followed behind and the tea tray appeared almost immediately. The tray carried small cakes and a flagon of lemonade besides the tea.

"I think you deserve to share this Martha. Tea or lemonade?"

Martha's face glowed and her eyes shone. "Lemonade please. One of the footmen said it's good working here, my lady. I like the housekeeper. She's a lot better than Mrs Powell, the witch."

"You shouldn't refer to anyone like that, Martha."

"I don't see why not. She hated you and she's in league with that Lady Lovell."

Georgie forgot all her scruples about encouraging servants to gossip. "Do you mean the mother of Cuthbert Lovell?"

"Yes. Mrs Powell used to work for her you know." Martha scowled.

Georgie stared at Martha. "Are you sure?"

"Yes. Ask Mr Jepson if you don't believe me. I wouldn't be surprised if she's still working for Lady Lovell."

The hot water arrived before Georgie could reply. If it was true it might help to explain Mrs Powell's attitude. Martha pulled out the peach coloured gown for her to change into. It wasn't a day gown but it would have to do. She made her own way downstairs as soon as she was ready. An elderly butler jumped to attention.

"Let me show you into the drawing room, Lady Hargreaves. I'll send Mrs Mills to you."

Georgie sat down, heart beating furiously. She must get on with this housekeeper. Mrs Mills entered almost straight away. Georgie immediately forgot her own worries when she noticed her careworn appearance.

"There's no need to stand on ceremony, Mrs Mills. Would it be easier for me to meet everyone in the servant's quarters?"

Mrs Mills hesitated and then smiled. "Yes, it would. We're rather shorthanded to open up the house."

Georgie followed her down to the housekeeper's room. Servants were scurrying about and the ones in the kitchens looked frantic. Mrs Mills lined them all up and Georgie went along the line exchanging a quick word with each one. Martha was right. Despite how busy they all were they seemed a lot happier than the servants at Hargreaves Hall.

"If you would show me back up to the drawing room, Mrs Mills, I'll let you all get on with your work."

Georgie came to a decision when they reached the hallway. Max would have to accept her role in making domestic decisions and she needed to start now.

"I don't want you all being overworked. We won't need a grand dinner this evening. I can see you're stretched. I would be grateful for your help in employing what extra servants are necessary."

"Bless you, my lady. Mr Jepson said you were kind. I could send straight around to the agency we use and have some candidates to interview fairly quickly. We can manage a proper dinner on your first evening here."

Georgie noticed the butler trying to catch Mrs Mills' attention. He coughed loudly. The door to the drawing room opened. A middle-aged lady, a vision in apricot satin, stepped out. Her features were softer than Max's but Georgie would have recognised her as his sister even in a crowd.

"There's no need to worry about providing dinner this evening, Mrs Mills, Lord and Lady Hargreaves will be dining with me."

Mrs Mills dropped into a curtsey. "Thank you, Your Grace. Will you be requiring tea, my lady?"

Georgie quaked. This must be Augusta, Duchess of Cathlay. She forced a smile and dropped into a deep curtsey. "Tea would be excellent and some more of your cakes please, Mrs Mills, if you have any left. Would you care to join me in the drawing room, Your Grace?"

Augusta inclined her head and went into the drawing room. Georgie studied her exquisite gown as she followed in her wake. The Lovell sisters certainly knew how to dress.

Augusta walked in to the centre of the room. She turned and gave her a half smile. "We meet at last, Lady Hargreaves. As I'm sure you've realised, I'm Augusta."

"I'm Georgina but everyone calls me Georgie. Do please take a seat, Your Grace."

"Thank you. We don't stand on ceremony in this family, everyone calls me Augusta." She sat on a sofa near to the window and indicated the space next to her.

Georgie joined her. A knot of tension twisted her insides, so much rested on this meeting. If Augusta didn't believe her story then Max never would. Augusta's expression seemed determinedly neutral.

"I've heard several versions of your meeting with my brother. I'd like you to tell me what really happened."

Georgie gave her an outline of her escape from the Huttons and how Max had rescued her from the barn. She couldn't bring herself to mention her encounter with Max at the Golden Cross.

"Why did you agree to my brother's outrageous proposal? Were you afraid of a possible scandal?"

Georgie jumped, although the question was spoken in a gentle voice. This was plain speaking. She met Augusta's gaze, which was fixed firmly on her.

"No, it wasn't that."

"What then?" Augusta's voice was sharper this time. Her expression was neutral but her gaze was fixed firmly on Georgie's face.

Georgie squared her shoulders. Why had she agreed? Heat surged to her cheeks as she remembered the fiery response Max had induced in her, both in the inn and when he had carried her back to Hargreaves Hall. The strength of him had wrapped itself around her frozen self like a blanket. She glanced up to see Augusta staring at her. She would have to tell her as much of the whole as she could bear if she was to be believed.

"It's hard to explain. He asked me when I was still recovering from my ordeal. If I'd been fully recovered, I don't think I would have let him talk me into it."

"He's handsome, charming, wealthy and a Marquess to boot. Do you expect me to believe that you would need talking into a marriage with him?"

"No, I suppose not, because I don't understand it all myself." She thought for a moment. "I knew it would be cold in those barns but I couldn't see well enough in the snow to be sure of finding the vicarage and my strength was fading. My legs were frozen by the morning when Max found me and I couldn't walk. He picked me up and threw me over his shoulder as if I weighed no more than young Peter. I wanted that strength. I'd lost everyone who was dear to me and the world had become a frightening place."

"So why would you want to refuse him?" Her voice was calm but she looked wary.

Georgie closed her eyes for a moment before she ploughed on. "I was too drained to make that sort of decision. If I'd been fully restored, I would have resisted the temptation to seek safety in his arms. I was brought up in a family who held strong views on the importance of love in a marriage." A spurt of anger ran through her at Augusta's sceptical expression. "We didn't even know one another, although I suppose in families like yours arranged marriages happen all the time."

Augusta studied her, her haughty expression proclaiming her every inch a duchess. Georgie tensed, ready to defend herself, until Augusta broke into a smile.

"I'm glad to see you have some spirit. That may have been true in previous generations but not now. This brings me to the question that really matters. Are you physically attracted to my scapegrace brother?"

Georgie gasped. She stared at Augusta who regarded her steadily. "Yes I am. That probably had a lot to do with my decision."

"Thank goodness for that. I would hate to see Max in a loveless marriage." Augusta's eyes narrowed, studying her. "Now tell me what else happened. All of it."

Georgie kept her eyes on the floor and stuttered though a

halting description of their encounter at the inn. She grimaced and looked up. "I'm afraid someone saw Max kissing me."

"I thought there was something you were holding back. Don't look so embarrassed, it wasn't your fault. I heard from Eliza that Max went home early from Simon Pryce's house party because of a row with his Aunt Selina." Augusta frowned. "That woman is a menace. I see now why Max offered you marriage. I was afraid he had made the offer simply to get back at his aunt."

There was a knock at the door and a maid came in with a loaded tray. Georgie concentrated on pouring the tea.

Augusta sat back with her cup and absentmindedly nibbled on a cake. "Before we go any farther, I should apologise for calling unannounced like this. I'm not normally so ramshackle but we're in a serious situation."

She put her cup on a side table and caught one of Georgie's hands. "All sorts of lurid stories are flying around the Ton."

Georgie gasped. "How could there be? We've only just arrived."

"I don't know, we only arrived yesterday ourselves. I came here looking for clues. Cathlay was passing when your carriage pulled up and he came straight home to tell me."

"It has to be Mrs Powell. Mr Breakwell escorted her to London when Max dismissed her. My maid insists that Mrs Powell worked for lady Lovell before she moved to Hargreaves. If she's correct and Lady Lovell is in London it makes perfect sense."

"Mrs Powell was the housekeeper at the Hall as I recall. Why get rid of her?"

Georgie felt heat rush to her cheeks. "She thought I was a woman of ill repute when I arrived. Even after I married Max she was so insolent Eliza advised me to tell Max to dismiss her. I was afraid she'd be angry enough about losing her job to stir up trouble. We agreed to leave her in post for a while longer and then Max decided to dismiss her straight away without consulting me."

Chapter Twenty Four

Max ran up the stone steps to his club and entered the marble floored entrance hall. He handed his outdoor clothes to a porter. He needed some time to think before he went to see Augusta and there might be a friend or two about who could tell him if news of his marriage had reached London. There was a hum of voices in one of the saloons, which was surprising so early in the year. He walked in and the room fell silent. Oh Lord, his hasty marriage must be the latest on-dit in Town. Hardly surprising after what he had overheard in Porchester.

The tall figure of Gervase, Viscount Ashbrook, jumped up from a dark leather armchair near to the roaring fire and walked towards him. Max was too stunned to move until Brook, as his friends called him, grasped his arm and propelled him out of the saloon into a smaller, unoccupied, room. Brook stopped to ask a porter to mind the door and then shut it firmly behind them.

Max walked across to the fire and crossed his arms. "I was afraid there would be rumours but it seems it's worse than I thought."

Brook grimaced. "I know you hate gossip. Lady Lovell was very vocal in her criticism after you left Simon Pyrce's house party. Simon's uncle, Welford, managed to get her away from everyone and I hoped he had quashed any gossip. Then I arrived in Town, after a family Christmas at my sister's place, to find you had been tricked into marriage by the daughter of a lawyer's clerk." Brook laughed. "That's the most repeatable version. There are others involving abduction and irate fathers and I don't know what."

Max ground his teeth. "What! Georgie was brought up by her uncle, now deceased, who was a clergyman and she was happy to accept my proposal."

He ran a finger inside his collar, which suddenly felt tight. Had she been happy to accept or had he forced her hand?

Brook's mouth dropped open. "You are married then?"

"Yes. To Miss Georgina Sherborne. We married the day she reached her majority. It's a long story but she ran away to avoid a forced marriage."

Brook held up a hand. You can tell me another time. Our priority is to stop the rumours. Do I detect the work of Lady Lovell?"

Max considered. There had been local talk but the villagers had been too happy that he had married someone known to be good natured for it to have turned vicious.

"I think it has to be. There is the complication of Georgie's guardian, a distant cousin, and her lawyer friend who Georgie is afraid of. Although, I can't see what they would gain from spreading gossip."

"They sound unsavoury. I'm still working for the War Office when they need me. I'm officially in London to open up Ashbrook House for Mama but they want me to oversee a secret investigation, which had to be put back until next week. I've got investigators kicking their heels. Send the details around

265

of Lady Hargreaves's former guardian and this lawyer and I'll have them looked into. We can't have them making trouble on top of Lady Lovell's efforts."

"Thanks, Brook. I'm going round to see if Aunt Selina is at home. I'll try and persuade her to say no more. The Cathlays should be in London any day now and Augusta might have some ideas."

Brook put a hand on his shoulder. "Gossip like this is your worst nightmare, isn't it? We'll all stand by you."

Max couldn't look at him. His voice shook. "I'm glad you're in Town. I'll catch up with you tomorrow."

Max strode out into the hall. He reclaimed his coat and gloves and ran down the stone steps to the street. He marched off in the direction of his aunt's London home, head down to avoid eye contact with anyone who might know him. His head was spinning. Before he met Georgie, he would have agreed with Brook that being the butt of gossip again was his worst nightmare. But it wasn't. Being rejected again was. He could only hope he hadn't ruined his relationship with Georgie beyond repair.

A young footman answered the door when he arrived at the house Selina shared with Bertie.

"The Marquess of Hargreaves to see my aunt."

"I'm afraid she isn't at home, my lord."

"She'll be at home to see me." Max strode into the hall.

The footman stared at him, looking puzzled. "She won't, mmy llord. She's not in London."

"What!" Max's voice dropped down to a growl. "I don't believe you for a minute."

Another footman joined them. "It's true, my lord. Mr Lovell is in residence but he's gone out for the evening."

Max shrugged and walked out. He wasn't going to bandy words with servants but he'd thought Selina had more courage than to refuse to see him. Ah well. Perhaps it meant she realised she had gone too far and the talk would die down. He reached his house and ran up the steps. A footman took his hat and coat and he noticed a fine, fur trimmed pelisse. Who on earth could be visiting them? He could hear voices in the drawing room and ran to investigate. Augusta was chatting, apparently calmly, to Georgie.

They hadn't noticed him and he edged into the doorway to hear his wife tell Augusta about Mrs Powell. They seemed to be on friendly terms. Max stepped into the room and they both looked up at him.

"I'm sure Selina is behind the rumours I heard in my club, Augusta. My cook recommended Mrs Powell to me. Charles had gone to visit his sick uncle and I didn't bother to check her references. Jepson told me, on the way here, that Mrs Powell was dismissed by Selina and asked Cook to recommend her to me. I expect Selina heard I was looking for a housekeeper and asked Mrs Powell to try and get the job. Mrs Powell saw an opportunity to cause trouble and went straight to Selina. My stupidity has caused an enormous scandal and I don't know how to right it."

"Oh, sit down Max." Augusta waved him to a chair. "Everyone knows Selina lives to denigrate you."

"You don't know the worst of it."

"I do. Georgie has told me everything. As long as you persuade her cousin to confirm your story of a longstanding engagement, your drunken assault will be ignored."

Max winced. Put like that it sounded awful. "It won't be enough Augusta. It's the talk of the town and the country after

267

what I overheard in Porchester."

"It's not like you to be so defeatist, Max. Now I know Selina is behind it, I'm sure all will be well. I'll take Georgie shopping tomorrow and see how the land lies. Cathlay wants to talk to you tonight. We dine at eight, don't keep us waiting." Augusta swept out of the room in a flurry of apricot skirts.

Max moved towards Georgie. She looked exhausted and who could blame her. "Georgie, I owe you an apology." His shoulders slumped. How could he have been so stupid?

"Not now, Max. You believed I'd schemed to force you into marriage, didn't you?"

He hung his head. What could he say?

"I need to lie down for a bit before we go out to dinner."

"Forget Augusta. We'll send a message and dine at home if you're tired."

"The servants already know we're dining out. There are so few of them they're exhausted getting the house ready at short notice. It wouldn't be fair. Besides, whatever Augusta said to you, she looked seriously worried to me. We should do what she says."

He started to argue.

"For goodness sake, Max. Her husband is a prominent politician. How would an unresolved scandal affect him?"

Georgie walked out.

Max stalked across to the window and stared out at the rain splashing off the pavement. What a fool he was. He had better start listening to Georgie. That said, if things were too bad, he would take her back to Hargreaves Hall and to hell with the Ton, Augusta and everyone else. As long as it wasn't too late to make things right with Georgie, he didn't care about them.

His biggest fear was Georgie getting the cut direct. He didn't mind for himself, he deserved it, but Georgie had already suffered enough at his hands. Seeing her talking to Augusta had opened his eyes. Her reaction after Mrs Powell's dismissal hadn't been guilt. It had been anger. She hadn't flown into a rage or anything so melodramatic. She had quietly gone about things as best she could, burying her anger. What sort of man did she think he was?

He sat in a chair with his head in his hands. That day in the library he had been so angry she had flinched away from him. Did she fear violence? How would he ever make it up to her? She was right, of course. They had to work with Augusta and try and face the scandal down. He sat bolt upright. Augusta had been on the best of terms with Georgie. Why had everyone but him seen what a good person she was? He didn't deserve her.

There was one thing he could do. It would be humiliating and it might not work but he had to try it. That footman had said that Bertie was in Town. He would hunt him down and beg him to make his mother retract all her accusations. Bertie's father had left everything to him, some in trust until he was thirty, but both properties were his. Selina was in his power if he could be persuaded to exercise that power.

He jumped up and then sat down again. It was more than likely true that Bertie was out. He had to obey Augusta's summons to dinner. She was in the best position to protect Georgie in places he couldn't go, like the dressmakers and milliners. He needed her help. He knew most of Bertie's haunts and should be able to track him down later.

* * *

They arrived at the magnificent Mayfair residence of the Duke of Cathlay at eight o'clock sharp. Cathlay was his usual urbane self but Max was under no illusions. They were the only guests and he would get a grilling once the ladies left them to their port. He sat through all five courses of the meal with all the patience he could muster.

The ladies withdrew and Cathlay passed him the port. "You're in some difficulty then, Hargreaves. Augusta tells me Georgina is a fine young woman so I expect it will be worth the trouble. She's very prettily behaved but rather quiet for my taste."

Max flew to Georgie's defence. "She's tired tonight and it must be a shock for her to find out she's the subject of wild gossip. She's never moved in fashionable circles and ..."

Cathlay raised a hand. "I'm glad to see you standing up for her. Augusta says she has plenty of spirit and the courage to escape from an attempt to force her into a marriage for her money. Selina's a meddling piece. She always wanted your father, you know, but she was much too young for him. Once he met your mother that was never going to happen."

Max was momentarily diverted. "I never knew that."

"From what m'father said about her I think the woman is a little unhinged. All this business about Bertie being your heir with you not yet thirty proves it if you ask me. Still once everyone knows she's behind the rumours it will all die down." He leaned closer and gave Max a sympathetic smile. "I shouldn't worry too much."

It was past midnight before they were able to leave. Georgie stumbled as they reached the coach. He put his hands around her waist and lifted her in bodily. The feel of her under his hands sent shockwaves through him. She was gossamer light.

He doubted she had gained any weight since moving in with him. She must have been too upset to eat properly. Now he thought about it, ever since the Mrs Powell episode she had picked at her food at dinner. Even tonight she hadn't eaten a lot. Guilt gnawed at him anew. He would make it all up to her somehow.

Jepson regarded him with a thunderous expression as he changed into more subdued evening clothes. Perhaps he ought to go to Georgie, but she was exhausted and a good night's sleep would do her good. The sooner he found Bertie the better. He would buy his help if he had to. He ran downstairs and threw a dark evening cloak on top of his outfit followed by dark gloves. He selected a walking cane and tested the mechanism. A wicked looking blade slid out silently when he found the raised bit in the handle. Knowing where Bertie was likely to be, he couldn't be too careful.

He felt tired himself and he could be in for a long night. He decided to start at the venues in the more salubrious parts of town and work downwards. His luck was in. He found Bertie at the second place he tried, a gambling hell. Max shuddered at the smell of alcohol and stale bodies. The walls of the main saloon, where he found Bertie, were decorated in shades of red and gold. The amount of gold making the effect seem tawdry. Bertie was at a table against the wall, raking in a large amount of money. Damn, if he was in funds it would be harder to buy his co-operation.

Bertie spotted Max straight away. He stood up and left the table.

"I wouldn't have expected to find you here, cuz. I heard you had a lovely new wife to keep you occupied."

There was a ripple of laughter from Bertie's friends and Max scowled.

"I would appreciate a word with you, Bertie."

"Walk back with me then, Max."

Bertie sounded completely sober, which was promising, if unusual. His friends muttered their disapproval.

"I've lost enough money to you lot in the past. I'm going home a winner tonight."

Max followed him out into the hall. The family resemblance was strong. Bertie had the deep blue eyes and height of the Lovells but his hair was lighter. They collected their outdoor wear and made their way into the street.

"What are all these strange rumours I'm hearing, Max?"

Max checked no one was in earshot. "That's what I want to talk to you about. It's true I've just got married but all the outlandish rumours are being spread by your mother."

"Ah, from Simon Pyrce's house party?" He sounded sympathetic. "I've told her to stop thinking about me being your heir and let it lie for years. She's made herself a laughing stock."

Max decided to tell him at least some of the truth. "The problem is this time there is some substance behind her nasty gossip, enough to be dangerous. My wife deserves better than to have her reputation ruined when she's done nothing wrong. I know you won't want to get involved but I'm begging for your help."

"I don't see how Mama's outburst at the party could have caused those sorts of rumours. From what I heard people were laughing at her as usual."

They arrived at Bertie's house. "Come on in, Max. I have some good news for you. Although in the circumstances it might be bad news."

He sounded puzzled and Max allowed himself to be ushered

indoors. Bertie took him into the library and offered him a brandy. Max refused. He needed to keep a clear head. Bertie wasn't making any sense. He sat on a comfortable looking, leather armchair near the fire. This must be a room Bertie used regularly to have a fire burning so late.

Bertie poured himself a drink and dropped into the chair next to Max, stroking his chin. "I wonder if that housekeeper I made Mama get rid of, after I caught her whipping the parlour maids for the second time, could be involved? She was here the other day looking for Mama. Awful woman but incredibly loyal to my mother. There was quite a scene when I insisted on dismissing her."

Max leaned towards him. "That would be Mrs Powell. My cook recommended her to me when I needed a new house-keeper. If I'd known she had worked for you I would never have taken her on. I knew your mother was behind this mess."

"Woah there, Max." Bertie raised a hand. "If you've got rid of the Powell woman, I expect she went to one of Mama's cronies when she found out Mama wasn't in London."

Max banged his fist onto the arm of his chair. "Doing it too strong, Bertie, if you expect me to believe your mother isn't in London."

Bertie raised laughing eyes to his. "You can believe what you like but Mama should be in Northumberland by now. I have some news for you."

"Northumberland? I'm sure that's a place she has always longed to visit!" Max rubbed the back of his neck to ease the tension in his shoulders.

Bertie laughed. "Mama doesn't mind where she goes as longs as it's in the company of the Earl of Welford. The reason she wanted an invitation to stay at Hargreaves wasn't to do with me, whatever she said. She wanted to be close enough to Welford's Kent seat to visit him. When he realised that, he offered her marriage as long as she stopped hounding you. Turned out he'd been interested in her for ages and had a special licence ready, with a view to proposing at the house party."

Max's mouth dropped open. "I don't believe it."

Bertie picked up a newspaper and threw it at him. "Read the marriage announcement."

Max stared at the announcement in The Times. "They were married on 29th December in London."

"That's right. We came back here for the ceremony and they set off for Welford's Northumberland estate the following day. Welford told her she had to promise to drop this silly feud she's had with you. He whisked her off for a bit so she wouldn't be tempted."

"She couldn't have spread these rumours. Oh Lord, Mrs Powell must have found someone else to do that."

"I'm not the villain you think I am, Max. I hope we can become friends without Mama's silliness. What can I do to help?"

Chapter Twenty Five

Georgie dragged her tired body upstairs. At least Max knew the truth now. In a way she felt worse. The more she thought about it the angrier she was with him for not trusting her. Did he think honour was only for the aristocracy? She should never have married a man so far above her in status. A yawning Martha appeared out of the dressing room when she entered her bedroom. Mercifully, she wasn't inclined for conversation. Georgie accepted her help to undress and sent her off to bed.

She snuffed out her candle and climbed under the covers. Now that Max knew she was innocent he would want to resume the relationship in the bedroom. She was so tired she wasn't sorry he had gone out. If he came to her later, he would get short shrift. Fear clutched at her chest. Had he rushed off to a London mistress for comfort? That would be unbearable. He ought to be here begging her forgiveness for doubting her and helping to ease her fears about how she would go on in London. It would serve him right if she showed herself up for a country bumpkin and he became a laughing stock.

If only she could fall asleep. Augusta had promised she would arrive unfashionably early for their shopping trip and she seemed the sort of person to keep her promises. At least she would be properly dressed but she would have much rather waited for Eliza to help her. It suggested Augusta had plans for her entertainment. She would do the best she could. If Max wasn't there to support her, he couldn't complain if it all went badly. It wouldn't be fun trying to face down the gossip with people she knew, let alone complete strangers.

* * *

Georgie was finishing off her breakfast in the smaller of the two dining rooms when Augusta was shown in. She jumped to her feet. Augusta asked a hovering footman for another coffee cup and waved Georgie back to her seat, taking the one beside her.

Augusta poured her coffee and waited for the footman to leave the room. "Where's Max? I was hoping for his escort."

"He went out as soon as we arrived home last night and I haven't seen him since." Anger made her waspish.

Augusta smiled at her. "That's the spirit, get angry with him, he deserves it. I have a feeling you've been giving him far too easy a ride. If you're angry with him let him know in no uncertain terms. Otherwise, you'll never get him trained." Augusta's eyes twinkled.

Georgie was too stunned to reply.

Augusta burst out laughing. "You think I jest? Men are still naughty little boys at heart. You need to give them boundaries in the same way you would with a dog you're training. The trick is to let them think they're in charge at the same time." She downed the last of her coffee. "Let's make a start. We have a lot to do today."

An impressive town carriage, drawn by four matched bays,

was waiting outside. A liveried groom held the door open for them whilst another handed them in.

"Max said he would have a phaeton made for me and teach me to drive a pair."

"Did he? Well that's something. That will be perfect for driving in the parks but you will need a town carriage as well."

"We may have one I suppose. Max said he was living in his bachelor quarters up until now so Hargreaves House hasn't been used much since your mother died. I know he intends to buy some more horses." She hesitated. "I mustn't stay out too long as Mrs Mills is hoping to have some prospective servants to interview this afternoon."

"We'll be as quick as we can but you must have some new clothes before we can take you about."

As she had feared, it seemed Augusta intended to introduce her to her friends. The clothes would have to be made so she would have a few days respite. They pulled into a street lined with shops. She could see at least two milliners and a modiste. The carriage drew to a halt. She let out a pent-up breath. The modiste appeared to be closed. Augusta rapped sharply on the door and they were invited inside.

A diminutive little woman, with bright black eyes, came out of a side room to greet them in heavily accented French. Augusta seemed to understand every word and replied in rapid French. The woman took Georgie's hand and pulled her into the centre of the room. She switched to English.

"Lady Hargreaves, it will be a pleasure to dress you."

Georgie started to stammer out her thanks but the woman turned back to Augusta.

"First we must find something for her to wear today." She opened a door into what appeared to be a workroom and disappeared.

Augusta patted her hand. "You won't recognise yourself when Madame Duval has finished with you."

Three young women appeared, all with clothes over their arms. Madame went with her into a changing room and poked and prodded as she tried them all on. An assistant wrote down measurements. Within minutes a richly embroidered cream day dress and a warm pelisse in an unusual shade of pale green were taken off to the workroom. For the next hour she was shown patterns and had fabrics draped all over her until her head ached. Augusta translated as Madame fired questions at her.

Eventually both ladies went quiet for a moment. "That should be enough to be going on with, Georgie. Madame says the first day outfit will be ready for you to try on in a moment. She'll have the first evening gown sent round before dinner."

Georgie drew Augusta to one side. "I lost quite a bit of weight with my cousins. It would be wasteful to buy too many clothes at once in case I put it back on again."

"Very true, my love, I'll tell Madame we'll leave it at today's order for now. Don't blame me if that starts a rumour that you are enceinte."

Georgie stared at her and tried to will the heat in her cheeks to go away.

Augusta laughed. "It might not be a bad thing if it does. They say the best way to dispel a rumour is to give the Ton a juicier one."

The day outfit arrived and fitted Georgie perfectly. She couldn't resist a glance in the looking glass. A stylish stranger looked back at her. So much for expecting a respite before any of the clothes arrived. Their next visit was to a milliner, where

Augusta saw a friend and introduced her. Georgie was aware of curiosity in the woman's face but she was perfectly amiable. Augusta helped her to select several hats. They returned to the coach loaded with parcels. A footman rushed forward to take them. Augusta certainly lived in high style. Would Max be the same?

Augusta opted to follow her in when they reached Hargreaves House. "I want to catch a word with my brother."

* * *

Max woke up with a start at the sound of his bed curtains being pulled back. He turned over in bed and groaned. What was Jepson doing waking him up so early? He felt as if he had hardly slept.

"My lord, you have visitors. Viscount Ashbrook and Mr Bright are waiting for you in the library."

Max sat up and shook his head in an effort to throw off the last dregs of sleep. "At this time of the day?"

"It's nearly noon, my lord. They said it was urgent."

"Send a message down to say I'll join them in twenty minutes." He was fully awake now.

Max ran down the stairs at a quarter past noon. He strode into the library to find his visitors deep in conversation. Brook spotted him first.

"Here you are at last. I came around for the details of Lady Hargreaves's guardian and her lawyer friend. Mr Bright was already here."

Max waved at Mr Bright to keep his seat and took the chair opposite to them.

"Lord Overton's groom, trained by me, traced the two men

who tried to cause a disturbance at your wedding to London." Mr Bright smiled. "My men are watching them and I've told Lord Ashbrook everything we know so far."

Brook broke into a broad grin. "I'm delighted to say that the two of them are working for Mr Fitzpatrick. A dangerous character, suspected of being involved in a smuggling ring and a friend of Mary Hutton."

"Good Lord, what is there to be delighted about in that?"

"With the information Mr Bright's team have gathered, we should be able to throw Fitzpatrick in prison for years for offences unrelated to his smuggling activities. You don't need to know what else I have in mind but we won't have to involve Lady Hargreaves in any way."

Max turned to Mr Bright. "Good work. Nat is lucky to have you. What were the men intending to do at our wedding?"

"They were trying to capture your wife. Mary Hutton thought her birthday was Christmas day. The snow stopped them finding her any sooner but when they realised what was happening, they decided to try and stop the service on the grounds she was a minor."

There was the sound of a scuffle in the hallway. The door to the library opened and a sturdy looking man, aided by a footman, dragged a fashionably dressed young man in by the points of his overlarge shirt collar.

Mr Bright jumped up. "What have you got here, Fallon?"

"Mr Algernon Hutton, Sir. We've been tracking him. I saw him come to the door and grabbed him." Fallon let him go and he sprawled at Max's feet.

Hutton stood up and brushed at his pantaloons. He held out a letter to Max.

"My mother made me deliver this. Before you say anything,

it's nothing to do with me so you can ignore it."

Max tore it open with a wary eye on Hutton. "It seems Mary Hutton has heard about the rumours around us and is threatening to make them ten times worse with a claim for breach of promise against Georgie if I don't pay her a large sum." Max's voice rose. "How can you say this has nothing to do with you, you miserable little guttersnipe."

"Because she can't do anything without me. I'm engaged to someone else, a widow. She's sold her business and home to a friend of her late husband's. We're escaping up north where Fitzpatrick, my mother's lawyer friend, can't find us. I had to agree to deliver this so he wouldn't suspect anything."

Max looked at Brook. "Do you think this is a trick?"

"I don't know. What do you think, Fallon?"

"It could be true, Sir. He's been coming and going to the house of a widow in Gracechurch Street, whenever that Mr Fitzpatrick hasn't been around."

Max ground his teeth. "He deserves to be thrown in jail for how he treated Georgie but we don't want any more scandal."

"That's what I'm thinking," Brook said. "With the help of Mr Bright and his team we'll take him in charge until we have Fitzpatrick under lock and key. If his story is true, we'll send him and his prospective bride on their way."

Mr Bright grinned at him. "I've rounded up several good lads, my lord. We're only too happy to help."

"Excellent. You can safely leave it all with us, Max."

Chapter Twenty Six

Georgie and Augusta ran Max to ground in the library.
"Well, Max, we have your wife looking quite lovely," Augusta said.

"She always looks lovely but now she looks modishly lovely."

He gave her a warm smile and Georgie caught her breath. He seemed pleased with himself.

"She does indeed. I think you need some time on your own, but first tell me what you've been up to, Max."

"Quite a lot. I managed to track Bertie down last night. You will be amazed to know that Selina is now the Countess of Welford."

"Really? That's good news but why is she still spreading rumours?"

"She isn't. They've gone to Northumberland. Bertie said Mrs Powell came around looking for his mother. He's probably right that she's gone around some of Selina's cronies. He's promised to do all he can to scotch the rumours."

"Not sure there is much he can do but even so that's good of him. I never thought he was as bad as you painted him."

"I'm coming to that conclusion. He suggested the marriage announcement, which he finally remembered to put in The Times for Welford the other day, might help us."

Augusta chuckled. "He's right. It's bound to create quite a stir."

"I had another piece of luck. I went around to my club yesterday afternoon and found Brook."

"You mean Viscount Ashbrook?"

"Yes. He and Nat's Mr Bright have got together. It turns out that Mrs Hutton's lawyer friend, Fitzpatrick, has been involved in criminal activities. Brooks got contacts. He's going to see he's put in prison. With him out of the way I suspect Mrs Hutton will leave Georgie alone."

Georgie pulled a face. "Awful woman. What about Algernon?"

"He won't trouble you. He's about to marry a widow from Gracechurch Street, but keep that quiet for now. I've spoken to him and his mother doesn't know yet. I was tempted to pull him limb from limb but we can't afford any more scandal." Max grinned.

Augusta laughed. "It sounds like you have it all under control, Max. We're having a small dinner party tonight."

"I'm sure Georgie would prefer to stay quietly at home tonight, Augusta."

"Cathlay has invited people who will be delighted to meet your new bride. We will expect you no later than nine o'clock. Georgina has an evening gown arriving later." Augusta swept out of the room. "I'll see myself out," she said, over her shoulder.

* * *

Georgie's mind was racing. Max was with Bertie when she suspected him of visiting a mistress. He pulled her down onto

283

a sofa and dropped a kiss on her forehead.

"I'm sorry, Georgie. I should have trusted you. Will you forgive me?"

Augusta's unusual views on dealing with husbands came back to her. Perhaps she should be more forceful with Max. At the very least she must be honest with him if she was ever going to have peace of mind.

"I hope so."

Max sat up straight. "I don't understand. Either you will or you won't."

"It's not as simple as that and it's time we were honest with each other. I want to be a good Christian and forgive you but I can't be sure I'll be able to. It hurts that you didn't trust me."

Max jumped up and walked around the room, running his hands through his hair. "I'm so sorry. It sounds stupid, but after Lavinia I was looking for problems where there were none. I ought to have told you what happened. I was barely twenty and madly in love, or so I thought. We were betrothed and then I found her in bed with another man. A man I thought was my friend. I was furious and the humiliation was dreadful. Even worse than my sense of betrayal."

"Oh, how awful for you."

Max sat back down. He took her hand and caressed her palm with his thumb. Georgie shivered and Max smiled at her before he continued.

"It got worse. She wanted the money and position I brought with me but she didn't want me. She wouldn't release me from the betrothal, confident I would be too humiliated to want the scandal to get out. She miscalculated. I jilted her. The scandal was dreadful but all my family supported me. I pushed you for an early wedding because I couldn't bear the thought of a long drawn out engagement and the inevitable speculation about whether I would come up to scratch the second time."

Georgie studied his face. "The trouble is we don't know each other, do we?"

"I suppose we don't. Can we start again and put that right? I do know that you're everything I've always wanted in a wife."

She longed to believe him. He looked sincere. "Are you sure? You became distant days before you dismissed Mrs Powell."

"You seemed scared of her and from something you said I began to wonder if she was blackmailing you."

"I wasn't scared of her but the things she said to me when I first arrived were awful. At the same time, my arrival was rather odd and many people would have wondered. I felt it my duty to be fair to her. My aunt campaigned against servants being dismissed on a whim."

"Which was why you were angry at me dismissing her out of hand?"

Georgie nodded. "Even after we were married, she was insolent towards me but I felt guilty about her losing her job." She lowered her eyes.

She had also felt guilty because part of what Mrs Powell had said, implying she was nothing but a wanton, was probably true. Why else would she have agreed to marry an aristocrat she knew nothing of if it hadn't been for the glorious sensations he aroused in her?

"You didn't have anything to feel guilty about. I noticed that guilt and was worried it meant you had cheated me. I've lost count of the number of women who have tried to trick me into marriage, but that's no excuse."

He looked contrite but could she believe him? Was that the only reason for his withdrawal after they started to plan the move to London? She longed to ask him but couldn't find the courage. "I suppose I can't blame you for doubting me after the things Mrs Powell said that day."

He caught her gaze. "Can we start all over again, Georgie?"

Somehow Georgie found the strength to look away. She had to be sure of him before she let down her guard. She didn't want to be hurt anymore. "Yes, but let's take it more slowly this time. I'm feeling exhausted. I think I'll take a nap before I dress for dinner."

* * *

Max watched Georgie leave the library. She did look tired but that guarded look he'd taken for guilt was still there. Something was troubling her. If he hadn't been such an idiot as to doubt her he would have noticed sooner. He didn't want her to be bothered by anything ever again. She said she wanted to take things more slowly this time. The inevitable press of engagements in Town, often keeping them apart, was a difficulty now rather than a relief.

A thought occurred to him. He walked around to the Mews and was fortunate to find Larkin sitting on a pile of sacks, sorting and cleaning the horses' tack. He nodded as Larkin jumped up and touched his cap.

"Did you send that message to your uncle?"

"I did, my lord. I sent one of our grooms off first thing. He should be back tomorrow. I asked him to have any pair uncle thought was suitable for a lady's phaeton and a horse for you to ride sent up straight away, on approval."

"Well done, Larkin. Before anyone in Town tries to take you off my hands, would you like the post as our head groom at

CHAPTER TWENTY SIX

Hargreaves House? If you accept there will be a large rise in your pay."

Larkin grinned. "Thank you, my lord. I'm happy to accept."

"Good. Come on, we're going to look at carriages now."

They took a Hackney carriage to the carriage maker in Lambeth that Larkins recommended. Max walked around looking at a few completed vehicles followed by a company clerk.

"These are good quality, Larkin. I'm of a mind to order a new curricle to keep in Town."

"If you'd be happy with a phaeton, Sir, we have one already made." The clerk sniffed. "The purchaser changed his mind. He said it looked too much like a lady's carriage."

Max went to inspect it. "This is a well-balanced vehicle. Do you think it would be suitable for a lady, Larkin?"

"It would depend. She'd need to be able to handle two horses."

Max turned to the clerk. "I want a phaeton for my wife. Would you reserve this for me until tomorrow so I can bring her to look at it?" Max pulled out a guinea.

"I'm sure that could be arranged."

"Good. I'll order a curricle for me as well."

Max arrived home in better spirits. Teaching Georgie to drive a phaeton with two horses up front would take time, time spent together.

* * *

Max knocked the connecting door to Georgie's bedroom. Martha let him in. Georgie was standing in the middle of the room and turned as he entered. He rocked back on his heels.

She was a vision in cream muslin, embroidered with silver thread around the hem and bodice. The new gown was the work of a master. Red highlights gleamed in her chestnut brown hair under the candlelight. Heat rushed to his groin at the sight of her. With an effort of will he managed to ignore it.

"Georgie, you look wonderful." He held out a rosewood jewellery box. "I intended to give you these for your first ball but I thought you might want to have them tonight."

She blushed adorably and accepted the box. "Thank you, Max." Her eyes opened wide when she opened the box and the diamond set was revealed.

It had been more than worth what had seemed an extortionate price at the time. "Would you like me to fasten the necklace for you?"

Georgie nodded. "Yes please."

He fastened the clasp, breathing uncomfortably fast in response to her nearness. She shivered as his clumsy fingers brushed the sensitive skin of her neck. He could swear she was as affected by their close proximity as he was. He dropped a kiss on her cheek before leading her to the mirror.

"What do you think, sweetheart? I saw these when I bought the pearls for your wedding present."

"They're lovely. They bring out the embroidery on the dress. I don't know how Madame's staff worked so quickly. There's an evening cloak to match."

"Trust Augusta to know the best places, you look beautiful."

"Thank you. I only hope Eliza won't be offended that I didn't wait for her."

Despite the blush tinging her cheeks she was determined to stay on a business like footing it seemed. He supressed a sigh, how could he have been so foolish as to doubt her. He didn't doubt the hurt he had caused her. It was there in her eyes, every time their glances met. It was a barrier he had to surmount but he must be patient.

* * *

The horses Larkin had hired to pull the town coach proved not to be the matched beasts he had been promised. It was already a quarter of an hour past nine o' clock when they pulled up at the bottom of the steps to Cathlay House. Max felt Georgie tense by his side. He gave her hand a squeeze.

"Don't worry. It always pays to be last to arrive when you're the star guests."

"I hope we aren't." Georgie laughed out loud. "I was hoping to stay hidden for as much of the time as possible."

Larkin opened the door. Max jumped out and lifted Georgie down beside him. She threaded her arm through his and they climbed the stairs. Max felt his own stomach tighten. A lot was riding on the evening. Augusta must have been impressed with Georgie to throw her straight to the lions like this. The thought gave him a warm glow. Augusta's regard was never given lightly.

A footman relieved them of their evening cloaks and the butler showed them into a drawing room lined with blue damask wallpaper.

"Lord and Lady Hargreaves."

Max fixed his features into a smile and led Georgie forward. He glanced around the room. There was a clerical gentleman he didn't know, two of Cathlay's colleagues in the Lords, all with their wives, and two couples he couldn't place. They stopped before Augusta and Cathlay. He gave Georgie's hand a squeeze and released it before bowing low. Georgie picked up the cue from him and went into a deep curtsey.

Cathlay's deep voice boomed out. "There's no need to stand on ceremony here, Hargreaves."

Augusta stepped forward to perform the introductions. Georgie's face lit up when Augusta announced the newly promoted Bishop of Harminster. The bishop patted her hand.

"Georgina Sherborne, I didn't recognise you when you came in but I can see it now. My word, the Marchioness of Hargreaves. Of course, your aunt was very friendly with Lady Wakeley, wasn't she?" He drew his wife forward. "It was that committee for building the new orphanage if you remember."

Mrs Matthews swept Georgie into an embrace. "Yes, they were good friends. It's wonderful to see you again, Georgie, if I may still call you that."

"Please do. Lady Wakeley can remember meeting me when I was younger but I know Lady Overton better."

"Ah, yes. You moved near to her, didn't you? We did miss you and your aunt when you left Canterbury. We must have an exchange of news later."

Augusta finished the introductions and led the way into the dining room. Max admired the skilful way she manoeuvred Georgie so that she was seated between the Matthews. Georgie appeared happier than he had seen her since before Mrs Powell's dismissal. He relaxed a little and was ready when the Countess of Haxby seated on his left, the wife of one of Cathlay's political friends, started probing. The woman was something of a gossip, presumably why Augusta had invited her.

"It's lovely to see you caught at last Hargreaves. We none of us had any idea you had someone in mind." She smiled at him.

Max could see her watching him with the intensity of a barn owl watching a mouse. "Georgie's aunt died at the beginning of summer and there was no question of her marrying then. It seemed best for her to start thinking about matrimony once she was out of mourning." He gave the Countess his blandest smile.

"Of course. Will Lady Overton be coming to town for the season?"

Max laughed. "The Overtons are expected soon, I believe. Lady Hargreaves will be able to tell you more precisely, they were planning some serious shopping expeditions once she arrives."

There was a general murmur of laughter from the gentlemen.

Cathlay glanced across at Augusta at the other end of the table. "In which case, my dear, you will not be popular with Lady Overton."

Augusta laughed. "Dear Georgina did warn me but she only bought a few things to replenish her wardrobe today. There will be plenty of shopping left for Eliza to help her with."

Max turned to the lady on his right who seemed a good-natured soul, if a little overawed by the company. The countess wasn't finished with him. As soon as there was a break in their conversation she pounced.

"I understand you had a quiet wedding, Lord Hargreaves, with only two of your sisters present."

"Lady Hargreaves is still not entirely over the sudden death of her aunt but she felt something of a burden staying with her only relatives, some distant cousins. We could have asked Lady Cathlay to take her in. However, with two sisters in the north of Scotland and two expecting additions to their families it would have been for some months."

Max glanced at Georgie and smiled. She lowered her eyes demurely but not before he saw a spark of comprehension in them. Good girl, he was lucky to have such a quick-witted wife. Now the Ton would all be watching to see if Georgie produced an eight month baby. He felt heat rise in his cheeks at the thought, unwittingly reinforcing the impression he was trying to give of an impatient bridegroom.

"I see how it was. I had thought dear Lord and Lady Cathlay spent Christmas at their estates in Berkshire." The countess studied Augusta who carried on chatting to Mr Matthews, appearing unconscious of being the subject of conjecture.

"They did. Lady Hargreaves conceived the idea of marrying on her birthday on Christmas Eve. I'm afraid the weather was against us and our messenger didn't get through to them. With all the preparations in hand we decided to carry on with the wedding."

Max shrugged his shoulders and raised his eyebrows at the countess, a challenge in his eyes. She had the grace to blush and changed the subject. He was glad when the meal ended and Augusta invited the ladies to leave the men to their port. He gave Georgie an encouraging smile before she followed Augusta out of the room. Would the countess have the nerve to try questioning Georgie? He could trust Augusta to intervene if she did.

The Earl of Haxby addressed a remark to him. He struggled to focus his attention on him with his mind on Georgie.

"What was that, my lord? I'm afraid I was wool-gathering."

Haxby slapped him on the back. "Who can blame you with such a lovely young wife to think about?" The man looked distinctly uncomfortable. "I was just saying not to mind my wife. She's an incurable romantic no matter how much I tell her it's unfashionable."

"Indeed." Max gave him a tight smile and inclined his head. If he hadn't been trying to hide something, he would have been angry at her impertinence. His jaw set. He was angry anyway. Haxby eyed him warily.

Cathlay caught his eye. "We were wondering if you intended to take your seat in the House now you're comfortably settled, Hargreaves."

"That's something I hadn't thought about." Max grinned at his brother-in-law.

There was a rustle of laughter around the table.

"I must discuss it with my wife but perhaps I will. We live in strange times."

This had the desired effect and the conversation turned away from his affairs to a general discussion on politics. When Cathlay suggested it was time to re-join the ladies he joined step with Max and let the others precede them. He nodded at his library and Max followed him in, shutting the door quietly behind him.

"You did well to keep your temper there, Max. The Countess of Haxby is the worst sort of gossip but her husband is a decent sort. I think we shall brush through this unscathed." He gave Max a hard look. "Which is just as well as there are important measures afoot and I want to be there to help them along."

"I'm sorry." Max hung his head. "I see now that it would indeed have been better to place Georgie with you. I was being selfish. I knew Augusta would want to wait until everyone could be there."

"No harm done. A long engagement would have been uncomfortable for you, although Augusta is very upset at missing the wedding. Never mind, she's impressed, delighted even, with Georgina."

Max smiled his gratitude. Cathlay could be tough but he was fair. "I suspect Georgie will want me to take my seat in the House. She has very strong moral values."

The muscles at the back of his neck tightened. How could he have been so blind as to doubt her honesty?

"Excellent. Why don't we go and consult her now? It would be useful to have you with us quickly."

Max agreed. He followed him out, grinning to himself. It would consolidate his personal position in society and Cathlay, the wily old fox, had finally persuaded him to take up his seat after years of trying.

He scanned the drawing room and relaxed when he saw Georgie chatting happily to Mrs Matthews. Augusta had the countess hemmed in at the other side of the room. Cathlay sat down beside Georgie and Max stood on her other side.

"My dear, I have persuaded your husband to join us in the House of Lords. He has agreed as long as the idea has your blessing."

Georgie's head dipped momentarily. From where Max was standing, he was sure she was hiding a grin. They needed the Cathlay's support but everything had its price.

"He most definitely has my blessing, Your Grace. There is much that needs to be done."

One of the political wives sitting nearby turned towards them. "Dear Lady Hargreaves, I should be delighted to invite you to my political salons if you're interested."

Georgie didn't hesitate. "I would be delighted. I've been chatting with Mrs Matthews about which charities I would like to support."

Max exchanged glances with a beaming Augusta. He put a hand on Georgie's shoulder. "I'm glad you want to follow in the tradition of charitable works started by my mother. When you make your choices, I would be grateful if you would give a thought to the local charities she was involved with."

The conversation turned to other subjects and Georgie seemed to be perfectly comfortable with so many older people. Hadn't she said her aunt and uncle were a lot older than her parents? It was probably something she was used to, but he was pleased to see she wasn't overawed by such illustrious company. Max was wondering whether they could decently leave when the Countess of Haxby tried another attack.

"I was at a dinner with a friend of Lady Selina Lovell the other day." The Countess gave a false sounding laugh. "Such lurid tales she was telling me. I understand you had to dismiss your housekeeper."

Two spots of colour invaded Georgie's cheeks and Max held his breath.

Georgie raised both eyebrows at the countess. "We did indeed. I'm afraid we didn't suit. I wasn't happy with the way she bullied the maids. I won't have it in my household."

Mrs Matthews jumped in before the countess could reply. "You sound so like your aunt, Georgina. She was always championing the welfare of servants."

"What a refreshing attitude, Lady Hargreaves," the Earl of Haxby said.

Augusta smiled sweetly at the Haxby's. "Your dinner companion couldn't have been a close friend of my Aunt Selina, Lady Haxby. She is, of course, the Countess of Welford now. I believe they have retired to the country for a while. Northumberland wasn't it, Max?"

"So Bertie told me."

Lady Haxby sat back, open mouthed. "That must have been a surprise for you all."

"Those who know her well could tell you it was only a matter of timing." Augusta gave her another sickly-sweet smile.

Lady Haxby looked as if she was gathering herself for another line of attack. Lord Haxby put a hand under his wife's elbow.

"This has been a lovely evening but we have an early start in the morning. I think it's time we left." He bustled his wife out.

Lady Wendover, one of Augusta's friends, laughed once they had closed the door. "Trust Maria Haxby to try to stir things up. You've sent her away with some fresh news though, Augusta."

Augusta smiled. "We were as surprised as anyone else but I wasn't going to let Maria know that."

"Very wise. I'm sure it wasn't Selina's intention but she has helped you out by getting married. The Ton will be agog." Lady Wendover looked around the room. "I take it the rest of us are happy to quash any nonsense we hear about the Marquess and Marchioness of Hargreaves?"

There were murmurs of agreement. The party broke up soon after leaving them with the Cathlays and the Wendovers. Lady Wendover turned to Max.

"I'm pleased to see you with such a lovely wife, Hargreaves, no matter what the manner of finding her." She smiled at Max. "Trust us to see off any gossip."

Chapter Twenty Seven

Georgie collapsed onto the seat of their coach. Max didn't look to be in any better case. He mopped his brow as he took the seat next to her.

"You were brilliant, Georgie. I think we are in the clear with Augusta's help."

She leant back against the squabs and closed her eyes. "I like Augusta. She's absolutely furious with you by the way."

She heard Max sigh into the darkness as their carriage moved off. "I knew she would be and I realise now I've been extraordinarily selfish. I was so pleased at the thought of avoiding gossip by having a quick wedding but it's backfired on both of us."

He took her hand and she couldn't stop a shiver running through her at his touch. She might still be angry but her body craved him more than ever. She moved until she could feel the warmth of him pressed up against her side. He dropped a kiss on her forehead.

"Georgie," his voice was deeper even than usual, a sensual rumble, "at the risk of sounding as if I'm only after your body, do you think we could resume relations?"

"That depends." Augusta had said to be firmer with him and keep him guessing. Georgie giggled. Not that she would have meant in this sort of situation.

Max shifted in his seat. "On what?"

She leant against him and whispered in his ear. "On what you intend to do to me."

An arm went around her and Max bent his mouth to hers. His other hand burrowed underneath her cloak and caressed her nipple through the thin fabric of her evening dress. When she thought she could bear it no longer he released her and pulled her onto his lap. With both hands free he started a double assault, caressing both breasts. She gasped with need and wriggled until she could feel the evidence of his arousal. Max groaned and she could feel him moving underneath her. The coach started to slow down before turning a corner.

Max lifted her back onto the seat. "We're nearly home. I'm so desperate for you I'm almost tempted to have the driver take us around the block."

Georgie laughed. "I know exactly what you mean."

She rearranged her cloak as the coach pulled up at the front of Hargreaves House. Max leant towards her.

"I hope your maid doesn't take too long to help you undress. I'll hurry Jepson up as much as I can."

* * *

Georgie sat on a chair in front of the fire wearing nothing more than a flimsy nightgown. She was doing this all the wrong way around but her need for him was all consuming. The door opened and she shuddered with anticipation, the rising tension pooling deep within her abdomen almost unbearable. Max sat on the edge of her bed, wearing his banyan and nothing else if the dark sprinkling of hair visible above it was anything to go by. Why didn't he take her in his arms?

"Georgie, I've been a prize idiot. I hope you can forgive me." His voice was gentle, more like the Max she had known to begin with.

He sounded as if he was trying to get into a discussion and her hurt was still too raw to cope with that. She immediately threw her nightgown off. Her tactic worked. He dropped his banyan and they fell into bed locked in an embrace. She raised her mouth to his and kissed him. Max returned his attention to her breasts and she turned her attention to the silky length of him pressed against her thigh. He threw back his head and bucked as her hand closed around him.

He pressed his hand between her thighs and slowly stroked her sensitive spot.

"I think you are ready, my darling."

She opened for him and he entered her in one strong thrust. Their need was so great there wasn't time for anything slower. They reached their release together and lay back exhausted. Georgie was wrapped in a warm glow. He had called her his darling. Perhaps he would grow to love her in the way she knew she already loved him.

This time he didn't immediately remove to his own room afterwards as he had before. He pulled her into his arms and when her head was resting on his chest stroked her hair. It was the most relaxed she had been for days and she felt herself drifting off to sleep. The next thing she knew it was dark and the bed felt cold without him.

* * *

She entered the breakfast room the next morning to find Max

waiting for her. There was an air of suppressed excitement about him.

"I've told the servants we are not at home this morning. Not even to Augusta. There are some things I want to take you to see. Come on, eat your breakfast. There is no time to waste."

Georgie munched her toast. She could get no more out of him and her imagination was running riot. Once she was ready, Max sent her to find a warm pelisse suitable for travelling in. He was waiting for her at the bottom of the stairs when she returned.

"It's a lovely day so I suggest we walk to the mews."

He opened a side door and led her through a surprisingly large garden for town. There seemed to be a kitchen garden as well as a lawned area. The day was bright and sunny. The plants in the kitchen garden were coated with a silvery layer of frost. Glistening apple trees rose above fruit bushes and herbs. Even the lawns shimmered in the sun. No wonder Max had told her to wear something warm. When they reached the mews, Larkin was waiting for them. He led out two beautiful matched greys. They were lively but they looked good natured. Georgie was entranced and edged towards them until she could pat the neck of one. She spoke softly to him and he nuzzled at her.

Georgie laughed. "Do you have anything I can feed them with?"

Larkin called to a groom who came back with two small apples from the stores. The horses munched on them happily as Georgie looked across at Max.

"They're beautiful. Are they for the town carriage?

"No, if you like them, they're for you. You did say you would like to try driving a phaeton, didn't you?"

"Yes, I've never driven a pair but I would love to learn how."

Max signalled to Larkin who took the greys back to the stables. "We've found a good carriage maker with a phaeton suitable for a lady already made. Would you like to come and have a look?"

"Yes please."

They waited for Larkin to bring out the town carriage. Max put his hands around her waist and lifted her in, laughing up at her as he did so. Max refused to tell her any more about the phaeton on the journey.

"Wait and see. I like it but it's up to you if we buy it. I've ordered a spare curricle." He looked around the coach as it rolled along. "We may need a new carriage as well. Now I'm committed to taking my seat in the house we will have to spend a fair bit of time in London. Modern coaches are better sprung than this one."

Less than half an hour later Max led Georgie into the yard of the carriagemakers. She stood for several minutes staring at the phaeton. It was superbly crafted. Max watched her with an anxious expression.

Georgie smiled up at him. "It looks well balanced and quite light for a vehicle like this."

"Shall we buy it?"

Hope filled her at the expression on his face. Finding love eventually felt a lot more likely.

"Yes please."

"I'll have Larkin fetch it home later."

He walked her back to their carriage. "I promise to teach you how to drive a pair. That will mean we make time to be together so we can learn more about each other as you wished." He gave a rueful laugh. "Things will be hectic soon, especially now I've promised to join Cathlay and his friends in the House of Lords."

Georgie laughed back at him. "It's the least you can do. I had quite a chat with Augusta when we went shopping. You wouldn't believe the trouble they've taken to smooth our way. It's not just because of Cathlay's position either."

Max declared all the travelling around had given him an appetite and they ordered a luncheon to be served in the breakfast room when they returned. They chatted and laughed and Georgie felt her day was still as enchanted as the frosty garden of the morning. Max broke the spell when the servants left them to their coffee after they had eaten their fill.

"Georgie, I know there are things you have held back from me. You don't have to tell me but I would love to talk about anything that is bothering you."

Georgie let out a breath through puffed cheeks. She was the one who had said they needed to be honest with each other.

"It's hard to explain. I was in turmoil after I agreed to marry you. I had gone against all my family's teachings on love and marriage but, with my defences lowered by exhaustion, I couldn't help myself. I felt so drawn towards you."

Max smiled at her. "I felt that pull between us too. I can understand you having doubts when we were strangers but there is something more isn't there? I can sense it."

"It sounds silly but Mrs Powell's attitude when I arrived affected me badly. She said such awful things and I began to wonder if I was a wanton," she studied the floor, "when I, when we, you know." She glanced at him and was surprised to see two spots of colour in his cheeks.

"If we're being honest, once my doubts about you crept in, I did wonder if your enthusiastic response meant you were more experienced than you admitted." He gasped. "I'm so sorry, Georgie. I've managed to insult you in every possible way now."

He tried to take her hands but she pulled them back. Tears threatened in earnest and she didn't want him to see. They fell on her skirt and she went to brush them away only to notice Max scrubbing at his own eyes.

"My darling, I've been so cruel. I'll make it up to you, I promise. I love you so much I don't want anything to hurt you ever again."

Georgie studied his face and burst into tears. Max pulled her into his arms and stroked her hair. "Don't cry, my love. I can't bear it."

"Oh Max, I think I've been in love with you ever since you carried me all the way to Hargreaves House, despite your sore head."

He nuzzled at her cheek. "I can beat that. I fell for a little brown nymph the first time I saw you. It's taken me a long time to realise it. My stupid fear of being tricked stood in the way. It was you who saved me, not the other way around. I love you my darling."

"It was just as much my fault, Max. I convinced myself a church mouse like me could never hold the attention of a man like you. I was worried about how you would feel if I didn't produce an heir."

"Oh Georgie, I love you. How could you think that? You are worth ten of me. I shall rely on you to help me know how to proceed in the Lords."

"That's not all. When you started withdrawing from me, as the move to Town drew nearer, I was convinced you would ignore me for a mistress when we arrived."

"You're the only woman for me, Georgie."

Max embraced her and set about proving it.

Epilogue

October 1807

It was just before dawn. Max paced up and down his bedroom outside Georgie's door. The servants had told him to wait in the library but he wanted to be nearby if she needed him. The cries of a baby reached him and he ran into her room without invitation. Georgie looked exhausted and triumphant all at the same time. They tried to shoo him out but he placed a chair by her side and held her hand, until a still crying bundle was placed in his arms.

He looked at the little red face in wonderment and passed the bundle over to Georgie at her insistence.

The doctor patted him on the back. "You have a fine daughter, my lord. Your wife needs to rest now."

Max stayed for a lingering look at the two of them. Georgie glanced up at him and smiled.

"I'm well Max. You can stop worrying. You look as if you could do with a brandy."

He dropped kiss on her forehead and obeyed orders. That was so typical of his Georgie. Always thinking of others first. He was such a lucky man. He decided against the brandy and threw himself on his bed fully clothed. At last he could take some rest, now he knew she was safe.

Later that day he was allowed back in to see his family. The baby was fast asleep in her cot by Georgie's side. He smiled at Georgie only to realise she was crying. He rushed to her side.

"What is it, my darling?"

"Oh Max, I didn't give you an heir."

He rocked her in his arms. "Georgie, I don't care about that. You're the most important thing in my life. I would be lost without you."

He stared at his daughter. "She's wonderful. What shall we call her?" He wiped away Georgie's tears and she smiled at him.

"My mother was called Caroline and my aunt was called Anne but I think we need Augusta in somewhere to make up for her missing our wedding."

"My mother was also called Augusta. Do you think Caroline Augusta Anne Lovell sounds suitable?"

"Perfect."

The End.

Afterword

If you loved 'The Marquess's Christmas Runaway', I would really appreciate a short review. This helps new readers find my books.

This is Book 3 of my Reluctant Brides series of stand-alone novels linked by character. The first two are:
A Good Match For The Major
The Viscount's Convenient Bride

For more information on my books please visit my website:
https://josiebonhamauthor.com

You will also find me on:
Facebook @josiebonhamauthor
Twitter@BonhamJosie

Printed in Great Britain
by Amazon